Foreplay for Murder

By: Dick C. Waters

*"Never throw a boomerang away...
It might come back to kill you."*

Dick C. Waters

Acknowledgment:
I thank Terri (Enos) Johnston for her friendship, support
and edits on this and my other novels.

"Scott Tucker Series" novels
Listed in the recommended reading sequence:

Branded for Murder
Serial Separation
Scent of Gardenia
Fragrance of Revenge

Foreplay for Murder*
(*The Adult version of Fragrance of Revenge)
Warning:
This novel contains sexually explicit material.
Content may be offensive to some people.
It is only intended for adult readers.

Author Page: http://www.amazon.com/author/DickCWaters

Chapter 1

I felt the cold damp air against my naked body. The boat raced and crashed against the heavy sea. My head bounced in concert with the boat's rise and fall and my butt was almost numb from slamming against the rough deck. My shackles clanked a steady beat in concert with the boat's nose dive off each wave's peak.

The boat engines' whine suddenly ceased. As it slowed, waves rocked the boat and splashed against it. The smell of rope was replaced by the familiar scent of Gardenia. I was still in darkness and couldn't see anything through the blindfold.

"Well now, look at you." Her breath was hot against my cold cheek. I felt her tongue as she lapped the tears escaping below the blindfold.

"Scott, do you fear the end?"

"I've made my plans…I'm ready."

There was no immediate response. "No, you're not ready at all—not from the looks of junior." Her hand grabbed my naked body. This time there was no reaction to her touch.

"I didn't wait all day for this." She moved her fingers, but for once my body was mine, not hers. She continued her usual best to get a response, but nothing was working in her favor. "Did I hurt you too much earlier?"

I tried to forget that torture.

Suddenly she yanked off my blindfold. "Scott, open your eyes…I said *open your eyes*."

She was kneeling beside me. She smiled and reached behind her and removed her blood soaked bikini top. She slid it down my body, but there was no reaction. "Scott, I have all night…you know I get what I'm after…sooner or later."

She leaned forward and started kissing and licking my body. My mind was thinking about the safety of my friends and their rescue.

1

Not getting the result she wanted, she pounded on my thighs. Then she pounded again and again. She screamed something, jumped up and rushed off. I barely had my breath back when she arrived waving a flare gun.

She pointed the gun at Denny, who was also lying naked on the floor, but he didn't move. "Scott, you will give me what I want or I will shoot him...*I swear.*"

I tried to recall the last time I heard Denny move. I hadn't heard any movement since she chained me here below deck.

"I'm not sure he's still alive, but do what you need to do. I'm going to announce to you and God, that I love your sister with all my heart. I've made my peace and now use that on me." She just stared at me. *"Do it,"* I yelled.

Her eyes opened wide. She turned and studied Denny's lifeless and blood-soaked form. Then she slowly turned her stare back to me. Her eyes looked like she was in a trance. Then the gun followed her eyes down to my groin. I saw her finger slowly squeezing the trigger. This was how my life was going to end.

For some reason, she let up on the trigger and laid the gun down on the wood deck. She got up and came back with a key, and started removing my shackles.

Two minutes later, with the chains still locked on my ankles and wrists, she had pushed me to the stern. The only sound was the waves slapping at the boat. I knew she had planned to shoot me minutes ago, but didn't want the flare to ignite the boat.

"Melanie, why are you doing all of this?"

She raised the gun to my head, but didn't answer.

"Melanie, I asked you a question...answer me...why are you doing all of this?"

Even in the limited moonlight I could see her eyes tearing up. "Scott, you have no idea how much I love you. From the moment we were at the warehouse, I realized what love could be like." Her hand was shaking and her finger was twitching.

I didn't understand entirely what she was saying, but this was my opportunity. "I know you do in your own way. You could really be a nice person, given the right circumstances."

"Do you love me?" She brandished the gun.

"No…but someone could love you. You need to give up this crazy vendetta against everyone. You have no chance of anyone loving you when you're like this." I could see the tears running down her cheeks, and her body starting to shake. "Melanie, do you remember your sister and your grandfather on his boat when you were growing up?"

Her expression softened, and she nodded.

"Wasn't that a great and wonderful time? Can you remember sailing on his boat, just the three of you? Wouldn't he be ashamed at what you've done?" I waited for the words to make any kind of impression. I could hear the distant whine of boat engines. "Why don't you be a good little girl and put that gun down?" She just stared at me. "Your grandfather is telling you to *put the gun down now.* Be that good little girl he remembered and enjoyed."

She was soon sobbing uncontrollably and bent over like she was going to be sick. The gun was still only inches from my face, but waving noticeably. She lifted her head and her expression softened. She wiped at the tears. She closed her eyes and bent her head. When she lifted her head again, I could see what looked like a little girl's innocent smile.

"Grandpa, please forgive me. I didn't do these things…*she did.*" She looked down at my naked body. "Scott, I'm so sorry this happened to you and the others."

The tears were cascading down her cheeks. For the first time, I really felt sorry for her.

"This…" Her voice softened. "This has gone too far. I can't let her do these things any more…please tell

Mercedes that…that a part of me loves her and wants her to forgive me. I hope you have a wonderful life together."

She suddenly swung the barrel toward my face. I flinched and yelled, "*No!*" Even with my eyes closed, the night sky seemed to explode.

* * *

"Scott…Scott, wake up. Wake up Scott."

I opened my eyes and another beautiful redhead with bright blue eyes was staring down at me. It was Mercedes.

"You cried out. You had that nightmare again, didn't you?"

"Yes. Only this time she was going to shoot me." I felt the sweat on my face and body. I went to wipe my forehead, but she beat me to it.

"Scott, this is exactly why I need you to give up investigative work. You were almost killed twice. You may not be so lucky the next time."

Mercedes stood beside the bed with her arms crossed. It was her bedroom, but it had become our bed for the last few weeks. She looked incredibly sexy with her long red hair hanging down only partially covering her breasts. She noticed my eyes moving down her body and she started to smile.

"You look incredible this morning." I reached for her arm, but she avoided my hand.

"Scott, stop. I'm worried about you. You've had nightmares almost every night since we returned from Bermuda. I can't do this anymore." She looked down at me and her eyes started to glisten. "I love you Scott, but I can't go to sleep each night wondering if you're going to have one of these dreams." I reached for her again. She avoided it and went to her side of the bed and sat down.

"Do you want me to leave?" She bowed her head and put her hand against her forehead. Her naked back was

4

stretched to its limit and I had to feel her. I slid over to press my naked body against hers. "Mercedes, I'm sorry. What do you want me to do…do you want me to go to my apartment?" I rubbed her shoulder and kissed her other one.

"Scott, please stop." I stopped, but the warm scent of Gardenia was captivating. In all our days and nights, I had never seen her cry. Now she was truly upset and I had caused it.

"Honey, what do you want? Help me please."

"Scott, I know you love me. You made that clear to me. I love you too with all my heart." She lost control again.

"That's why I can't let this continue any longer. I almost lost you twice. Do you know how crushing that is?"

I watched her study the ceiling. "Honey, I know it must have been tough on you. I owe you my life. You saved it twice. What do you want me to do?"

She swung around and looked right into my eyes. "What I want is for you to promise me that you will not get involved in any more investigations." She studied my reaction.

"Scott, that's not your forte…it's mine. I can't spend any more days worried about losing you. I might not be lucky the next time." Her tears were dripping onto my chest. "You want to know what I want…I want you to give up any investigative work and stick to your business improvement focus. Will you do that for me?"

I didn't answer her. I couldn't. She searched for my answer and then turned and buried her head in her pillow.

* * *

I spent the last hour on her couch trying to put the pieces of our conversation back together. It was her comment that she might not be lucky the next time that brought her to tears. In the years I've known her I had never seen her cry.

I was having a problem dealing with upsetting her. But, I couldn't ignore how much she loved me. I didn't mean to hurt her, but obviously my actions had and my returning nightmare brought her feelings for my safety to the surface.

I couldn't defend myself. Mercedes was right. I was never formally trained to do investigative work, and getting involved in investigations did put me in harms way. Her sister had two chances to take my life and if it wasn't for Mercedes' intervention, I wouldn't be here right now. I owed her my life, and although I haven't told her, I'm ready to give the rest of my life to her.

I unconsciously felt the scar on my abdomen. I didn't need to look at it to be reminded of the arrow carved there. Melanie thought it was so funny when she carved it, and I can still hear her words as she threatened doing something even more damaging to other body parts.

It's still hard to believe that Mercedes' sister could have been so different. It's no wonder why Mercedes gets so upset…looking at that scar is a reminder of how lucky I am to still be alive.

I know Mercedes wants me to promise to never do another investigation. I owe that to her, and I've made up my mind to tell her why I can't.

I considered going to my own apartment, but I would rather be here in the morning.

I went back into her bedroom and let my eyes adjust to the darkness. I gently pulled the covers back and smiled when I saw Mercedes' long red hair cascading over her shoulder and down her back. The limited moon light illuminated her contours. The sight of her naked body, even her back, caused my body to react.

I climbed under the covers and positioned myself lightly against her. I wrapped my arm around her waist and kissed her shoulder.

"Scott, please…not tonight."

I was glad she didn't send me away. I was glad she was still talking to me. I was glad to smell the wonderful fragrance of Gardenia. The thoughts of losing her were too much for me. I leaned forward and kissed her on the shoulder. I put my head on my own pillow, but kept my arm around her and my lower body pressed lightly against her.

The thoughts of losing my wife two years ago, the pain from my captivity, nearly losing my life twice, along with upsetting Mercedes and bringing her to tears got the best of me.

I took a deep breath, and said a silent prayer and gave thanks for still being alive.

I closed my eyes and took a deep breath, the sweet fragrance of Gardenia filling my senses, but then realized I still had a problem. Yesterday, I promised her father I would indeed investigate who was involved in blackmailing him. I tried to control my breathing and hoped my heart racing wouldn't be interpreted as something else.

What could Stephen Strong have done that he doesn't even want his FBI daughter to investigate much less know? What can I say when she brings up her request for me to give up investigative work?

Scott, you should never hurt the one you love.

Chapter 2

Mercedes must be still upset with me. Although her note indicated she had to go to the office today, I read between the lines. Recently, it hasn't been easy for either of us to get out of her apartment. One or the other picks up where we left off the night before.

Frequently, there's the soft, but insistent touch of fingers against skin—my body awakening before my mind. Then the wonderful feel of soft lips and an insistent tongue. After a heated engagement, our race to see who can commandeer the best spot under the shower head. Despite our intent to just shower, it is never just that.

This morning the shower felt cold and lonely. She already left for her office. For the first time, I felt like I invaded her space.

I thought about her request and realized I couldn't tell her what I was going to do for her father. I promised to help find who was blackmailing him and also promised NOT to say a word to Mercedes about it.

I felt the arrow scar and a smile crossed my face. Mercedes laughingly commented she would always know how to find my prize...the arrow pointing at it.

Immediately, I remembered her crazy sister carving my body with a fish knife that could have done even more damage. She knew it, and she relished the fear in my eyes as she purposely made me think of what she was capable of doing. She had me, and the others, right where she wanted us, and she was unfortunately good at commanding what she wanted from us.

Mercedes was right...I could be dead now. Or, I could be useless as a man. *Do I really want to do what I promised her father, or do I really want us happy for the rest of our lives?*

* * *

I hadn't smelled it before, but the scent of Mercedes' Gardenia perfume caught my attention as I wiped my face. I loved the scent and closed my eyes with the towel held tightly to my nose. I could picture Mercedes' soft body instead of the towel. *Although people say they love each other, I honestly can picture myself with her the rest of my life.*

I looked in the mirror and the smile was gone. I was trapped between trying to do the right thing for her father and her insistence that I just focus on business process improvement.

Mercedes often told me to take the frown off my face. She liked it when I smiled making the dimples prominent. She also commented that my blue eyes seemed to sparkle with a light from inside. Many times recently she would run her hands through my neatly combed blonde hair and tell me to go to her room and take off my clothes. That was often hard to do being seated in a restaurant. She also liked to see my face turn red, which she acknowledged with a wink and a lick of her lips. Later, when we arrived at her apartment, she wouldn't let me take off my clothes…commenting that she had waited all night to do that. Her red nails tracing the arrow scar would put a mischievous smile on her face.

I really missed being close to her this morning. I dressed in one of the fresh set of clothes I brought to her apartment. I made the bed, noticing it wasn't the usual shambles. *I guess I better plan on staying at my own apartment for the near future. Although she didn't specifically tell me to plan on that, I sense she needs a day or two to herself. Should I leave her a note? She'll know what's up when she notices what I've taken with me.*

* * *

I loved the feel of my ten year old '58 Pontiac. However, the engine's angry sound clearly showed how upset I really was. There wasn't much traffic on Memorial Drive this holiday morning. Stephen Strong wanted me to meet with him to talk about a plan for my investigation. Yesterday, there wasn't any problem with having a meeting with him, but today was a different story. *Should I tell him that I owe it to his daughter not to do his requested investigation?*

The lot could easily hold twenty cars, but today, due to the holiday there were only three cars in the lot. His office building was a two-story rustic brick structure. One side was devoted to his real estate development company and the other to his real estate business. His personal office overlooked the lot and entry, and provided an excellent view of the Charles River. I parked my car and looked up toward his office, but the smoke colored glass hid any sign of life inside.

There wasn't anyone at the reception desk, which wasn't a surprise. I took the stairs behind her desk two at a time and wondered why I was rushing. Despite all of the delay at Mercedes' apartment I was still ten minutes early.

I knocked on his door, but he wasn't inside his office.

"Scott, I'm over here pouring myself a cup of coffee. Would you care for a cup?"

I walked down the short hall to the coffee nook and spotted Stephen pouring a second cup. He looked different this morning. The tinges of gray in his hair at the back of his neck were the same, but he had khaki colored Bermuda shorts, boat shoes without socks. I hadn't seen him previously without a suit or a sports coat.

"Somehow I knew you would be early Scott. Did you come over from your apartment?" he asked, handing me one of the cups.

I could feel my face flush, but smiled and took the cup. "No, actually I came over from Mercedes' apartment." I'm sure he knew that, but was testing me.

He smiled without replying, sipping some of his coffee. I took the opportunity to retreat to his office. He followed, motioning me to have a seat in the sitting area.

"So, since you see more of my daughter than I do…how is she?"

I could feel the frown coming. "Well today I really don't know. When I woke up this morning she had already left for the FBI building." I paused checking for his reaction. He just nodded. "Stephen, I have something to talk to you about."

"That's why we're here. However, I sense something is wrong. Care to share?"

I took a deep breath and noticed I could even hear my exhale. "Stephen we had words last night." I took a long drink of coffee. "That's our first ever, and she was obviously still upset with me this morning…only leaving a note that she left for work."

He frowned and placed his cup on the coffee table and turned to face me. "It's about your doing this investigation isn't it?"

"Oh, I didn't even tell her about our discussion, but she doesn't want me near *any* investigations. She wants me to focus on safe things like our realty project."

Stephen looked up and out the window over my shoulder without commenting. I drank the rest of my coffee and decided on a refill. I needed to let what I said sink in.

When I came back in, he was standing looking out towards the Charles River. I could feel my hand shaking realizing the impact of what I said.

He didn't turn around to face me. "Scott, I've got a real problem. I have no one else to turn to for this investigation. I can't share the details even with you, but I can't possibly involve Mercedes in this. You're the right person to handle this." He turned and came back to the couch and sat down. "Scott, I'm sorry I've put you in this awkward position. You really care for her don't you?"

I swallowed and hoped only I could hear it. I hid quickly behind my coffee cup while I considered how to answer.

"Scott, you don't have to answer that…I already know the answer." He shook his head and added, "I don't want to do anything to ruin what you have, but what is happening to me, could actually negatively impact Mercedes. I can't share the details, but I must find whoever is blackmailing me, and put a stop to it." His face turned red and he walked over to his desk.

He unlocked and opened his center drawer pulling out a white envelope. "I didn't share this with you yesterday, but I want you to see how this could hurt Mercedes." He came back and sat on the couch as he handed me the envelope.

I opened it and read the typed letter.

'Mr. Strong,
I know what you did. I have the power to expose you and your secret.
I'm sure you're smart enough to realize what exposing this would do to you, your business, your status and your family.
Unless I receive $5,000 by Sunday midnight, I will contact the press to have this story published.
I will be in touch.
Mr. Know!'

I folded the letter, put it in the envelope and handed it back to Stephen. "That amount could buy a couple of Cadillacs or make a big deposit on a house. When did you get this letter?"

He took a deep breath. "Eight weeks ago. That was the first of three similar letters. I paid him what he requested, but he hasn't stopped." He pounded on the wooden coffee table and his coffee spilled over the top of his cup. "Scott…he wants another five tonight."

I was only half listening to his explanation of where he dropped the money.

He brought my attention back when he added, "If you don't help me, I'm going to wait for this bum and I'm going to end this once and for all."

Chapter 3

The office building wasn't busy today as she passed the security guard. "Good morning Ms. Strong. I didn't expect to see you today. Happy Fourth of July."

She regretted not smiling at him as she passed. "Yes and the same to you Mr. McNichols. Crime doesn't know a holiday."

He watched her long-red hair whip to the side as she turned quickly entering the elevator.

There were some typewriter sounds in the general office area as she unlocked her office door. She didn't feel like socializing this morning and threw the keys onto her desk. She turned and shut her door so quickly it made a loud bang. Although she had loafers on she was still tall enough to bow over the top of the five-drawer file cabinet. She closed her eyes and tried to calm herself.

Why had she left without speaking with Scott? She was upset with him, but she let her emotions get the best of her. That is so out of character for her. All she wants is for him to forget investigative work and focus on something safer. If anyone in the family needs to do investigative work—let it be her. Family?

Her heart was beating and she could feel a doozy of a headache coming on. She sat down at her desk and put her forehead on her arms. She could hear her deep breathing.

She has known Scott for years and they have never had words before. Even when she set up the elaborate snowed in Christmas Eve at that lonely cabin and he never made love to her, she didn't get upset with him. *Why now?*

The arrow on his abdomen was a constant reminder of how close her sister came to taking his life. She had two attempts to kill him or do him even more serious damage and had failed. If her own skills hadn't been that good she would never have rescued him. She worried that she wouldn't be that lucky a third time.

That is ludicrous since her sister blew her head apart with a flare gun. Scott told her that her sister changed into a different person right in front of his eyes just before she was going to kill him…and killed herself instead.

She felt her fingers running across the spirals on a notebook on her desk. The texture felt like Scott's arrow scar. The image of Scott's naked body tied to that dungeon bed with her sister torturing him was too much for her. She didn't want to be mad at Scott, but she didn't want him to be killed either. The tears were coming and she was glad she was alone.

Even with all the education she received at Harvard and training at the FBI academy, her gut told her that she had something to fear.

She pulled the small compact from her purse and touched at her makeup. Her complexion had a slight rose tint to it and she's learned how to wear just the right amount of makeup. It's obvious that she is more attractive than she gives herself credit for…she can tell by Scott's reaction that he likes what he sees. It's also very obvious he likes what he sees when she's without clothes. There's more than the arrow pointing.

Those thoughts put a smile on her face and her blue eyes seemed to brighten just like Scott's. Even though she didn't doctor her nails this morning they were in perfect condition. That's because she resisted Scott's attention last night. It was hard to do and she could tell by the slight pressure against her bare bum that he needed her. It reminded her of their time at the cabin when he didn't make love to her, but his body was telling a totally different scenario.

She thought of Scott's scar and her first acknowledgement which she referred to as a road sign pointing to Passion Street. One light nail scratch across the arrow was all it took.

She hoped Scott would be at her apartment tonight, as she really needed to make up for last night, but she knew better.

* * *

She realized she needed to get to work soon or she would be headed to either the phone to call Scott or to find him. She unlocked her file cabinet and pulled out the large file titled *Missing Citizens - Bermuda.*

Although they were successful finding Scott and the other captives, there were three women and one man still missing. The consolidated investigations led them to find the people involved with the sale of the expensive yachts. However, there was still a dead end as to where the four missing people on one of those yachts disappeared to.

The investigation now centers on Aruba and part of Venezuela. There's the distinct possibility the women were kidnapped and are now part of white-slave trade. However, they have no proof, only some witnesses that think they saw women being put ashore off a vessel thought to be part of a pirate ring operating in and around the Caribbean. The vicious nature of those involved caused people to ignore what might look like suspicious activity and to keep it to themselves.

She pulled pictures out of the folder and looked at the women. They were all young and attractive and would not have anticipated what they were walking into. The last confirmed report they had was when they took on provisions in Bermuda aboard the yacht "Import-ant" owned by one of the kidnapped but rescued men.

It was an easier scenario to grasp…women being kept for sex…than her sister keeping men for the same purpose. However, she did, and was indeed successful for almost two years. Fortunately, Scott wasn't her slave for that long. When she questioned him about what happened during his captivity, he danced around the details. Judging from what she knows and can see on his body, he suffered more than just the physical aspects of his captivity.

If Scott isn't there tonight she's going to really miss him. It has been very easy to get a sound night's sleep after hours of love making. She's going to really miss the beat of his heart against her back. She caught herself running her fingers along the spiral.

She got up to make a cup of coffee, but noticed her excitement showing plainly against Scott's white shirt. *See Scott, even when you're not right with me, you can still get me going. If you were really a detective you would know that.*

The phone's sharp ring made her jump.

"I heard you were in. Something's happened. Can you come up to my office?"

* * *

She didn't know her boss was in this morning. It must be something really important if he's in on a holiday. She loosened her blouse but realized that wasn't going to help the situation and just let it hang outside her jeans. She knew Scott would like that picture and hoped her boss was focused on business this morning.

"Come in Mercedes and have a seat." Even though they were almost alone in the building he got up and closed the door.

"Good morning Mercedes...I'm glad you're in. I would have been calling you anyway. I just received a telegram from our embassy in Venezuela that a woman believed to be one of the missing women from Bermuda was found murdered."

"Any other details?"

"She was found with her hands tied behind her back, nude and obviously tortured. She was killed by a gunshot to

17

the back of the head. As best they can tell without any identification it is Paula Scott's body. I'm trying to get dental records now, but I'm running into difficulty due to the holiday."

He stood and went to his blackboard. He wrote her name on the board. "Mercedes, if this is indeed one of the Scott sisters, this would confirm the earlier reports of the women winding up in Venezuela. Her condition might also bring credence to the notion that there's indeed a slave trade scenario. My concern is that with one of the women turning up murdered in this fashion, we might not have much time to find the others."

"I know what's coming next."

"I'm sure you do. You and I, along with Ralph, need to jump on the next available plane. I'm arranging tickets now, so by the time you pack and get to the airport we'll have what we need. We'll be meeting with Venezuelan authorities, but the communication I received is that they do not want us anywhere near *their* investigation. My hope is that they see you and change their mind. I'm sorry to say that, but those Latin men don't necessarily think with their heads…if you know what I mean."

"I have the folder on my desk so I will take it and head home to pack." She looked at him, and he looked like he wanted to say something more."

"If I might, what you have on will work just fine."

She could feel her face flushing. "I guess that's a compliment, but I'll pack some other things that might be also appropriate."

"Good. One other thing…are you and Ralph going to be okay working closely together again?"

She studied him for a moment before answering. "I can handle him okay as long as he's focused on the case and not on my pants."

"That is exactly why I asked the question. I can't afford not to have both of you with me, but I also can't afford to have you both together without me. He was noticeably out of control in Bermuda, and if it wasn't for your support, he would have been written up."

"Duly noted, and I will be able to handle him." She got up quickly and headed to the door.

"Mercedes…" She stopped and turned. "You are an amazing agent, and we benefit from your expertise." He paused. "However, it's plain to see how Ralph could get himself in trouble."

The comment caught her off guard. She smiled. "I thank you for both compliments. I'll see you at Logan in about two hours. Happy Independence Day…sir."

"Yeah, so much for a long holiday weekend."

Chapter 4

I realized that Stephen was desperate and might also be serious about confronting the blackmailer himself. Stephen shared that his wife is on some heavy-duty medications since Melanie killed herself. If Stephen was killed, or arrested for killing the blackmailer, his wife would surely have more serious problems.

Besides, I can't ignore his asking for help. He only wants me to find out who is doing the blackmailing. *Now that I think about that, then what happens? I'll just identify who it is and then see what Stephen plans to do. He already said he can't make this public. Now, I'm more concerned about my involvement. I better get some advice.*

* * *

I made my way around Harvard Square which was blocked off for the parade. Brattle Street had many cars parked along it since it was so close for people who wanted to see the parade. I parked behind the building, but was surprised when I saw Mike's car parked in one of the parking spaces.

I opened the front door which was unlocked.

"Is that you Scott?" Mike asked from somewhere inside.

"Yes it is." I walked towards his office.

"I thought I heard the roar of your car," he said holding his ears.

"Very funny. Happy Fourth of July, Mike."

"Yes and the same to you. I didn't expect to see you in today. I thought you would be enjoying a long weekend and your redheaded friend."

I gave that a quick thought and responded, "Yeah, me too."

"Oops. Do I detect a problem?"

I smiled and sat down. "You know Mike, I have a lot of respect for you detectives…you don't miss much."

"Scott, I'm about done here, and was about to leave. Do you have something you need to take care of, or do you want to join me for a beer?"

"I don't have anything in particular I was going to do. I was just coming into the office to get my mind off things." I stood up. "I would love to have a beer, or maybe a couple of pitchers."

"Lover's quarrel?" he said smiling and getting up.

"There you go again. Why don't I keep my mouth shut, and you can tell me what I should do?"

"Sure, after many years of marriage…buy flowers and a box of chocolates."

"If it were only that easy."

* * *

We walked around the block to the Harvard Pub. We spent many hours here talking about cases when we both worked on the task forces, along with just having a beer or two after work.

The entrance to the pub always surprised me. There was just a window and a door, but once inside, the short hall opened up into a large lounge area with high tables. The bar was off to the left side of the hallway as you came in. Today the lounge and bar was crowded due to the holiday. It didn't look like we were going to get our usual table or a table at all.

We stood at the end of the hall looking around. Mike's expression turned to a smile. I felt two breasts pressed into my back and arms wrapped around my waist.

"My, oh my, who would let you out on a long-weekend?" I recognized the sweet voice of Maggie.

I turned around to look down at Maggie's smiling face and breasts only inches from falling out of a much too small top. "Hi Maggie."

She looked up and smiled. "Yes Scott, they're still there." She looked down at her breasts and pulled them up with both hands. "That reminds me, you both still owe me a visit...you really need to see my dance routine. What else can I get you Scott...Mike?"

I was bright red and could feel it in my ears. "Any chance of a table?"

"Oh, you come see me dance and I'll get you a table right down front. Other than the stage it's dark in the club and no one would see your face light up like now." She turned to Mike. "I just love how I get to him. Happy fourth Mike." She did a quick look over her shoulder. "Just a minute, I'll be right back."

"She does like teasing you, doesn't she?"

"Yes she does, and she does a good job. I don't think I could ever see her dance routine. From that point on she would never be dressed again. There's not much left to the imagination as it is."

Maggie was waving to us from over near the far wall. We made our way through the crowded pub. "So, where's the redhead you guys are always flaunting?"

"She's working today."

"So, that's why you look like a lost puppy dog. I just love little puppies. You guys want your usual drafts, or can I get you one of our special pitchers?"

Maggie was not very tall, which was ideal for resting both of her breasts on the table, but she had one hand on my thigh. "I think we could use a pitcher." I answered with a voice that wasn't my own.

"I'll get you a pitcher and a *picture*," she said with a squeeze, and a big smile. She turned and wiggled away.

"You know Scott, she teases everyone, which is why the owner likes to have her waiting on tables. Being an exotic dancer leaves her very comfortable with her body. However, she *really* likes it when you come in here. I'm sure you've noticed that. What's up that you can talk about?"

I watched as Maggie headed our way with a pitcher and two frozen mugs in one hand and coasters in the other. She threw the coasters from about four feet away and one slid in front of Mike and the other slid off the table into my lap.

She placed the pitcher and one mug on the table and coaster, and then started to reach for the other coaster. "I guess I'm losing my touch, I can usually hit the table from six feet away."

Mike and I knew her ability with the coasters, and it wasn't an accident it was sitting in my lap. I picked the coaster up quickly and placed it on the table.

"Scott, you seem a little jumpy today." She put the remaining mug on the coaster and filled each mug. She reached around her back and placed something on my thigh. "That will give you a little preview of my routine, and I'm sure something to get you up and going in the morning." She winked.

I looked, and it was a picture of her doing a routine. I turned red, but didn't know if the picture was upside down or not. I didn't know what to say.

"Thanks for the compliment Scott. Keep that to yourself…okay?"

I put the picture in my shirt pocket. Then looked over at Mike and he was almost choking on his beer.

When Maggie left and I had downed half my glass of beer and felt I could talk in my own voice I said, "I do have something to talk to you about."

"Let's have it."

* * *

"I have a problem."

"Just one?"

"Funny man." I looked to make sure Maggie wasn't going to disturb us, or more exactly – me. "It involves Mercedes' father, Stephen."

"I take it it's not related to the real estate project you're working on for him?"

"I wish it was. No, this is much more serious, and you're the only one I think I can share enough of what's going on to guide me."

"How can I help?"

"Stephen has asked me to do a private investigation for him, but Mercedes is asking me to stay away from any future investigations. She doesn't know anything about her father asking for my help. She's concerned I almost bit off more than I could chew—"

"Did you call me Scott?" Maggie asked from behind me.

"As a matter of fact, would you please bring us another pitcher."

"Oh, just a pitcher…I thought you wanted…never mind, I'll bring you another. Gentlemen, need anything to eat?" She said it with a deliberate straight face.

"Mike, do you want some rings?" I asked.

"Sure, that sounds fine."

Maggie tugged up on the top of her outfit. "I'll be right back boys."

"Phew, where was I?"

"You were explaining your problem involving Stephen and Mercedes."

"Right. Mike, I need your advice as to what to do. I want to help Stephen with his investigation, but I also don't want to ruin my relationship with Mercedes."

"Is there any danger connected with the investigation?"

"There could be. Someone is blackmailing him and he wants me to find out who it is."

He studied me for a moment, and then responded, "Scott, I would say this could indeed be dangerous."

"Are you guys talking about me again?" Maggie asked as she came up from behind me.

"No we weren't…talking about you. You're not dangerous." I answered, and then immediately regretted the words.

"Well Scott, you might say that now, but if you saw me dance you might have another opinion. I'll let you think about that, and get your onion rings, which should be hot and ready by now." She said that in a normal voice, but then came over and leaned against me, and whispered in my ear, "Scott, I caught that no good husband of mine with one of the other dancers. We're now separated and soon to be divorced. Please come see me dance. Will you do that for me?"

I looked at her and she looked like her emotions were starting to show, her eyes sparkling. "I will seriously give that some thought."

She smiled and winked, and tugged at the top of her outfit and wiggled away.

"What may I ask was that all about?"

I took a deep breath before I answered. "She's almost single again and really wants me to see her dance."

"She's right Scott. Seeing her dance sounds more dangerous than the investigation, especially if Mercedes finds out about it."

"Mike you never answered me about the investigation. What do you think?"

"I think you should do as Mercedes asked and let our office do the investigation for Stephen."

Maggie arrived with the rings and another round. "I thought Scott could use another beer, so I brought both of you another." She reached between her breasts and pulled out what looked like another picture. She put it in my white shirt pocket and tapped on the pocket. "Just something for…later." She smiled and spun away.

I didn't dare look at what she gave me. However, I could smell the fragrance emanating from my pocket.

Mike watched the exchange and then asked, "Would you like to explain to Stephen why you can't do the investigation, and then mention our alternative? Do you really want to risk your relationship with Mercedes? If you want my opinion, don't get yourself involved. You can't afford to lose her, or worse, your life."

"So Scott, what will it be?"

Chapter 5

Dr. Adler looked at her baby picture which was now wrinkled from his handling. His life changed the day she entered his world. That was well over twenty years ago. She was covered in hair, which they thought she would have to live with all her life.

At the time she came to stay at the hospital, the disease called Ambras Syndrome was not well known. Her condition was later diagnosed as Circumscribed Hypertrichosis. However, when she reached puberty the hair regressed.

He spent years with her trying to deal with her emotional instability and lack of self-esteem. He used post-hypnotic suggestions to give her a better feeling about herself.

Despite her current beauty, he still needs to work with her so that when she looks in the mirror, she sees how beautiful she really is. All she sees is how she looked as a hairy monster. Despite all of his recent attempts, she has confessed that when she looks in the mirror, all she sees is the image of her earlier disfigurement.

He pulled one of the more recent photos of her. All of the lanugo hair has long since disappeared. Her body is the color of fine porcelain. Her hair is a bright red and has only been slightly trimmed since birth. He liked to see her hair partially covering her naked breasts, the long strands reaching almost to her navel. The triangle patch of hair where her thighs meet is a much lighter color and soft to his touch.

He has many Polaroid pictures of her naked body. When she's not actually with him, the pictures help him fulfill his other fantasies.

He still finds it amazing that she has never felt ashamed of what they do while she is under his hypnotic spell. For many years he has become her lover. He has contemplated sharing with her what they do together, but fears it would end his ability to continue. He can't tell a soul what he does with her, as it would mean he would be relieved of his managing the care facility and could also get him disbarred, and possibly arrested. He thinks often about the day he will share what they have been doing all these years. However, he's concerned his reward of her beauty and her body is too much to risk telling her.

He can't tell her about how he has fallen in love with her, and he certainly needs to maintain the ultimate of discretion from the other caregivers at the institution. All they know is that for years he signs her out of the facility to his home to help her transition to the outside world. His fabricated reports talk about her progress toward that end.

* * *

They spent hours in this secret room in his basement. During the day, light would filter in from the two windows high on the basement wall. At night, light from the small lamp on the nightstand would cast a soft glow on her body. When he planned this room he purposely located it at the back of the house, making sure it was away from any people passing by on the sidewalk.

Now, the cool air of the room was sensual against his naked body. He stood against the foot of the bed, closed his eyes and pictured her once again naked on the sheet covered bed. Her ankles restrained by the ropes at each corner. Her wrists slipped into the other ropes at each bedpost. She could normally remove her wrists anytime she felt the need. She never did, but this time he made sure she couldn't. The white of her body against the black sheets was an erotic sight.

He could hear his rushed breathing and his heart pounding. Despite all the things he normally does with her, now he was doing the things he really wanted to do. *He imagined her shock of what he was doing and her predicament registering in her wide eyes—this time she was trapped.*

In spite of how much talent she had learned in the fine art of lovemaking—it wasn't enough to satisfy his cravings. He was going to make her pay for what *she* had created. He had always made sure he didn't leave any scars on her body, but this time he didn't care.

She had always been a willing student, but this time she was crying out for a different reason. The vision created the release his body so needed.

* * *

Minutes later he opened his eyes and realized what he had done. In spite of all of his medical training and credentials he couldn't control his behavior. In just a matter of hours he would have the real thing for three whole days and nights.

Why couldn't he wait? Will this be the weekend he fulfills his most wicked desires, or will he be content for the fire inside her body, the warmth of her mouth, the soft lips and exploring tongue, mixed with the bite of her teeth? Why is that not enough?

He was getting erect again, but this time he had to wait. He had trained her well, but he had created a monster within himself. He wasn't proud of his behavior, but he had gone too far and was lost forever. His guidance had succeeded in creating a girl, no a woman, capable of satisfying both their needs.

He knew deep inside him it was getting harder and harder not to fulfill his deepest fantasies whether she was willing or not.

Chapter 6

His good fortune was when he was able to copy and read Doctor Adler's files on the beautiful patient in room four.

He learned enough to be dangerous, but most importantly he learned enough to get rich.

He made more money in the last few weeks than he made all last year. Tonight he was going to add more to his bank account.

However, despite his ability to manage to pull off the extortion of Stephen Strong, which had no end in sight, his real interest was in the beautiful redheaded patient named Alexis. He also learned the good doctor was aiding her in adjusting to the real world for her future release. *I bet!*

His gut told him that more was going on than what was in the file. She's much too beautiful to ignore, and he was sure that the doctor was engaging in other activities while she was in his personal care. His plan was to find out what was really going on at the good doctor's house.

The doctor also made another mistake. He gave him a key to his house to get some files he had left behind, which he needed for a meeting. He pulled the key copy he had made and looked at it. *Chris you are a smart lad indeed.*

Recently Alexis has been giving him signs she wants more than a nightly bed check. He's even managed to check her out while she takes her shower. Although she has a private room, he has pass keys to all the patient rooms. His nightly visits have gone on for weeks. He's the only caregiver on duty at night so his only fear is that she will see him.

If I were the doctor, I know what I would be doing with her. Right now she's third on the list. The money collection is first, a visit to the doctor's house second and just maybe more details of Alexis will surface.

He is still trying to put all of the pieces together, but the most important thing is that he knows Stephen Strong is a rich real estate developer, and is quite content, it seems, to keep giving him money. *Maybe it would be best to see if he can afford ten thousand dollars. If Stephen cuts off his willingness to fork over the money some time down the line, at least his bank account will be much larger.*

He was working a different shift this weekend. Today he was working noon to 9 pm. While he sat at the duty desk waiting for the doctor to sign Alexis out until Sunday night, he remembered his visit to her room last night.

The shower in her room is located to the left as you enter her room. With her bedroom door shut to the hall, she doesn't need to shut the door to her bathroom. She should, but she doesn't. She leaves it slightly open. *Was she doing that for him?*

Last night her shower routine was very different. He closed his eyes and recalled what he observed.

When he first saw her she had already washed her hair and was rinsing the soap from it. She had her long red hair in both hands and was pulling her hands along the strands under the spray. Even her naked back was sensual. Her hips flared presenting the best ass he's ever seen. He could only see the side of one ivory breast.

She finished rinsing her hair and soaped a face cloth and turned with her back to the spray. Her long red hair reached almost to her navel, only covering one of her breasts. She closed her eyes and soaped her face, and then her arms. She was obviously in no rush to leave the comfort of the warm water.

He had a bulge now just thinking about the magnificent erection he had in his hands last night watching her. She put her head back and rinsed her hair, the water washing over her face. Then she washed each breast very slowly, almost like she loved the feel of the cloth. Her eyes were still closed. He was in the dark hallway, but he noticed her rose buds standing at attention. It was an incredible sight.

He looked around now to make sure he was still alone at the duty desk with no one watching him.

The amazing thing was that she still had her eyes closed, almost like she was letting a lover wash her body. *Boy could I do that for you.*

He closed his eyes again and picked up right where he left off. She washed below her breasts and then her stomach and reached around to wash her butt. She stopped suddenly, and opened her eyes, and he thought she could see him standing there partially naked. However, she reached for the soap and soaped up the facecloth.

She did each leg, front and back, and turned under the handheld sprayer still hanging on the wall. She then started to wash between her legs, but her back was to him. Her legs were slightly apart and she was in no rush. She had her left hand against the wall but he could tell this was more than just a wash. Her right hand was moving keeping beat with his.

Then she turned and looked at the slightly open bathroom door, and for a second he thought she saw him and what he was doing. However, if she saw him she gave no indication and resumed her washing. A minute later she dropped the facecloth and had a finger doing a special wash. She smiled and put two fingers into the folds and her thumb against her special spot. His breathing sounded like a freight train but he didn't care.

She bent slightly at the waist and looked like she had bitten her lip. She turned and grabbed the hand-held unit, adjusted the spray nozzle and directed it where her fingers had been. Over and over she moved the vibrating spray across her special part. He couldn't stop but tried to capture his release. Two seconds later he saw her climax and almost collapse.

He had never witnessed her doing that before.

She turned the water off and stretched her arms above her head. He remembered the panic as he tried to wipe himself and get his pants up. In that moment he had the feeling she knew he was there, giving a hint of a slight smile.

"Chris, are you okay?" a deep voice asked.

He opened his eyes and the doctor was standing in front of his desk with Alexis slightly behind him.

"I'm sorry doctor. I didn't hear you approach."

"I'm leaving now with Ms. Strong. I need to sign her out."

"Right," Chris replied. He stood there looking at Chris. "Oh, I'm sorry." He opened the 'sign out register' and turned it towards him.

"One other thing Chris. I forgot to lock my office door. Would you keep Ms. Strong company for a minute while I go lock it? Please help her with her coat too. Thanks."

"Sure no problem." He felt uncomfortable coming around the desk to be that close to her. He smelled her fragrance as he held the coat for her arms. She put her long hair over the back of her coat and turned quickly.

She looked right into his eyes like she was searching his brain. Then she looked down to his pants. "I see you are as excited as you were last night. Thank you for my coat and for your *visit* last night." She looked over in the direction of the doctor's office. "Now unless you want to lose your job, you will keep your visits between us, and you will do as I say next time."

He didn't say a word. He was still trying to process what he just heard.

"Are we all set here?" Doctor Adler asked.

"Yes doctor. Chris is an excellent caregiver. We're all set now."

"We'll return Sunday evening. See you then?" Doctor Adler said and grabbed Alexis' arm and guided her away.

"Have a nice holiday weekend Chris, and I'll see you Sunday night too," Alexis said, looking over her shoulder and winking at him.

"Enjoy the holiday weekend both of you." He watched them leave through the front door. *Now, who is blackmailing whom?*

Chapter 7

She couldn't hold back the smile. The look on Chris' face was priceless. He had no idea she knew he was there last night. Now she has power over him. He's not bad looking and has some other special gifts. However, Sunday is a long way off.

She felt the pressure of Dr. Adler's hand on her arm guiding her down the walk. She learned that he was twice her age. He was never married and lives alone in a very large home. She's learned the routine well.

He signs her out for whatever time he has available. They go to his house mostly, but every once in a while he takes her out to a nice restaurant. The last time was very nice as it was a seaside restaurant. They sat outside and watched the activity in the small harbor.

She stopped and looked back at the care facility. The bright-spot lights lit up both the sign in the front yard and the house itself. She thought of it as a house, since it's been her home for all of her life. 'Lighthouse Manor' still has a nice ring. 'We care when you need us to' was printed below the name. The white columns on either side of the front porch gave the Georgian colonial an impressive and inviting entry.

"Alexis, what are you looking at?" Doctor Adler asked.

"I've spent so many years looking at the inside of this home; I just wanted to commit the outside to memory."

They silently stood on the brick walk looking at the building. Alexis knew the inside like the back of her hand. There were ten patient rooms; four on the first floor and six upstairs. Off the front entry was a nurses' station which was open to the main entry hall that had double doors to the main living area and dining room beyond.

At the end of the main hall was the library which doubled as Dr. Adler's office. There were rest rooms to the left of his office. The kitchen was across the back of the building out of sight. Patient rooms were along the left of the hall; hers was across from the nurses' station.

"Alexis, are you alright?"

"Doctor Adler, you've shared much with me for over twenty years, and you're almost like a father to me, but you've never told me about my parents." She looked at him. "Why haven't you told me the rest of my story?"

* * *

She no longer rode in the back of the Cadillac, but now sat in the passenger seat. However, the front seat could easily seat three people comfortably. He never answered her question, but had nodded his head and quickly ushered her to the car.

Someone had to be paying for her care, which she knew had to be expensive. There were seldom ten patients at the home. Even if the building were paid for, there were considerable expenses involved running the facility. She decided to find out more about her parents and who was paying for her care, especially since he avoided answering her. *He's been out of character since she asked the question.*

She could tell he knew she was staring at him. There was something about him that interested her. His hair was black without any sign of gray. His hair was full and was always well groomed. She wondered if he went to the same hair stylist that came to the facility. *Maybe she went to his home and did more than style his hair. She sensed some jealousy.*

He usually wore gray slacks like now, with a dark-blue blazer over a white shirt. Most of the time he would wear a tie, but usually when he was picking her up, he did not have one.

His chin was long and square and when she had the chance to fix on his eyes they were a deep brown and reminded her of maple syrup. He was what she considered handsome. She thought of the hair stylist, and now wanted to run her fingers through his hair and make him more like a human than a statue.

She thought about Chris' frequent visits and liked seeing his private parts. She even caught Dr. Adler in the shower one morning and watched for several minutes. *She wondered if all men did what they did.* She felt a strange sensation between her legs and wished she could touch herself. *Would she be able to get Chris to touch her body now that she shared that she knew he was watching her?*

"A penny for your thoughts?" Dr. Adler broke the silence, and looked at her.

She could feel the heat on her face, and knew he couldn't tell she was blushing because of the dark car interior. Despite her condition she smiled at him. "Maybe I should share what I was thinking." She weighed the risks. "Do you think I'm pretty Dr. Adler?"

"Alexis, we've discussed your looks many times. You still deny what I keep telling you. You are no longer the ugly child who came to live at the home. I've shown you the pictures of how pretty...no, how beautiful you are. You need to understand what a beautiful butterfly you've turned into." He looked over again briefly, and she turned towards the side window.

"If I'm as beautiful as you say I am, then why am I still at the home, and how come...no never mind."

"Alexis, maybe riding in the car like this...you can share what you resist sharing when we're talking in my office. Tell me what you were thinking, please."

She wanted to tell him what she was going to ask, but she liked what she had, and didn't want to jeopardize it.

"Alexis, we've spent years together. You must know by now that you can say anything, or ask me anything. Please tell me what you were also going to ask me."

She turned quickly to face him. "So, if you think I'm so beautiful how come you can ignore it so well?"

Chapter 8

Mike was not in favor of my doing the investigation. I wasn't at all surprised. Mike knew about those other times I could have lost my life. The idea of Mike doing the investigation was appealing. However, I had made the commitment to Stephen and had to at least attempt to identify the blackmailer.

I headed to my apartment to change into some darker clothes. I had decided to go to the drop location to see if I could spot who was picking up the blackmail money. Stephen told me he was going through with the drop, but indicated he was losing his patience.

I called Stephen hoping to catch him at his office.

He answered the phone, which didn't surprise me. "Hi Stephen, Scott."

"Hi Scott. Have you decided to help?"

"Let's just say that I'm going to go to the drop location tonight to see if I can learn anything. We'll discuss things later. Are you still going through with the drop?"

"I don't have any choice at this point in time, but putting all those green hundreds in the bag…well, as I said, I'm losing my willingness to continue this. At some point, one of us has to stop, or be stopped."

"Okay. I'm willing to help tonight, but…let's just see how tonight goes."

"Thanks Scott."

"Now, let me see if I got the details correct. You go to the Dudley Street station and as you enter, there's a column with the street name sign on it. It's the only column someone would see leaving the station. In front of it is a metal bench. You stand on the bench and put the bag of money behind it on the metal cross rail. Is that correct?"

"That's correct Scott. The station is not in the most desirable section of Roxbury, and is normally pretty deserted at night. However, you need to be careful that nobody sees what you're doing."

"Do you have any suggestion as to where I can watch who picks the money up?"

Stephen didn't immediately answer. "Good question. Let me think about that for a second."

I was getting concerned Stephen hadn't thought about that.

"Well Scott, you need to be close enough to spot someone standing on the bench to get the money and close enough to see if you can identify the person. However, you need to be far enough away not to be seen yourself, or be seen hanging out in the area."

I immediately thought about the Mission Hill gang that was involved in kidnapping men, and some women, for the torso killers. I recalled being held captive by one of the women and got a chill up my spine. That was one of the reasons Mercedes wanted me to stay away from investigations.

The choice of a location so near the gang's area raised my suspicion as to whether this gang was involved and seeking some revenge.

"Okay Scott, here's what I suggest. The station closes at 9 pm, which is why I'm to make the drop at 10 pm, which means the main station is locked, but the entry area still has access to the flyers and other schedules. If you wait in your car across the street you can see who comes and goes. Near midnight there shouldn't be anyone coming and going except the blackmailer. You should be close enough to see who it is."

I was considering what he offered.

"Scott, maybe we should meet and go together in your car?"

"As much as I would like the company, I think that's too risky."

"Scott, I'm going to put in a good word for you with Mercedes. She needs to know—"

"No, Stephen." I interrupted him immediately. "Please do not say anything to her about me. She would be much too interested in why you offered."

"Scott, do I sense a problem?"

I took a deep breath. "Let's just say she's concerned that I should focus on business things and not things that could get me killed."

* * *

I changed and was going to head over to pick up some of my things at Mercedes' apartment. I was really hoping to run into her and try to smooth things out between us. However, I realized I should scout out the Dudley Street station to know what I was going to do, and where I needed to park.

It was a short ten minute drive from my Brookline Village apartment to Roxbury and the Dudley Street station. My white '58 Pontiac Bonneville convertible was not very inconspicuous. Late at night, it was going to get even more questioning looks, especially since I was white too.

I drove by the station and noticed there were people entering and leaving even though it was a holiday. I turned up one side street beyond the station to come back to the station—wrong thing to do. It seemed like everyone was on the front steps or on the sidewalk and I was the afternoon chicken dinner. I didn't care about turning around. I was headed out of there.

My heart was beating and I was thankful I managed to get back to the station without losing my car or my life. I parked the car across from the station entrance. I estimated it was about forty feet from where I was parked to the entrance.

There was a light pole with its globe still intact, so I assumed there would be some light to help me see who would be taking the money. If I backed up just a little I could see if someone stepped up on the bench near the entrance. I had a plan and wondered what it would be like near midnight tonight.

I quickly got back into traffic and headed the fastest route out of this area to Mercedes' apartment near MIT.

* * *

I pulled in front of the building and the door man greeted me. "Hello Mr. Tucker. Will you be parked for the night?"

"No Harold. I'll be leaving shortly."

"Why don't you use the receiving area, there's no deliveries expected today."

"Thank you Harold." I discreetly handed him a folded dollar and got back in my car. I pulled around the side of the building and parked on the down slope area to the receiving docks.

I was coming around the building when I saw Mercedes looking fine as usual in one of my white shirts and a short black skirt. She was standing in front of her apartment building looking at her watch. I was about to call to her when I noticed her turn to a man exiting the front entry door with two suitcases.

I recognized Mercedes' white luggage and the man...it was Ralph. I remember Ralph from Bermuda, and he was involved with Mercedes while they were investigating the missing men there.

Mercedes said there was nothing between them, but I could tell from his actions that he didn't see it that way. Despite her saying that nothing happened, I could tell he at least had tried.

He came over to a waiting cab, handed keys to her, and put his arm around her while helping her into the back seat.

He couldn't help but notice that her legs went a long way up under her skirt.

"Shit…shit," I muttered to myself. It's a holiday weekend and she's headed off with him. Where the hell are they going? I tried to remember our last words last night, but I couldn't remember saying anything that would have resulted in her running off with him.

The cab pulled away along with a part of my life.

* * *

I entered the apartment to get what I came for. I went in the bedroom and found the bed a mess. I searched my memory and could almost swear I had made the bed before I left. *Could they have gone to bed before they left?*

I sat on the bed and gave some more thought to our discussion. I felt real guilty planning to do the surveillance this evening. I'm doing what she specifically asked me not to. I love Mercedes and she's said she loves me. *Now I wish I had said more things to her last night.*

The thoughts of her going to bed with Ralph were absurd. I grabbed one of my suitcases in the closet and started to put some shirts and pants in it. I went over to the dresser and took out socks and underwear and added those. Then I took my shaving stuff from the bathroom. The other things I had at my own apartment, but the shaving stuff was only here. I closed the suitcase on the bed and lifted it off.

I noticed something other than crumpled sheets. I moved the top sheet and found a pair of boxers.

"Shit…shit…and triple, shit." I don't wear boxers.

Chapter 9

Mercedes left no note, the bed was a mess, boxers were left between the sheets, and I saw them leaving together with suitcases.

Despite what it looked like, this didn't make any sense to me.

Mercedes might have been upset with me about my doing investigations, but she didn't know anything about her father asking me to do an investigation for him. *Or, did she?*

I tried to recall last night's conversation after my nightmare. Maybe I talked in my sleep about his request for me to do an investigation for him. I found myself sitting on the bed still holding the boxers. *What would a true detective do in this situation?*

I turned the material inside out and shook it over the off-white bed cover. The sheets were black so I knew I wouldn't be able to see anything. I wanted to see if anything appeared, but I really didn't want to see anything.

There on the bed cover were two short black hairs. My fear was confirmed. Ralph had indeed been with Mercedes in bed and nude. I threw the underwear, which hit the bedside lamp knocking it off the nightstand. The shade hit the wall and the lamp base bounced on the rug.

I stood and pulled the bed cover off to the floor and then the top sheet. I felt the bottom sheet to see if it was warm, but it felt cool. I rushed into the bathroom and found two wet white towels discarded in the corner.

Mercedes always hung her towel over a hook or at least over the shower rod. Now I knew the naked truth. They made love in bed and showered together. As hard as it was to believe Mercedes could actually do that with someone else…the facts didn't lie.

* * *

As much as I tried to deny the facts there was no other explanation. If Mercedes really loved me, she might have just been vulnerable today. I just couldn't accept what I had seen. Then it hit me.

She knew I still had a key and would find the condition of the bedroom, the bathroom and worse his boxers. She did this on purpose to send me a message. *I got it.*

I didn't know why I was rushing around the apartment getting *all* of my stuff together, but I was. They were not coming back anytime soon. I felt like a ton of bricks was lying on my chest—it was so hard to breathe. My head was spinning with images of Mercedes and me at the cabin, with her in a towel too small for the task. Those images were quickly replaced with Ralph in bed with her and then in the shower.

I thought we were in love and would be together for the rest of our lives. That's what we had talked about. I still couldn't understand why this had happened…but it did. The worse part was that she knew this would almost kill me when I found her apartment this way. *I really had misjudged her. Maybe she's more like her sister than I ever knew.*

I tore the bed apart and punched the two pillows before throwing them across the room. I realized the mess I made and sat down on the naked mattress. There was no way I could blame Ralph for what happened. He would be defenseless to resist her beauty. Even to this day I'm surprised she's not married or at least engaged.

I fell back on the bed and tried to calm down. I was still in shock, but now I knew I was going to help Stephen with his investigation. I didn't care how dangerous it would be. Being safe didn't matter any longer. *Why did I think I had Mercedes all to myself?*

I opened my eyes and looked at the mess in the bedroom. My clothes were all scattered everywhere. The last time I saw such a mess was when we came into her bedroom and couldn't wait to get our clothes off and feel our naked bodies touching. My hand brushed against my shirt pocket.

I pulled two pictures out. One was the one Maggie had given me showing her dancing at her club. The other I hadn't looked at. I looked at it and it had her phone number on the back and 'please call me' written below it. I turned the picture over and it was a XXX rated picture of her with a dance pole. I stared at the picture too long, and realized Maggie sharing this picture with me told me how she felt about me.

* * *

It was only 9 pm, and I was headed up Mass Ave in the direction of Harvard Square. My stuff was thrown in the trunk and the back of the car. Harold, the doorman, saw me throwing my stuff in the car and just shook his head, and didn't say a word. *Yes, Harold things have changed considerably…you won't have my tips any more.*

My hand was shaking, but it wasn't nerves from what I was going to do near midnight. It was what I was doing right now. I had time to think about what I was about to do, but I was mad enough now to do it.

I could only imagine Maggie's eyes when she spots me watching her dance. Is this really fair to her? Why not? She had more than gone out of her way to indicate she likes me and most certainly wants me to see her dance…and I would say, more than that.

* * *

It took a minute for my eyes to adjust to the dark interior. It was not only dark, but the smoke filled my nostrils and made it hard to breathe. It was crowded in the strip club and the men shouting over the loud music made me consider what I was doing here.

I was about to turn and leave when fingers gripped my shoulder. "Would you like a table near the stage?"

I turned to the voice and was greeted by a petite blond whose assets were much too large for her frame. I tried not to stare and noticed her smiling as my eyes went to her face. "Sure, thanks."

She led the way to one of the two remaining tables near the stage. However, they were on the side near the wall, not front and center. That was fine with me. I had never been in a strip club before, and wished now that Mike was with me. I was glad the eyes were not on me, but on the ebony creature almost fully naked on the stage.

"What would you like to drink?" she yelled to me as I sat down and turned almost nose to nipples.

"A draft would be fine." She started to move away. "Oh, is Maggie dancing tonight?"

"Who?"

"Maggie."

"Oh, you mean Bubbles."

"She's scheduled at 10. Do you know her?"

"What?"

"Do you *know* her?"

"Yes, I know her from the Harvard Pub."

"Okay, I'll tell her the blond guy from the pub is here."

"No…no that's not necessary." However, she had already left.

What the hell am I doing? I looked at my watch and I had twenty minutes until she appeared.

Vickie was back with my beer and told me the amount. Her name was on her bow tie, which I tried to focus on instead of other things. I gave her a five and told her to keep the change. She did a slight double take and I realized she appreciated the large tip.

I was impressed with the next dancer and her routine. She was a tall redhead and her body reminded me of Mercedes. When she removed the last of her outfit she was completely bare. Her final routine was to scrunch down and pick up bills standing on end. I was glad my view was limited, but my mind was racing. She took her time leaving the stage.

My mind was thinking about what Mercedes had done, and what she and Ralph might be doing.

There was a drum roll from somewhere and a leg appeared from between the stage curtains. The curtain became part of the next dancer's act. Although she had an outfit on, her use of the curtain was erotic. Even I wanted to see what the dancer looked like. She tumbled out from behind the curtain, landing with the pole between her legs.

She slithered up the pole and then swung around facing me. It was Maggie. Her arms were over her head hanging onto the pole, and she gave me this big smile. She mouthed 'thanks for coming.' She did some other things with the pole and I was mesmerized. I also had to adjust my excitement, which she observed and smiled and winked.

She danced around the stage, and men were inserting bills into her top and what you might call a bottom. Then she came over to me and went down on her knees and moved like a kitten stroking its body against a leg. I went to insert a bill in her top, but as I reached the top disappeared. She threw the top in my face. The five dollar bill was still in my hand when she flipped over and picked it out of my hand with her toes.

She was back to the pole and the rest of her act was a blur. However, my body was reacting to her performance and I was surprised at how well toned her body was.

Although she had large breasts which she flaunted at the pub, they were worth the visit, and she will never be the same at the pub again. I'll remember her final move for a long time—she put her toe into the bottom of her g-string and slipped it off. It took easily over a minute to complete the removal, much to the men's enjoyment.

Before she left the stage she came over and posed in front of me. I thought she wanted her top back and I went to hand it to her, but she shook her head and once again mouthed 'thank you' and dove under the curtain. I heard the applause and added mine.

I was on my third beer and checked my time. Two hands covered my eyes and breasts greeted my ears. I looked up to see Maggie's big smile. She slid her hands around my shoulders and sat on the chair next to me.

"Thank you for *coming* to see me dance," she said, the smile frozen on her face.

"You were amazing."

"Were?"

"Okay, you are amazing."

The waitress came over and Maggie shook her head. The waitress quickly turned and left.

"Scott, I hope you really liked my routine. But, I have to admit, I never thought you would come. Are you okay?"

Maggie had a white cut off T-shirt which barely covered the tops of her breasts. She caught me looking at her top.

"You like?"

I took a deep breath and could feel my face flushing. I looked away for a quick second and realized many of the men were watching us. "Maggie, you are incredible."

"Thanks Scott. Was that my routine, or my body, or both?"

"Everything."

"Did my second card do the trick to get you here, or is the redhead giving you a problem?"

I could feel the emotions of the early evening coming back, and looked away.

She put her hands on my knees, well actually a little above my knees, and bowed down so we were nose to nose.

I could see the tears forming in her eyes. The music had stopped between acts and we could hear each other.

She spoke, but the tears were rolling down her cheeks. "I know I really don't have a chance with you Scott, we're from different worlds, but I want to thank you for coming. I can tell something's bothering you. Would you like to have coffee when I'm done? I have one more routine to go tonight close to midnight."

I surprised myself and wiped her tears away. "Maggie, this isn't fair to you. Something did happen with Mercedes and me, and I think she's seeing someone else."

"Scott, I think you need more than a coffee. I'm willing to benefit from what happened, regardless of where it leads. Wait for my last routine. I want to hold you tight. I need you too." She leaned over and kissed me.

I couldn't resist her and enjoyed her kiss.

"Maggie, I'm sorry but I do have something to do around midnight. If I didn't I could really go for holding you tonight."

She studied me and was doing a mind read on my brain. "That's one of the nicest things anyone has said to me recently. Thank you, and thank you for coming tonight. I'm sorry you're concerned about Mercedes, but I'm glad you came. You're a special man Scott…and I would like to be part of your life, in any way I can. You have my number, and you know where I work." She rocked slightly and her tears flowed again.

She got up quickly and bent and hugged me, and her fragrance was as intoxicating as her routine. She reached for her discarded top, and left quickly without saying another word.

Now I was even madder. The last thing I wanted to do was to upset her. I thought she was just being a tease, but now I knew differently. *What the hell am I going to do about it?*

Chapter 10

It was close to midnight on a holiday night. The money drop should have been done two hours ago. He parked on an adjacent street to walk to the Dudley Street station. Of all the places in Boston to pick, this might not be the best choice, especially carrying money. However, it is what it is.

Chris came around the front of the station and tried to casually check who might be around. He saw no signs of any activity that might give him a reason not to pick up the money. He darted inside the station entrance. The light from the lamp pole outside was sufficient to light up the small waiting area.

He jumped up on the metal bench and reached over the familiar sign. The bag wasn't there. His immediate reaction was that someone had seen the drop and had taken the bag of money. He felt around the area, still nothing. He moved down the bench and felt the other side, his hand touched on a paper bag. He looked around one last time and pulled the bag out.

He wanted to get out of this area as soon as his feet would accommodate. He stuffed the small bag under his dark sweatshirt and headed out of the station. There were three men in dark clothes crossing the previously deserted Tremont Street. He didn't like the looks of the men or their focus on him. He turned and headed around the building to his parked car.

He could hear the beat of feet hitting the sidewalk and without turning, started to run. He considered throwing the bag of money over his shoulder, but that was something that he wasn't quite willing to do. He could see his car parked on Columbus Ave, but he would have to cross the street. He heard the whoop of a police car, but didn't turn to see what it was doing.

He unlocked his door and threw the bag on the passenger side floor. He started the car and pulled out onto the road and noticed the police talking to the three men across on the adjacent corner. One of the men was pointing at him. He headed up Columbus Ave, but really wanted to be headed in the opposite direction to Dr. Adler's house in Chestnut Hill.

He could hear sirens in the distance behind him and turned off Columbus, but didn't know what street he was on. He knew he was headed west, which was the right direction. The neighborhood was not well lit and the street narrow since there were cars parked on both sides. It was definitely not the place to stop or break down. He noticed the blue lights flashing off the buildings around him and in the rear view mirror saw the cruiser continue on Columbus.

His heart was pumping and he wondered if he should select a different location for a money drop next time, even though this could be his last request for money.

He was coming up to a stop sign and slowed. Four men jumped out from both sides of the street from between parked cars. They were intent on his car and now waiting for him to stop. He wasn't going to take the chance and gunned the car almost hitting two of the men. They immediately starting running and he thought they might be headed to their own vehicle.

He had wanted to turn at that intersection, but now he was in a similar neighborhood. A car was pulling out onto the narrow street ahead of him and he saw headlights in his rear view mirror. He gunned the car again and almost hit the front fender of the car as he passed. The car stopped dead in the road, the driver probably in shock. The other car's headlights were behind it now.

* * *

Fifteen long minutes later he was parked around the corner from Dr. Adler's house. Most of these homes had garages and long driveways, so parking was easy. However his car was noticeable along the deserted street.

He opened the bag and felt the hundred dollar bills. He closed the bag and pushed it under the passenger seat. There was no one on the street, which was not a surprise since it was after midnight. He turned the interior light switch off and opened the car door. Two minutes later he was at the good doctor's house, but the lights were all off.

Chris knew the layout of the house having been there once before. He thought about using his key, but decided to go around the back of the house to be sure there were no lights on in the rear. He took his time making sure not to hit anything. When he came around the back of the house he noticed a glow on the grass. He silently headed to the light source.

It was coming from two basement windows. He checked the rest of the house out and there was only a light coming from an upstairs room. He went over to the closest basement window and peered in. The light was coming from a small lamp on a nightstand. Then he saw a nude figure on a bed.

It was Alexis, and she was naked and tied to the bed posts. Her ankles were being held by ropes. There were ropes also at the head posts. Although the window was covered in dust he could make out her features. Her long red hair was spread out covering the pillow and the top of the sheet above her head. She had her eyes closed and looked like she was in pain.

He tried to see if there was anyone else in the room, but he couldn't see that far beyond the foot of the bed. Her body glistened in the faint light of the room. She was covered with sweat, but she looked as stunning as she did last night. He saw her body move suddenly and then saw what had hit her.

It gave the impression of a dozen separate shoelaces all attached to a single cord. Oh my God, she was being whipped. The separate strands moved down her from her breasts down between her legs and then down one leg. It disappeared quickly and then came down across her flesh again. He thought he heard her scream, but couldn't be sure. The whip's motion traced the same movement as before only this time it slipped down her other leg.

He moved to the other window and looked down into the room. This time he was near her head and could see another leg near the foot of the bed. He strained against the far side of the window and saw the good doctor. Doctor Adler was naked as she was and was obviously enjoying what he was doing, judging from his erect penis.

He looked back at Alexis and realized her hands weren't tied, but were holding onto the ropes. She was free to let go and stop this at any time. The lashes crashed against her body, but it looked like she was either trying to move away, or trying to reach the tendrils. It was an erotic sight especially knowing she seemed to be enjoying the abuse.

He lost count of the number of lashes, but even with the dirt covered window he could see the red marks on her pure white body. He was very excited himself and remembered watching her shower the night before. He wondered if they had been doing this or similar things for the hours since they left the care facility.

He thought about his next actions. *If I entered the house and went downstairs and confronted them, would they include me in their fun? If I just watched them could I learn more about what motivates Alexis? He remembered her comment to him about keeping his visits between them, and doing what she says next time. Could he now turn the tables on her, and have her do what he says?*

The doctor's sudden move brought him back to reality. He climbed on the bed and soon had his head between her legs. He watched him for several minutes and then watched her let go of the ropes and pull his head further into her body. A minute or so later she was writhing on the bed with her hair flashing from one side to the other.

He heard her yell out and the good doctor moved his body up across hers and put his hand momentarily between them. They were locked together and soon both were soaking wet and spent. She dug her nails into the doctor's butt. He thought he could make out her tongue wetting her lips. He could only imagine what was on *her* agenda. Her head rolled towards the window, her eyes opened and she smiled.

What magic did the doctor have to get someone so young and beautiful to give herself this way? He was going to find out.

The window was now fogged, but he didn't care…they weren't the only ones wet and spent.

He had seen enough.

He had also discovered another way to make some money.

Chapter 11

I got a good look at the blackmailer's face. He spotted the three men walking across the street towards him and froze. Now that I knew what he looked like, I could tell Stephen about him. It would be up to him to figure out who it might be. At least it's not a female. It had crossed my mind that maybe he had a lover who was getting back at him.

I didn't like the looks of those guys either and waited for them to get away from the station. I was certain the men were intent on having more than a conversation with the other white man in their village.

I started the car and got my white ass out of there. I had lots to think about while I drove. I have a woman who knows me, never saw me privately; but I think really wants me to be more than a friend.

Conversely, I have a woman who knows me quite well, wants my body, sees it quite often, but I think is sending me a message that she doesn't want me anymore.

My problem is that I love Mercedes, and still can't believe what I saw with my own two eyes at her apartment. The fact that she left her apartment in that manner told me she wanted me to find the evidence and get the message.

Regardless, she's with Ralph at this moment. I have Maggie's number and could be with her tonight, but I have to think that out. The good news was that I made her day, and the bad news was I didn't make her night.

Stephen asked me to call him at the office tomorrow even though he expressed his desire to know who this person was tonight. He said it would be too risky to call tonight as his wife is still recovering from all the trauma of her daughter killing herself.

I looked at my watch and it was just before 1 am. Maggie would be just changing from her last routine. I considered changing my mind and heading to the club, but that is like convicting Mercedes before she proves herself innocent.

Scott, you are being such an asshole. You never were good with girls and you certainly need to learn more about women.

Despite what you want to believe, she went to bed with Ralph, during the afternoon when she knew you would be gone, and even if she didn't realize he left his boxers in the bed...she left the bed messed up and the evidence of their shower. And, most of all...I'm now guilty of doing exactly what she asked me not to.

I'm in another investigation, and yes, she's right, it could be dangerous and I might even...I didn't even want to think about those consequences.

* * *

I pulled into the driveway at my apartment. Mrs. Abbott, who is my landlady, is sure to know about my frequent absences from my apartment. It's pretty hard for her not to, since she leaves the paper on the stairs for me each morning. This is when I wish there were many apartments in the building. She's very smart and even if there were other apartments, she would know about my being elsewhere.

I parked and entered the front door as quietly as I could. There were yesterday's papers sitting on the first step. I knew without even looking that 'Dear Abby' and the crossword puzzles would be missing. I could feel my first smile of the day coming on. Even though I tried my best to be quiet, the stairs gave my presence away. I unlocked my door and closed it very quietly.

Once the light was on, I looked around the apartment as if it was my first time seeing it. It was neater than I remember it. There were some work projects on the round table to my right. The sitting area was to my left and the couch looked very inviting. Despite my bedroom down the hall, I spent many a study night on the couch. However, the only woman who was ever in the bedroom was Lisa.

It seemed all of the time I spent with Mercedes, it was at her apartment. I have to admit that her abode is much more impressive since it's in a high-rise. It just hit me that maybe Mercedes felt that being in my bedroom here might bring back memories of Lisa.

Lisa stole my heart and was my first love. We enjoyed our love affair, and our marriage. It was cut too short by the accident on a winter's night. I stayed away from Mercedes for almost two years following Lisa's funeral. Mercedes finally had to call me, and gave me hell for not being in touch with her. My falling in love with Mercedes was long after she had fallen for me.

I went in the bathroom and started to get ready for bed. I was surprised I hadn't needed to go to the bathroom before now, but I made up for lost time. I looked at myself in the mirror and as Mercedes would say, 'wipe that frown off your face.' I did look like I was carrying the weight of the world. Things could be much worse…*I wondered how.*

I emptied my pockets and placed the contents on my nightstand. I had one coin and it was a penny. I thought of my conversation from a long time ago when Mrs. Abbott told me the penny has two sides and it represents the day. You can have a 'heads up' kind of day, or it can be something else. She told me to always remember to make each day a 'heads up' kind of day.

I flipped the coin and turned it over and it was 'heads up.' *Now my job is to figure out how I can make it that kind of day. Why do I feel like Mercedes is going to call and explain things? I woke up yesterday morning having a nightmare, and it was kind of that kind of day. Maybe tomorrow will be a heads up kind of day.*

I was tired and turned off the light.

I don't know whether I just drifted off to sleep, or I was asleep for hours. I heard a ring, then another, and another. It was the phone. I fumbled for the receiver. "Hello."

Chapter 12

"Scott, I'm sorry to wake you. It's me."

"Mercedes…it's almost two in the morning. Are you okay?"

"Scott, I've been calling every hour for about four hours. Where have you been? I was worried about you."

"I'm surprised you're calling."

"I know I woke you. I'm sorry."

"It's not about you waking me…I know what happened."

"Scott, what are you talking about? You're not making much sense. I'm sorry I called at this hour."

"I saw you leaving with Ralph."

"That's why I'm calling. We were—"

"You don't have to explain. I know these things happen."

"Scott, listen to me...maybe I better call later. We were called out on the missing tourist case. We're in Venezuela. They found one of the missing women, and she was murdered. I thought you should know where I was."

"Thanks for letting me know."

"I can tell by your tone you're not happy with me…I'm sorry. I shouldn't have left for the office without saying goodbye, but I was still upset with you about our conversation the previous night. I'm sorry."

"Is that all you're sorry for?"

"Scott, have you been drinking, and where have you been all night?"

"Maybe we're even now."

"I was hoping you went to the apartment and got my note."

Scott didn't immediately respond. "I didn't see any note, but I got your message loud and clear."

"This is certainly not my Scott talking. Maybe I dialed the wrong number."

Neither said anything for an extended period.

"Scott, I'm sorry I had to go out of town, but it couldn't be helped."

"There are many things we have no control over. I'm sure what happened yesterday is one of them."

"It's very late. I know I caught you at a bad time. You must be having another of your nightmares, as I've never heard you talk to me this way."

"I really thought we had a future together...but now I'm not sure."

"*What? Scott, you're making no sense at all.* I'll call later and we can have a more sensible conversation."

"You can call, but I probably won't be here. I hope Ralph is going to take *special* care of you."

"Are you jealous? He's just a work associate."

"Is that what you call it these days? I'm sure he appreciates the extra work benefits."

She couldn't believe her ears. Now she was the one having nightmares. She started to cry, but tried not to let him hear. She was losing control and hung up the phone.

* * *

Her heart was beating a mile a minute. She never anticipated Scott's reaction to her leaving. She was confused and replayed the call in her head. She left him a note, but he never saw it. He said he got my message loud and clear.

Scott never talked to her this way. Yes, she was short with him about his doing further investigations, and yes, she did leave without talking to him. It was obvious he was jealous about Ralph, but why? He said he saw me leaving with Ralph. So, why didn't he say hello?

The whole conversation was a total disconnect. *I left him a message, didn't I? Yeah, I put it on the dresser. How could he have missed it?*

So, if Scott saw me with Ralph it had to be either in my apartment because we arrived separately, or, it had to be when we were leaving in the cab. She played back their departure. She was waiting at the curb for Ralph to bring down her luggage. The elevator was busy so he said he would wait for the next available one.

He came down no more than five minutes later. He came over to the curb, gave her keys back, helped her into the cab, and the driver put her two suitcases in the trunk. So, if Scott saw her with Ralph, that's what he saw.

She thought about her short skirt which Ralph paid special attention to when she got into the back seat. Well, she knew he wasn't actually paying attention to the skirt but was checking out her legs. *Is that what Scott is upset about? Ralph got a peek at my legs. That reminded her of the night he saw more than that part of her body. However, Scott knows nothing about that.*

Think Mercy, what could Scott be so upset about? Maybe he thought we were going away for the weekend together. However, she just told him where they were and why. He wouldn't continue to be upset, and would have been glad to hear they were on FBI business.

Scott didn't see my note. Ralph locked the door to my apartment when we left and had the key with him, which he gave me when we met on the sidewalk. No, Ralph wouldn't have done anything while he waited for the next elevator.

I'm going to kill him.

* * *

The next morning they had planned to have an early breakfast in the main hotel dining room. She wore one of Scott's yellow shirts with her black lace bra and another short black skirt. That should give the local police something to focus on.

Ralph came in the dining room and spotted her. He had a newspaper under his arm and slid into the booth.

"Good morning Mercy," Ralph said, but his eyes were focused on her chest.

She held two fingers by her right ear. "Good morning Ralph. How many fingers did I just hold up?" she asked.

"What? I didn't see you holding up any fingers."

"I thought so. I want to ask you—"

"Would you like to order now?" the waitress asked.

They both ordered, but Ralph was interested in the waitress's motion away from the table.

"As I was saying, I want to ask you about our leaving my apartment."

"Yes, what about it?"

"When I left on the crowded elevator, and left you for the next elevator…did you go back into my apartment?"

"Yes, I did. Why?"

"What did you do that for?"

"I left our itinerary on the coffee table, and had to go back for it."

"Why didn't you tell me you went back into the apartment?"

"What does that matter? I didn't give it another thought."

She looked at him, and even though he didn't look guilty, she thought he was concealing something. "Did you do anything else in there?"

The waitress brought their coffee and juice drinks.

"Before you answer me, you better not lie to me."

"As a matter of fact I did do something else." He paused. "I used the bathroom one last time."

She studied him while he prepared his coffee. "Ralph, you wanted to be a friend. If I find out you did more than what you just said…you can forget being a friend. Do you understand me?"

"Wow, you can really be a hellcat in the morning when you haven't had your coffee."

She now knew he was hiding something. "Do you remember what kept you from being written up for sexual harassment in Bermuda?" She pointed at him. "Answer me!"

"Okay Agent Strong, it was you not putting things in writing."

She was about to warn him again when their boss arrived at the table.

"Aren't we formal this morning? So, what didn't she put in writing?"

She started to prepare her coffee. "She told me what time to meet this morning, but I forgot. I guess I needed it in writing. We did get in pretty late last night," Ralph offered.

"Good morning Agent Strong, you look like you need more than coffee this morning. Didn't you get a good night's sleep?"

She looked at him. "As a matter of fact I was awake most of the night." Then she gave Ralph the evil eye.

"Is there a problem here?"

"No sir, nothing that I can't handle."

Chapter 13

I was tired, and needed a coffee. It was warm in the apartment and all I had on was my sweat pants. I retrieved the newspapers, made my coffee and sat down on the couch. The news came on the TV.

'Investigators have reported the discovery of a body, believed to be one of the missing women from Bermuda. Officials from the FBI are now in Venezuela where the body was found. Although still speculation, authorities believe the three missing women may have been kept against their will as part of a high-end-slave-trade rumored to be operating in the Caribbean area.'

That's why Mercedes was called away so quickly. Well, at least she's not spending the weekend with Ralph as part of a holiday weekend getaway.

What I don't understand is why she didn't seem to understand why I was so upset. She left me the message about what happened at the apartment…no note, messed up bed, boxers between the sheets, and showered together.

I played back what I witnessed at her apartment. I saw Mercedes standing on the sidewalk looking at her watch. Ralph was coming out the doors with her two suitcases. He handed her keys and helped her into the cab. The cab driver added her luggage into the cab. His luggage was *already* in the cab.

He came to pick her up and had access to her apartment. Maybe Ralph left me the message and not Mercedes. It fits, and that is why Mercedes was so confused with my responses.

If his suitcase was already in the cab, they didn't have time to go to bed, and take a shower together.

You son of a bitch Ralph. You still want her to yourself don't you? I hope I didn't screw myself with her.

The phone's loud ring made me jump.

..*

"Hello."

"Hi Scott, it's me. Good morning."

"Good morning Mercedes."

In concert we both said, "I'm sorry."

We laughed, and then we both said, "I figured it out." And, we laughed again.

"You first," I said.

"No, you better go."

"Okay, let me tell you what I found when I got to the apartment yesterday." I went through spotting them on the sidewalk and getting into the cab. Then I told her about the condition of the apartment.

"I'm going to kill him," she responded.

"I thought you were going away with him for the holiday weekend. The fact that you didn't clean up what happened, I mean what looked like what happened in the apartment, made me think you were really upset with me and running off with him."

"Now I know why you were so short with me on the phone. I suspected something when I talked with Ralph this morning, but this goes beyond what I ever thought he would do. I'm still going to kill him…or worse."

"Mercedes, calm down a minute. If he went through that much trouble to split us up, can't you imagine how much he likes you and wants you?"

"I guess you're right, but I'm still going to find a way to get even. I love you Scott."

"I love you too."

"So, where were you last night that I couldn't reach you?"

"Do you want the bad news, or the bad news?"

"I'm not sure. What is the first bad news?"

"Remember Maggie from the Harvard Pub?"

"Yes, and you better not have spent time with her."

65

"Define 'time'?" She didn't respond. "Given what I thought happened with you two, I went to see her dance."

"And?"

"And she was good."

"How good?"

"Unbelievable."

"Are you talking about her dancing, or something else?" I didn't immediately answer.

"So, what is the other bad news?"

"I can't say."

"What do you mean you can't say?"

"You'll only get mad at me."

"Oh Scott, tell me you didn't."

"I didn't."

"Then why can't you tell me?"

"I'll tell you later, when we're together."

"You're right Scott, it will be later…much later."

I heard the click and the dial tone.

I don't know what is worse…her thinking I spent time with Maggie, or my keeping the secret of doing her father's investigation? I guess the good news is that she didn't have sex with Ralph. *Oh shit, she thinks I did with Maggie, and now things are reversed. Will she now spend time with him to make things even in her mind?*

* * *

I pulled into Stephen's parking lot. It was a Friday, but it was the day after the 4th, so it was a long weekend for most people. The only car in the parking lot was Stephen's.

As I went up the stairs I could smell the freshly brewed coffee. I entered Stephen Strong's office.

"Well, what is slowing you down this morning?" Stephen asked turning in his chair from the window to face me.

"I don't understand."

"Well Scott, since I've known you, you take those stairs two at a time. So, what has got you down today?"

I knew I couldn't share what had happened with Mercedes. "I got to bed late last night."

"Yeah, I hoped you were able to spend enough time to see who's behind this scenario. Coffee?"

I started to get up, but Stephen held up his hand. "I'll get it, while you think about last night, or this morning."

A minute later Stephen handed me the cup and I tried to take a sip, but the cup was shaking too much.

"Would you like something a little stronger?"

"I could use it, but no thanks."

"I got a good look at the blackmailer. He came out of the station and spotted three men coming in his direction from across the street…he was motionless while his brain kicked in."

"Tell me about him."

I took a deep breath, but my mind was going back to my last conversation with Mercedes. "I would say he's in his mid-thirties, about six feet tall, slender build with brown hair and good looking. He wasn't what I had pictured. I thought I would see an ugly creep with a beard. I could id him again if I saw him. I didn't get a look at his vehicle as he went around the building on foot followed closely by the men."

"Anything else?"

"Yeah, the area he picked is like asking for trouble. I think he might reconsider his choice after last night."

"So, you think he might continue this blackmail scenario?"

"Is there anything that would make him want to stop?"

"I guess you could be right, given the fact he hasn't stopped already."

"Where do we go from here?"

"Well, if he doesn't ask for any more money, this might be the end of it. However, if he asks for more money, that's a different story."

"Stephen, maybe if you gave me a clue as to why you are being blackmailed I could figure out who might be behind it."

I watched him get up and go to the window. *Maybe he's going to share something.*

"Scott, the only thing I'm going to share with you is that it is a family issue, which if it got out, would not put me in good light with the public and my family."

"Stephen, did you have an affair?"

He took a deep breath and turned. "Yes, but this is not what this blackmail is about. That was for your ears only."

"Now you've only got me more interested in what someone could have over you. At some point if I'm going to really help you find out who's behind this, you've got to give me a little more information. I think I can help, but not given the situation as it currently exists."

"I appreciate what you're saying, but my wife is in no condition to have another scandal come to life. I will promise you this—if this continues I will give you a little more to go on, or I will take this into my own hands and end it once and for all."

"How's my firecracker of a daughter treating you?"

Chapter 14

He managed to take another roll of Polaroid pictures, but he had exhausted the poses he could put her in.

Alexis wanted so much to reach the pinnacle of beauty that she willingly posed for his picture taking. His ability to hypnotize her and create this other world for both of them was something he wished he could write a paper on.

However, it was his secret. If he could write it, he would title it 'Climb the Heights.' Those were his magic words to open her up for this amazing world of endless sex. He realized he was now lost forever, he could never relinquish her back to the normal world. They would grow old together, but he also realized he had fallen in love with her.

Soon he would say the words to bring her out of this fantasy land. She might question the strange marks on her body, but he had all the answers.

She had so much beauty and talent he wished he could share it with the world. However it was his prize and his prize alone.

He wondered how he could get her to conduct the other fantasies he so desired. Currently she was the object of the many scenarios he could conjure up. She played her role so wonderfully, with never a hesitation. He was going to find a way for her to put him as the object. He had to in order to fulfill those other fantasies. One in particular was to have the roles reversed and to have him tied to the bed.

He opened the door to their special room. She was still tied to the bed, but asleep. She should be after their hours together. This was the first time he wanted to shower alone.

He closed the door and went to the bathroom which was down the hall from the bedroom. The cool air felt good on his still naked body, and he was surprised he was getting excited again. He turned on the light, and then the shower but left it turned to the cold side. The shower was a walk-in shower and large enough for a wheel chair to maneuver. He moved the sliding shower door and entered.

The spray hit his body like ice picks and he recoiled until he became accustomed to the cold and the sensation. He quickly washed his hair and was tempted to rinse with warm water, but resisted it. He thought he heard something and paused, but then resumed his washing.

The images of Alexis were too recent and too strong and he found himself paying particular attention to his body's reaction. He dreamed it was her that was washing him and punishing him with the icy spray. He had the real thing only a few feet down the hall, but despite his soreness and the cold water he was lost in the fantasy of being her prisoner.

The shower door slid open and brought him out of his fantasy.

"Why Doctor Adler, you look like you could use some help there," Alexis said with a smile, and stepped into the shower with him.

He moved his hand away and reached for her immediately. *"No," she barked.* She moved into the cold spray like it didn't exist.

"You shouldn't be doing that to your body. It's my turn. Turn around and back up to the wall. Now raise your arms and put the back of your hands up against the wall." The hand held spray nozzle was just over his head and spraying her body. He saw her breasts now beet red from the ice pricks. "Stop looking. Close your eyes and don't move."

She moved the bar of soap up and down against his Adam's apple. Then she moved the bar across his lips. In some fashion she was torturing him. The feeling was erotic. The thoughts of being her prisoner were even more erotic. She slowly washed his shoulders and his arm pits. He could feel the cold spray bouncing off her body onto his. Then she moved the soap bar across his chest and back and forth across his stomach and navel. His body was anticipating her intimate touch, but it didn't come.

"Open your eyes and watch me," she commanded.

She was in no rush. He was enjoying the sight, but his arms were getting sore. He went to move his arms down, and she jabbed him with the soap bar. "I didn't tell you to move. Keep your arms up above your head."

He put his back to the wall and looked at her for some sign of whether she was still hypnotized. She moved her hand and the soap back to her body and resumed her washing. He realized she was enjoying the reversed roles very much. His dream was coming true.

"Now close your eyes doctor." A minute later he heard soft sounds coming from deep in her throat. He jumped when she started washing his body. They had showered together, but this time it was different.

"Do you like having the roles reversed?" she asked, in a sexy voice.

When he didn't immediately answer her she got his attention. "I asked you a question." He quickly realized he had lost all control of the situation.

"Yes." He forced an answer.

He lost all track of time, but knew if the water was warm it would have been cold by now. He considered whether he liked this situation or not, and realized she held his fate. He felt he could trust her, but at times he wondered really what he had created.

"You're hurting me," he finally spoke.

"I know I am. Do you really like having the roles reversed?"

"Yes, very much."

He knew he had lost all control, and he knew she recognized her new power.

Time was passing and he was trying to commit all of this to memory. All his senses were flooded simultaneously and although his fantasies were being satisfied, he realized he had created a monster. He was caught between being a researcher and a subject. His mind was reeling, and his body was not his any longer.

"You really love this, don't you?" she asked, bringing him back to reality.

"Yes."

"What other things can I do for you?"

"Do you really want to know?"

"Does that answer your question?"

"Yes. I'll share them, but not here, and not now."

"You my fine doctor...you are not in control any longer...I am. I can tell you're going to love the role you're going to play."

He could barely sense the cold water spray, his body was numb now. He didn't care. He was in love. He was in love with a creature he had created. He wanted to tell her he loves her, but he couldn't. He didn't care about anything any longer. He had transitioned to the object. He loved it and he could tell she loved her new role too.

Chapter 15

She had him right where she wanted him. She liked this new power she had over him. He couldn't control things any longer, and she really liked being able to dictate what they were doing. She had some surprises for the good doctor, but all in good time.

She knew she was learning some new tricks, and the old ones were also good and she loved having multiple climaxes.

Although she was much occupied at the present time, she couldn't get a new conquest out of her mind. It wasn't the doctor, it was Chris.

When he watched her the other night and she saw what he was doing, she had an incredible climax. She smiled remembering his predicament.

Her nails dug into the doctor's flesh and her teeth made him jump. She thought she heard him scream, but she really wanted to make Chris scream. She now had the power over both men, to get them to do whatever she wanted. She smiled at the thoughts of Chris being unable to resist her.

The good doctor's movement brought her back from her fantasy. She let him try to resume control of the situation, but knew he couldn't any longer. It was exciting to watch what she had created. This new power was going to be so much fun.

They had showered many times together, but this is the first time it was on her terms. At this moment she wanted what she couldn't have. She wished she was watching Chris. She wanted his hands on her body, and she wanted to reach out and touch his.

She felt sorry for the doctor, but watched in amusement. They had gone full circle. This is how she found him when she opened the shower door. She wondered if she should just leave now and return to the bedroom. *No, that's not as much fun as controlling things here. "Stop."*

He didn't answer, but moved his arms up over his head and resumed his earlier position. She watched him close his eyes. *He was now hers. She could demand whatever she wanted, and it looked like he was powerless to do anything about it.*

"The choice is yours. However, you need to tell me exactly what you want me to do." She wondered just how much power she had at this moment. *Could she actually get him to beg for what he wanted?*

"Doc...you need to tell me exactly what you want."

Although he didn't respond, his body reacted to her words.

"Doc, I'll do whatever you want, but you have to tell me what you want me to do." The ice cold spray caused her to finally want some warmth.

She saw him take a deep breath. "I want your..."

"I'm listening," she said and waited. Although he couldn't yet say the words...she had him where she wanted. "We're making progress here, good progress. Tell me Doctor Adler, what do you really want?"

He yelled his answer and in that moment their roles officially changed.

She had some surprises for him, but all in good time...all in good time.

Chapter 16

He dumped the bag full of money on his bed. He wished it was Alexis he was dumping on his bed. The scene of her with the doctor was still fresh in his mind. She was an incredible sight.

He spread the loose bills across the bed cover and instead of feeling the money he was feeling her. Then he recalled what she said, '…unless I want to lose my job, I better keep my visits between us, and I will do as she says next time.' His hands were enjoying feeling the money on the bed, but his mind was playing those words and what they meant.

She's not upset with my visits and she wants them to continue, but she wants me to do what she says. He closed his eyes and fell back against the pillows. *What does she have in mind? I can think of some things, but I can't afford to lose this job.*

He thought of the money spread out on the bed. *How could he also blackmail Doctor Adler? He would need to be discreet, or the doctor would fire him.* He saw the doctor's checking account balance on his earlier visit to his house and knew he could easily afford a few thousand dollars. The doctor couldn't afford to lose his job at the care center.

He thought about the file material he had copied, but had never read the entire file.

He planned on making a deposit of the money over the next few days and had put most of it away in stacks of $900, withholding enough of the money to buy a new Stingray. That should help his love life some. He quickly pictured Alexis riding in the convertible with her long red hair blowing in the wind. Despite his attempt to think of her with clothes on, she was indeed naked.

* * *

He pulled the folder from his bottom drawer and started reading the material he had passed over. There was a recent newspaper article about missing US citizens in Bermuda. The article was actually several articles all stapled together.

A few minutes later he had put some of the pieces together. Mercedes Strong, who was Stephen's other daughter, was an FBI profiler who helped locate the men and one woman who were still being held prisoner in a dungeon like facility. Two men were also killed by a Margaret Orion.

He held the other newspaper article and he was looking at two pictures of Margaret Orion; one after her plastic surgery and one before. Her name was really Melanie Strong. However, he was looking at Alexis' picture. Melanie Strong and Alexis Strong were twin sisters. *Twins.*

He was getting excited about the details in the file. Doctor Adler was closely following the Strong family and especially this Melanie character.

As he read the full material in the file, he was able to fill in all of the details. Mrs. Strong gave birth to twin girls. However, one of the twin girls, Alexis, was stricken with a deformity – hypertrichosis.

Hypertrichosis was described as a covering of hair on her face and other parts of her body. He had made copies of the pictures in the file and saw how she arrived at the facility, and progressed over her early childhood. The doctor's notes indicated she lost the hair around the time she entered puberty. There was a picture labeled 'Alexis at 13 – loss of lanugo hair.'

He had never been at the facility when she was this age. He studied the picture for a few minutes and then put it aside noting that it was something special.

After a few hours he now knew the Strong family secrets. Actually, it wasn't the Strong family secrets, it was just Stephen's.

There was communication in the file that Dr. Adler was to keep the twin birth a secret and that included never informing Mrs. Strong of the twin births. Stephen indicated that the deformity would crush his wife and he wanted Alexis' birth to be kept secret from everyone.

There were some legal documents in the file, but he couldn't totally understand what they meant. He assumed they were to satisfy any state birthing requirements.

However, there was a contract in the file that described Alexis' care and annual payments, which increased every two years. The payment this year alone was twenty-five thousand dollars.

However, there were two bank accounts noted in the file, one to the care facility and one to Dr. Adler. The good doctor was receiving a separate payment each year of twenty thousand dollars. He was getting paid and having sex with her…what a deal.

Chris took the picture of Alexis at thirteen and the newspaper picture of Melanie Strong and contemplated more than his next move.

Chapter 17

I was really missing Mercedes and found it very difficult to deal with the loneliness of my own bed. I was trying my best to fall back asleep. The phone's sharp ring didn't create the normal confusion at this early hour.

"Hello."

"Hello Scott, its Stephen. You sound like you were awake."

"You caught me awake. Its 6 am, what's up?"

"I need to talk to you right away. Something important has come up. Can you meet me at my office?"

"Sure, just give me a few minutes and I'll be there."

I heard the click in my ear. It must be real important judging from Stephen's behavior.

* * *

After Mercedes' upsetting call at 2 and Stephen's at 6, I was feeling the effects of little sleep. I drove over to Stephen's office building, but don't remember the drive at all.

His car was the only one in at this hour, but it was Friday of the long holiday weekend, so I wasn't surprised. I looked up at his office window, and even though it was smoked glass I could see him standing watching my arrival.

"Good morning Scott." He pointed to the couch area. I was surprised there was not the usual offer of coffee. I needed it badly this morning.

"I'm sorry Scott. Would you like a cup of coffee?"

"I can wait a few minutes. You look like you need more than coffee."

He threw the folded piece of paper at me. "I've had it Scott. Read that. I'm going to kill this son of a bitch. He has got to be stopped."

It was a simple note:

'I know more than I did before.

The price of my being quiet has just gone up. I want $10,000 to keep quiet. You need to leave the money in the usual place and manner by midnight Sunday.

If you fail to do that, I will tell your WIFE what you did, and then alert the newspapers.

Mr. Know'

I passed the note back to Stephen. He immediately went over to the bar and poured himself a drink and downed it, and poured another. "Are you up for a stiff one, Scott?"

"Sure, but not Scotch."

He poured about two inches of what looked like bourbon in a small glass, and then went back to his own glass and added some more.

I waited for Stephen to add something.

"I suppose you're wondering why my wife is now being mentioned?"

"I noticed that."

Stephen's face was red and he looked like he was going to squeeze the life out of the glass. "Okay Scott, here's the awful story, but you have to promise you will keep it to yourself. When you hear what I have to say, I know you'll know why you can't tell even Mercedes."

* * *

He spent the next hour walking me through what happened with the twin birth, the twin with the disfigurement, hiding the twin births from his wife and finding a facility to take his twin daughter. He said his wife has had some mental breakdowns, and finding out she gave birth to a baby in this condition would have severe repercussions.

For years Stephen has supported her care and has also provided an incentive for the doctor to keep things under wraps. He hasn't had contact with the doctor for years.

However, he makes sure the annual payments are made to two separate accounts.

I was still wondering if Mercedes had a twin sister.

"Scott, Melanie's twin sister is Alexis."

Stephen's voice sounded like he was in a tunnel. The image of Melanie was consuming my brain, and what she had done to me. I thought the nightmare of my two captivities was over, but I was immediately living the pain and the memory of almost losing my life twice. The room was spinning and I wondered if the drink this early in the morning without much sleep was the cause.

"Scott…Scott are you okay?"

I blinked a few times and tried to focus, but Stephen's face was fading in and out. I felt a chill and a clammy feeling. *Melanie is going to get me again.*

Stephen went over to the bar and came back with a small vial and put it under my nose. It smelled awful. He took the glass from my hand just as I was about to let it go. My mind went to Mercedes' request that I give up investigations, and I'm now wondering if it's too late to do that.

I could hear my own breathing. Stephen was just watching me and not saying anything. The room stopped spinning and I could now see Stephen waiting for me to come back into the room. The only problem is I never left.

"Scott, are you okay now?"

I took a deep breath and looked at him and then at the glass. "I guess I should have eaten something this morning. I didn't sleep very well last night."

Stephen left and came back in the room. "This might help, but it's not that fresh." He handed me a doughnut along with a bottle of Coke.

"Thanks." I ate the doughnut without stopping, and then drank the coke. "I'm okay now."

"Scott. I wanted you to know what was going on and why, but I'm going to put a stop to it now. This can't go on.

I can only support this extortion for just so long. My wife is going to find out if this keeps up, and all of this will crush her."

"Stephen, I want to involve Mike Miller in this. This is getting out of hand."

"No. You can't. I owed bringing you up to speed on this, but I can't let you tell anyone else about this."

I could see he was like a cornered rat. "Okay, then give me one more chance to find out who this guy is. Please."

"Okay then. Sunday night better tell us both who this guy is, or he won't see much of next week."

Chapter 18

I realized how desperate Stephen was to get this guy out of the picture. I think we both realized that this was going to continue until he was physically stopped. I've got my one chance to find out who the guy is, and couldn't blow it.

Stephen also made a good point. Since he was being blackmailed about his twin daughter—the man must have some knowledge about her. He suggested that the man might be connected to the care facility. Based on the man's description, Stephen ruled out that it was the doctor who he is paying behind the scenes.

I now had the address of the care facility, which I considered progress. The thought of someone at the care facility blackmailing Stephen has considerable merit. Chances are the person is not making a large income, and these recent amounts would add a considerable increase to his annual income.

I headed back to my apartment to give some thought to how to tackle this investigation and specifically what to do Sunday night. I also needed to get some rest knowing that I was going to be up late tomorrow night.

* * *

I picked up the papers Mrs. Abbott left on my stairs. It was almost 9 am, but it felt more like midnight.

I glanced at the front page of one of the newspapers and read the introduction to the story about the body of one of the missing women being found in Venezuela. Yup, that's where my Mercedes is off to. Reading about the possibility of a slave-trade gave me immediate concern for Mercedes' safety.

Then I thought about her not being alone, and being closely guarded by Ralph. Maybe by now, he was guarding her much too closely. I saw how her apartment was left, and it was obvious they had gone to bed together, and showered. However, Mercedes would have realized if she didn't clean up her apartment, I would have noticed what they had done. Her attitude on the phone didn't sound like she had left me a message.

I decided to head back to bed, but wanted to shower first. This time I was going to take a warm shower and get relaxed to get a good few hours sleep.

I didn't remember much about getting in the shower. I was doing things automatically. The warm water turned cool and I tried to warm it up. However, the ice cold water reminded me of the nightmare of being held captive by Melanie.

Although in her own way she said she had fallen in love with me, it was not really love, but a means to satisfy her appetite for sex. Having kept several men captive at the same time helped diffuse her craving, but she was still quite adept at getting my attention.

I felt the scar on my abdomen. I can remember her cutting me and the look in her eyes as I thought she was going to do something far more disastrous. Melanie knew she had my attention, and she got off on the control she had over me. Even though I tried to will my body not to react to her insistence, she was much too adept at getting the response she wanted. However, I'm alive and that's water under the bridge.

Mercedes has found a love of my scar, and tries to make light of it. However, she can't imagine what it was like to be defenseless, literally to be in the hands of a madwoman with a knife.

Now to think there's a 'new' potential Melanie waiting out there, I wanted not to put myself anywhere close to Alexis. I tried to reason that Alexis had a totally different childhood and early adult life and couldn't possibly be the monster her twin was. I felt a chill across my body and it wasn't caused by the cold water.

Alexis couldn't possibly be the monster her twin sister was...could she?

Chapter 19

"Paddy, its Mike. I'm at the office going over some of our investigations. I had a question to ask you about the Nielsen investigation."

"Good morning Mike. You're in on a holiday weekend…not that I'm surprised, but I thought you and your family were headed out to the Cape."

"We were, but our kids came down with what's going around. We thought it better to stick around. I thought I would take the opportunity to clear some things off my desk. Do you have any plans for the balance of the holiday weekend?"

"No, not really. We have company coming tonight for dinner and some cards. What did you want to ask me about the Nielsen investigation?"

"Never mind…I just found what I was looking for. I'm sorry. I should have just opened my eyes more."

"Did you hear the news about the body found in Venezuela?"

"Yes, I heard it. It doesn't look good for the other missing women, does it?"

"You know Mike, I had my doubts about whether we would ever find those people, but I think the women are indeed being held as part of the slave-trade. Now that one was found murdered, I wonder if the others will turn up the same way, or was this being sent as a warning to the others."

"I should call Scott to see if Mercedes is involved."

"Have you heard from Scott?"

"Yes, as a matter of fact, we had some drinks yesterday morning at the pub. He is…never mind."

"What were you going to add?"

"I can't say."

"Is, is a powerful word. Is he doing something he's not supposed to be doing?"

"Interesting you should ask it that way. Okay, without telling you the details, Scott is about to get himself into another investigation."

"I thought we had an understanding that we do the investigations, and he takes care of the business process side of our business."

"Yes." Mike thought about his response. "He's caught between respecting a request to help, and Mercedes strongly requesting he never get involved in any more investigations."

"So, does this involve Stephen Strong?"

"Why did you mention him?"

"Scott doesn't have too many other people that might make a request of him like that. So, it does involve Stephen?"

"I didn't say that."

"Yes, but you didn't need to confirm it. Can we take this over for him?"

"I wish we could, but I don't think he will consent to it. I'm going to give it another shot, but I'm not too confident that he will take our offer to help. We almost lost Scott twice already. I would hate to see him get in over his head again."

"Mike, Scott's doing some good things for the office, and we owe it to him to keep him away from things he shouldn't be involved in. Can we do anything behind the scenes, if he doesn't allow us to help?"

Chapter 20

Maybe it was because she was missing Scott so much, but she was enjoying the police captain's obvious interest in her assets. Ralph went off with one of the central police officers to view some related files on human trafficking.

The captain confirmed, "Ms. Strong you have come to the right place to learn about what might have happened to your citizen. Please sit down." He pointed to a seat across from his desk in his large office.

She sat down, but the overhead fan was not doing much to combat the humidity within the police station or his office. She watched Captain Chavez wipe the sweat on his brow. "Captain, now that it was confirmed that the body is that of Paula Scott, we know that she was brought to Venezuela. We're concerned for the safety of her sister and that of Ms. Quinlan, along with Mr. Damelio. I would like to know your thoughts on what happened to her." She was talking to his eyes, but they were riveted on her chest.

"I'm sorry Ms. Strong that our office is so oppressive. The humidity here is hard to deal with. Can I get you something to drink?"

"No, that's not necessary." She was surprised that he spoke English so well. She wondered what his background was.

"I suppose you're wondering why I speak English so well?"

"Yes, I was surprised." She wasn't surprised that he moved slightly to get a better view of her legs. She felt it in her best interest to allow him the benefit of her short skirt.

"I was educated in the states, and moved back here with my parents who were Venezuelan citizens. That was about twenty years ago." He moved even closer to his desk. He wiped his forehead again, but he was not hiding his interest in her body.

"That's very interesting. Where did you live in the states?" She could feel the perspiration on her chest, and put her thumb in between her two top buttons to wipe the moisture.

"We lived in Texas…Houston area to be more exact."

Mercedes watched him studying the outline of her black bra. "Very interesting. I need to ask you for your opinion of what you think is happening with our missing citizens." She undid the top button on her yellow shirt, which was starting to soak up some moisture.

"Well, you read the report on Ms. Scott. She was found nude and tied up, and she had been tortured. She was a very pretty woman, just like you." He let the words linger, and then added, "The other two women are also young and very attractive. Maybe we could examine the file together…let's say this evening at your hotel?"

"Thank you Captain Chavez for your offer. However, my boss is here and we have limited time for our investigation. If I can't learn anything from talking to you, I'm sure Mr. Gordon will be talking with other officials. Maybe we need to make some progress while I'm here." She crossed and uncrossed her legs on purpose, hoping to entice him to spend more time now with her.

He smiled and didn't immediately reply, but his eyes did. "Yes, why don't we spend a few more minutes?" He got up and came around to her side of the desk and seated himself closer to her.

It was so obvious that it caused her to smile. "Thank you Captain."

He resumed talking, but she knew he was obviously enjoying a closer look at her body, or what he could imagine she looked like under her slightly wet clothes.

"Although there is no actual evidence that Ms. Scott was connected to what is happening here in Venezuela, my thoughts are this."

She watched him take a deep breath and she was glad she had put on additional perfume before they left the hotel. The scent of Gardenia works many wonders. She thought of Scott and how she would like to be with him at this moment.

"Young women are being kidnapped and held as part of the slave trade here in our country. Young attractive white females are very much in demand. Countries such as Saudi Arabia and Yemen pay a large sum of money for such women. Pirates operate in the Caribbean area and when they find a vessel alone on the sea, they commandeer it, usually kill off any men aboard and rape the women continually until they're brought ashore."

She acknowledged, "Yes, the 'Import-ant' was last seen in Bermuda with Mr. Damelio and the three women. They would have been in the Caribbean, and could have encountered pirate activity."

"I think it would be certain that they did. I wouldn't be at all surprised if the pirates have eyes in Bermuda and ports in the Bahamas and other places, making note of interesting targets leaving port. I don't see a ring on your finger, are you not engaged?"

"No, I'm not."

"American men must be so behind the times, that they allow someone of your beauty to remain *free.*"

She noticed how he mouthed the word while licking his lips. "Thank you again, Captain. I noticed how interested you are in my…presence."

"Perhaps I can show you some of the possible places where these women might be held against their will."

She felt her skin crawl, and knew he was just looking for an opportunity to get his hands on her body. "Perhaps those locations were overlooked in your original investigations?" She noticed his expression change. "I would like to see where you are considering, but I would like my partner to accompany me."

"I see." He sat back and altered his view slightly. "What we think happens when the women are brought into the country, is that they are forced to sign some false paperwork showing they owe a large debt. Maybe for their rescue." He smiled. "The debt is so large that in order to pay for it, they are forced into being a 'domestic servant' and as such are paid for their sexual services to their new owner, and possibly a much larger circle of friends. It's not a pretty picture, but when they tire of them, they are sold to those foreign countries, which could care less about how they were treated."

"That does sound like a solid scenario."

"The ones who manage to avoid the local forced labor, shall we say, command an even higher price. I'm sure you can appreciate unspoiled goods, versus abused ones. I'm not sure why Ms. Scott was tortured, but maybe that is how the owner made his money, or got his kicks…or both."

She noticed how he was perspiring, and wanted to wipe the moisture forming again on her neck, but resisted the temptation.

"Ms. Strong, I must admit that you yourself are quite the beauty, and we don't see many redheads around these parts. You really should utilize our services while you are in this country, as there are many men who would pay a hefty amount for you."

"Thank you Captain Chavez for the compliment." However, he was insinuating she whore herself.

There was a knock on the door. The captain got up to open it, and looked like he had a pistol in his pants pocket. He didn't try to conceal the affect she had on him. When he opened the office door, Ralph was standing there with another officer.

"Are you ready Agent Strong?" Ralph asked.

"Yes." She got up and let the skirt slip to a more proper place. She held out her hand to the captain. "Thank you for your insight, and we will be talking further." He shook her hand and then held it with his other.

"Once more Agent Strong, I urge you to consider our services, and protection, while you are doing your investigation. I'm sure your group is on someone's radar at the moment. Please let me know if I can be of any service to you. Regardless, be very careful where you go, and don't go anywhere alone."

Chapter 21

Her new found power over the doctor was providing more rewards than she had anticipated. She liked being the center of his past attention, but this role reversal was incredible.

He shared his desire to have the roles reversed, and she was an excellent student. Hours ago when they first got started, she took it slow and followed his commands for what he wanted her to do to him. He was enjoying the attention and her body told her how much she liked it.

When this all started, his ankles were tied like hers had been and his hands were holding onto the headboard ropes. He wanted her to use the whip device on him, which she obliged. However, her reluctance to really whip him caused him to yell at her. That was his second mistake.

His first was allowing her to actually tie his wrists. Something happened as soon as he was immobile. She didn't totally understand the transition, but she loved her new found power. The doctor was caught between enjoying her attention and wanting to be released. She wondered if he finally realized her true condition since she failed to react to his hypnotic trance termination. However, his constant pleas to be released forced her to gag him.

She remembers that moment very well. His eyes got big as saucers and she believes he finally realized what he was getting himself into. He truly panicked when she sat on his thighs and reached behind her exposing the straight razor.

She opened the razor and studied the blade. His head was rolling from side to side. She looked at his manhood and in one quick motion cut one of his pubic hairs. He looked so relieved. He watched her split the hair with the razor.

She jumped off the bed and came back with the blindfold he used on her. She could see he realized he had lost all control and was showing honest concern. She put the blindfold on him, but he was resisting. She picked up the razor she left between his legs. She put the back of the razor between his legs and he immediately froze.

She enjoyed shaving him clean. He didn't dare move an inch, but it was obvious by his erection he was in some way enjoying this. It was more work than she anticipated and she cut him more than once. The taste of his blood was metallic, but not offensive. She could also tell her attention had him ready to explode.

Receiving punishment is not as much joy as giving it. She may never relinquish this control again, and she realized if she did, she might truly regret what he would do to her.

Despite how the doctor feels, she has found new ways to punish him and reward herself. She experienced several orgasms over the last few hours. He had no way of knowing what she was going to do to him next, or what she was doing to herself.

She stopped punishing him and just looked at what she had done. He was covered in red welts from his forehead to his feet. She wanted to roll him over, but was concerned he might overpower her. She opted not to at this time.

"Oh, wow just look at you. You're covered with red marks." She touched his forehead, cheek, neck, chest, stomach, lingering at his penis and testicles, then his thighs and feet. "Are you hurting?" He didn't move his head. She reached out and grabbed him. "I said are you hurting?"

He quickly nodded his head. She released him.

She climbed onto his thighs. "Poor baby…let me kiss away your pain." She started at his forehead kissing and licking her way down his body. When she got to his prized possessions he was more than ready to explode. She decided to go lightly because her body was more than ready to feel him inside her.

She adjusted her position and felt him inside her. He had trained her to do Kegel exercises. She did two and he exploded and she did too. She collapsed onto his chest. His heart was beating like crazy. "Doctor Adler, are you a happy boy now?"

He nodded. They still had many more hours to spend together and she had a major decision to make about which one she was going to kill. With all this new experience she couldn't get Chris out of her mind. *She wanted to use these new techniques on him. But how could she?*

She felt the moisture oozing down the inside of her thigh. She smiled at what she had accomplished and what the future was going to be like.

She wiped herself. It wasn't exactly what she expected…it was blood.

Chapter 22

He felt her heart beating against his chest. Although he was in some pain and had feared what she was originally going to do to him, especially with the straight razor, he had a feeling of exhilaration. He could smell her hair with her head on his chest, and there was a strong scent of Gardenia.

She had more than fulfilled his fantasies. He was amazed by how she took control and what she did without his instructions. He wanted to go to sleep and didn't care that he was still tied, gagged and blindfolded. His biggest concern was that she failed to react to his attempt to break her trance.

There was no way she could have been faking being hypnotized all those times. It would have been impossible for her to willingly do all those crazy things he made her do. Or, was it?

* * *

It was easy for him to fall asleep. Being tied up reminded him of being in his crib as a child. His parents had buckled him into his crib each night. He had tried to rationalize why they did this, and he thought they might have feared his hurting himself somehow.

It felt like they had slept for hours. Alexis was still lying on top of him when he woke. He tried to take stock of the parts of his body where her body was against his. It was harder to do than he expected. He could feel her warmth, but he wanted to feel where her breasts were against his chest.

"Are you awake now Doctor?"

He responded with a nod of his head.

"Would you like me to remove the gag and the blindfold?"

He nodded again. He felt her push the blindfold up over his head and opened his eyes. She was looking right into his eyes. She didn't look like the same person he remembered seeing before all of this. She seemed to have a new sense of superiority.

She lifted his head and undid the gag. He watched her searching his eyes. He loved her, and now loved her even more. She kissed him with a passion he had never felt before.

"Are you happy now?" she said lifting herself slightly off his body.

"Yes…very. Are you?

"That was incredible. But look at you…you have welts all over you."

He realized he was still tied up. "Are you going to untie me?"

"Do you want me to?"

"Yes and no."

"I don't understand."

"I have to use the john."

She smiled. In that case—no."

"What do you mean?"

"I mean, *no* you can't go to the john."

"Alexis, I have to go. I'm going to explode."

"I already did." She reached between her legs and showed him the blood.

"Did you get your period?"

"Yes, but that is a good thing. I'm not pregnant."

He realized she never responded to his words which would terminate her trance. "Heights climbed." He looked for a reaction, but she just smiled.

"Say it again Doctor."

"Heights climbed…heights climbed."

"I'll say. I never had that many orgasms."

He could tell she was looking for a reaction. She's been faking being hypnotized all those many times. She did all of those things he thought she never would without being in that stage.

"That's right my good Doctor. I faked all of those many times you thought you put me under. You did some *very dirty* things to me." She reached down and grabbed him. "You were a very bad boy weren't you?"

His excitement started building. "Yes I was."

"Bad boys need to be punished…isn't that correct?"

"Yes, but I have to go to the bathroom."

"We'll take care of that." She slid off of him and stood beside the bed. "I'll be back in a minute. Don't leave and don't pee either."

* * *

She was gone for what seemed like an hour. He was ready to explode and tried to ignore the pressure on his bladder. *She said she was going to punish me, but is this what she meant?* He was afraid he couldn't hold it any longer.

"Tada." She jumped into the room.

He noticed she was holding a milk bottle, and knew what she was planning on doing with it.

"I'm glad you managed to hold it. I was starved and made myself something to eat. I also inserted a tampon. Want to see?"

He didn't answer and didn't need to. She jumped up on the bed and she was close enough for him to see the string. "Do you like what you see?" She stayed poised over his face and she turned her head to look at his lower body. "Oh, look at that. You do like what you see." She pushed on him with the milk bottle. "Oh well, lets see how we can do this."

She turned around, her thighs beside his head now. She stuck him into the bottle. "You better relax junior or we're not going to be able to do this without making a mess."

It was hard for him to relax with her parts only inches away from his face. He tried to think of other things, but it wasn't working very well.

"I guess given our positions it's hard for you to relax. Right?"

"Please, I need to go."

She moved off him and stood beside the bed. "Okay, now do what you need to do." He was inside the bottle which she was holding between his legs like it was a urinal.

He was still somewhat excited and as he started to pee it burned. He watched her eyes as he filled up the bottle. He kept going and going and wondered if the bottle was going to be big enough.

She went over to the dresser and he was shocked by what . she had in her hand.

"Please don't do anything with that." He watched her put the camera up to her eye. The camera made a click and the picture slid out. "Alexis, please."

"Please what doctor?" She bent down and took a close up. "These aren't the only pictures I took while you were sleeping. I'm taking them with me, so I can think of you when you're not with me."

"Alexis please. You can't. If anyone sees them I will lose my job."

"Exactly."

She looked at the last picture and showed it to him. "Don't you agree you look very sexy all tied up with a bottle of piss between your legs?" She watched as the other picture developed, turning it to orient it. "This one is a classic, no matter which way you turn it." She showed it to him and he immediately pulled against his restraints.

She removed him from the bottle and held it up to study the contents. "Wow, I guess you needed to go. Feel better now?"

"Yes. I feel better now." He watched her walk over to the dresser and put the bottle on it. He was glad she took it away.

"Now, my good Doctor, bad boys need to be punished." She came over to the bed and untied one ankle and then the other. "Right?"

This was his chance to take control.

"Now, put your legs over one another."

He hesitated and she took his breath away with a directed slap. He did as she instructed. She tied the ropes around his ankles. Then untied the rope holding his right wrist and tied it to the left bedpost, and then tied his left rope to the right one.

"Now roll over."

He hesitated and she quickly bit him. He rolled away and was now on his stomach.

She didn't say a word and just stood beside the bed. Finally she broke the silence. "Do you want to be punished, or should I just go upstairs and leave you?" She ran the whip across his shoulder and down his back over his butt.

She struck him across the shoulders. "It's your choice. But you can make me pay later if you want. What will it be?"

He felt his erection and moved his hips slightly.

She reached under him. "I guess I got my answer. You're such a bad boy and such a sick man."

Whack…whack…whack.

Chapter 23

Chris was working his Saturday evening shift at the Lighthouse Manor. Alexis' room across from his desk more than occupied his attention.

She wasn't due back until Sunday night with Dr. Adler. He couldn't resist the temptation of being in her room again. The other patients wouldn't think anything out of the ordinary and he could always offer a reason to be in there.

He opened the door to her room. The image of her taking her shower the other night came flooding back. He turned on the light in the bathroom and stood at the entry. She was an incredible sight and the fact she knew he was watching her that night excited him now.

More importantly, the comment she whispered to him about doing whatever she told him to do, increased his excitement. '…if I wanted to keep my job.' *That wouldn't be a problem. I wonder how far she would take that.* Well, now that he knew what the doctor was doing with her, could he use that to trump her threat? Thinking about that, could he even get Doctor Adler to allow him time with her?

He left the light on in the bathroom and went to her bedroom area. He felt the bedspread and pictured her on it the way she was at the doctor's. The next thing he checked out was her dresser drawers. He learned she was very organized.

Her jewelry, some cosmetics and personal items were in the top left drawer. Bras were in the second drawer, and panties and socks in the bottom drawer. There was nothing surprising about any of those. Then he spotted something black at the bottom of the pile. He pulled the item out and it was a pair of black panties. They were a thin transparent nylon, cut like a bikini bottom. He quickly opened the second drawer and found the matching bra. The doctor must have bought those for her.

Why didn't she pack those for the doctor's house? As a matter of fact, where did she get jewelry? He must have bought those for her too. This was getting more interesting by the minute.

He continued looking in her dresser. T-shirts were in the top right drawer, shorts in the second drawer. Sweaters were in the bottom drawer. He started to close the drawer and decided to see if there was anything on the bottom. He felt a solid item...a book.

He pulled it out and started looking at the contents. It was her diary. The first entry was when she was twelve.

'Doctor Adler took me to his house today for the first time. He said he was going to hypnotize me to help me with my therapy. He explained to me about the command that would put me under, and the command to bring me out of it – Climb the Heights and Heights Climbed.

He spent several minutes making me very calm and then gave me the command to put me under...but it didn't work. I was afraid to tell him I wasn't under, and then as time passed, I couldn't.

He had me take off all my clothes and then took pictures of me in various positions. Then he took off his clothes and had me do things to his body. They shocked me at first, but I have to admit I liked the feelings along with touching him. I have to admit I liked the feelings way too much and shouldn't have. I don't think I can ever tell him that I wasn't hypnotized especially since I played along with him.

I hope that this is something that continues between us. My fear is that he finds me ugly. I still have a thin coating of hair covering my body, but it doesn't seem to bother him. And, it seems to be decreasing lately. He says that it will completely go away someday soon. I think he finds me attractive, well, he constantly tells me that I will be very beautiful someday.'

He flipped the book to another page.

'Two months ago I turned thirteen. My body continues to have big changes. The ugly body hair completely went away about four weeks ago. My face has no signs of the ugly hair, but I still have a problem looking in the mirror. I still picture the way I looked with the hair on my face and body.

Doctor Adler told me that I continue to get more and more beautiful. He really likes me a lot. As I mentioned in an earlier entry two months ago, I started to bleed between my legs and panicked. When I went running to the doctor's office he took me back to my room and explained what it was. He said I was becoming a young lady.

When I was with him last night he commented on how my breasts were developing, and said that was another sign of how I continued to become a young lady. There's also a patch of red hair between my legs, which is almost blonde. He thinks he put me under and took more pictures of me without any clothes on. I can tell by his reaction he really likes how my body is developing. He's spending even more time with my breasts and touching me.

I find this hard to write, but I have to. When he believes I'm under he changes into a different person. At first it scared me, but now I would like to spend all of my time being the object of his experiments.

He left me alone for an hour and asked me to read a soft-covered book titled 'Candy.' I read parts of it and when he came back in I wanted him to play with my body. He refused and said I had to do what I wanted to my own body. I was uncomfortable, but since I was 'under' I had to do it. I did that before in my bedroom, but no one was watching me. I liked him watching and getting excited.

He showed me what he called the magic spot and within several minutes I couldn't hold back any longer and screamed. He laughed and laughed. Then he asked me to kiss him down there. Since then he really likes that and I have found some new tricks that I can tell he really likes.

He says it doesn't really hurt, but I can tell by the way he flinches, that it does. I have found a new secret weapon. If I tease him he isn't the good doctor any longer.'

Chris wanted to skip to the later pages, but heard something outside in the hall. He quickly put the diary back where he found it, closed the drawer and headed for the hall door.

* * *

The door almost hit him in the face as he reached for it. She jumped back not expecting him to be in her room. She closed the door behind her.

"What a surprise to find you in my room. It's not time yet. What were you doing in here?"

He noticed the bathroom light was still on. "I couldn't resist it any longer...I had to come in your room."

"That gives me an idea for later. However, Doctor Adler didn't see you and I think he's headed upstairs to see if you're there. You better leave."

He started out, but she jumped in his way. "Do you remember what I said yesterday?"

"Yes, how could I forget?"

"Good. Then I expect you back here later tonight. I had to come back early because I got my friend, but you can *come* later. Do you understand what I mean?"

"Yes. Did you have a good time at the doctor's?"

"That surprises me...you know what we were doing when you looked in the window." She put her arms out to the side. "Maybe I can help you later."

Chapter 24

I decided to check out the care facility address Stephen had given me. The money drop wasn't scheduled until Sunday, but I wanted to see if I could spot the guy who made the pickup the other night.

Even though it was a holiday weekend, the Saturday night traffic was lighter than a normal weekend. It was only a fifteen minute drive to Belmont. I parked across the street and up a few doors. I could see the front walk leading from the side parking area to the front door. The spot lights lit up the front of the building. It was a nice looking white Georgian Colonial with black shutters beside the windows and front door.

I soon spotted a Cadillac pull into the driveway. A man dressed in a white shirt, gray pants and a blue blazer got out of the driver's seat and went around and opened the front passenger's door. When they came around the back of the car I could see a tall woman beside him with long red hair. That has to be Alexis. However, I couldn't see the woman's face, but I saw Melanie's.

I got a chill up my spine. To think Melanie had a twin sister was almost like my captivity wasn't over.

The man held her arm and helped her up the front stairs. They stopped at the entrance and spoke briefly to each other. The man pulled her close to him and then opened the front door.

A minute later a light in the first window on the first floor went on. I imagined it was either an office or maybe her room. I got out of my car and went over to the parking lot. There was a gold Pontiac Tempest in the parking lot. I figured it was about a '63. I wrote the license plate number down and decided to write the Cad's down too.

I didn't know if the Tempest was connected to the blackmailing, but thought it would be good to have the plate. Mike might be able to research the license plates for owner and address info. *See, I already anticipate Mike helping. I'll cross that obstacle later.* I walked back to my car hoping no one had seen me.

About fifteen minutes later the same man came out of the building and climbed into the Cad and drove off in the opposite direction.

While I sat there I tried to think about the blackmailer. He, or she, had to be someone who knew about Alexis. The person most likely had to be someone who worked at the facility and had access to information that indicated Stephen was the father.

It could also be someone who wasn't connected to the facility, but had access to the doctor's files including Stephen's address. In fact, the person wouldn't know that this was being kept under wraps unless documentation showed that.

The image of the woman walking with long red hair hanging down the back of her jacket reminded me of Mercedes. She has no idea of what her father was keeping secret from her and her mother. Her image was replaced with the image of Stephen having an affair with another woman. The thoughts of Mercedes with Ralph in a foreign country came to mind.

Would Ralph try to seduce Mercedes? How could he honestly resist her? From the first day we were introduced in Paddy's office, I have been uncomfortable around her. She knows how to get me going. The image of her in that cabin dressed in a towel too small for the task came into view. *If I was Ralph, it would be very hard to ignore her. I don't think I could blame him for trying either.*

Chapter 25

Alexis put her back to the door and took a deep breath. The image of Chris doing the things she was thinking of was getting her excited again.

The front door opened and closed and she knew the doctor was leaving. He wouldn't be back until Monday morning. *Could she occupy Chris's time until then? Most likely not, but she could put a dent in his time. That made her smile, because what she had seen was not anywhere close to being dented.* She heard the sound of the Cadillac's engine.

She now had the power over the doctor, and the thought of having two men within her control caused her body to react. Then it dawned on her...*what was Chris doing in her room?* The light in the bathroom was on, but the shower is dry. She hustled over to her bed—no problem there. She opened her drawers. When she got to her bra drawer she discovered they had been moved.

The black bra was not folded the way she folded it. When she inspected the panty drawer, the black panties were also disturbed. She smiled, *that my dear Chris will cost you some pain.* Then panic set in.

She dropped to her knees and opened her bottom right drawer. She reached for her diary and quickly discovered he had indeed moved it. Those were entries she had not intended anyone to see. If he had read any of those he would know what she and the doctor had been doing, but worse, how she had been faking being hypnotized and her inner most thoughts of how she felt about what he did to her. The only thing in there is either private thoughts or things about the doctor. She didn't know exactly what she was going to do about his snooping, but he's gone too far now.

My dear dear Chris...at some point you are going to really regret what you just did. You have crossed a line and have no idea what I am capable of doing. The doctor also trusts me and lets me tie him up...you both have made some unfortunate mistakes.

She looked in her dresser mirror, and noticed, maybe for the first time, how beautiful she looked. She started to undress and knew what she was going to wear for Chris' visit.

Chapter 26

Max Gordon went off with two police officers to visit where the body of the woman was found. Although Ralph was with her all day, he seemed to be focused on their investigation and didn't give any impression he was interested in her.

The way the captain behaved looking at her in her sweaty outfit, she was very surprised Ralph wasn't paying much attention to her. She checked and the second top button on her yellow shirt was indeed unbuttoned. She knew her shirt was sticking to her bra and left little to the imagination.

It was now early evening and they had skipped lunch. The captain had given them three areas where they might want to investigate. Their police officers had questioned people, but nobody provided any information. The captain insinuated the locals would certainly want to spend time with her, and in the process might divulge some guarded information.

The police officer pulled the unmarked car into a parking spot. "Would you please give us a few minutes to discuss something in private?" Mercedes leaned over to the officer.

He nodded and left them alone.

Mercedes turned to Ralph. "You seem very distant today. Is it because of our discussion about what you did at my apartment?"

"You made it clear I was out of line. I'm giving you the space you want."

"Thank you." She wanted to say more to him, but hesitated.

"Are you worried that I didn't notice how beautiful you look and also how sexy you look in that damp outfit. And, if I might ask…why a black bra?"

"There's my Ralph." She thought about those words for a moment too long. "Max thought wearing an outfit to get the authorities' interest would be in our best interest. It worked.

The captain was about to cop a feel if we spent any additional time together. In fact, he suggested he come to my hotel to work on the case some more. I know what he had in mind."

"*Your Ralph, huh?*"

"That was a bad choice of words. I wasn't used to your not paying attention to me."

"So, are you saying you like my attention?"

"Let's just say I am used to it."

He turned in the seat to face her. "Do you know how hard it is to work close to a beautiful woman like you? You move in a certain way, and it takes my breath away."

"I think we better stop this discussion right now."

"No, you brought this up, and you have to know my side of the story. It was all I could do not to make love to you the night you had too much to drink and didn't remember what had happened. The next morning your expression was priceless when you thought we had indeed shared each other. But, we didn't. Mercy, its hard working with you, but it would be worse if we weren't together."

"Thank you for respecting me that night."

"Now you know why I sabotaged your apartment. I had hoped it would open the door for us, but I'm sorry. It was stupid of me. I also never thanked you for not filing paperwork of my harassment...so thank you again."

"Wow. I didn't expect all of that. I can tell how much you like me. I think you're an excellent agent and I enjoy working with you. I'll try to make it easier on you to work with me." She pulled at the front of her shirt, and buttoned the second button.

"Mercy, we're still trying to do our investigation here." He reached over and undid her shirt button. "Like I said its hard working with you, but you're right about how we need to get information from these locals. Leave the buttons the way they need to be, and I'll just try not to get hard...I mean, deal with it."

"I guess now we understand each other, and it's nice to know how you feel. However, my heart is with Scott." She smiled and closed her fist over her heart. She watched his eyes and his expression and knew what he was thinking without him saying it. She pushed him. "Let's get this show on the road."

It was plain as the nose on her face that when they approached their driver he had only seen her walking his way. *I guess the outfit will do the trick.*

* * *

"Miss, it is not good you go into cantina. Mr. Ralph and I go, and you stay in car," the police driver advised.

Mercedes studied the man, and knew he was just trying to be helpful and to protect her. He was dressed in civilian clothes to hide his identity. However, anyone looking at Ralph or her would know they were not from this country. Especially, since Jose was their interpreter.

"That's okay. I appreciate your advice, but I have to participate."

"Mercedes, maybe he is making a good point. If we find someone who wants to share information with us, then we can get you...to keep his interest."

"No. I don't think that makes any sense. I'll go with you."

"Then we're not going to go in there. Jose has told me privately that several women have gone missing in these three joints. They have never been seen again. Why don't we do this? I'll go in with Jose and if things look promising, I will come get you to join us. I promise."

"Okay, but you promised." She said the words, but she didn't feel comfortable about saying them. She grabbed the keys to the car and headed back.

It was an hour later when Ralph and Jose returned to the car. The broken glass next to the car immediately gave Ralph a feeling that something terrible had happened.

They both ran to the car and found it empty and Mercedes gone. There was no sign of any struggle, but obviously she hadn't left on her own.

Chapter 27

It wasn't a cold night, but a chill went up my spine. I
checked the car mirrors to make sure I wasn't in danger.
There was nothing, but I still had the strange feeling.

Despite my concern about Ralph, I couldn't help thinking
about Mercedes doing a murder investigation in a
dangerous place. I hope he's keeping an eye on her, but not
too close an eye.

Mercedes would make a perfect target for a slave trade
scenario. She would command a very high price and given
the fact she might have had only one lover, she would be
the cream of the crop. *Why the hell am I even considering
this scenario? If something awful were to happen to her I
would never get over it. Do your job Ralph, and just your
job. Have I been her only lover?*

I know I had to get used to her being in dangerous
investigations…that's her job and she's good at it. *If we got
married would she continue working for the FBI? Would
she alter her assignments if we had children? Would we
even have children?*

I thought of our conversation about my seeing Maggie
dance, and what she might have thought happened between
us. She did hang up on me. Maybe that would give her an
excuse to be with Ralph. No, she would be mad at him too.
What if they separated and did their own investigations. As
much as I didn't like the thoughts of them working closely
together, I didn't like the thoughts of her doing her own
investigation.

Speaking of investigations…what the hell am I doing?

The bright headlights shining on my rearview mirror and
racing up behind my parked car made me wonder if this
was the blackmailer. The car stopped right behind my car
and the blue lights lit up the neighborhood.

* * *

They didn't buy my story that I pulled over to rest for a minute. I should have thought about my answer before I said I just pulled over. Someone in the neighborhood spotted my white convertible and my checking out the care facility. I just hoped nobody at the care facility noticed the police action.

In a way, I was glad the Belmont neighborhood is where my car was left. If it was Roxbury who knows what would be left of it. I had never been in a police station before, so I was very uncomfortable. The metal chair in the small office was uncomfortable, and nobody has come in to talk with me for over an hour.

I gave them my license and registration, which they have not yet returned. My trump card was Mike Miller. I heard a key in the lock and turned to see a familiar face. It was one of the detectives on the task force.

"Well, Scott, what a surprise to have you in our precinct. What the fuck were you doing?" He threw the door shut and took a seat in the swivel chair.

"Hi Paul. I didn't expect to see you." Paul was our receptionist's boyfriend, Paul Brosque.

"You stole my line. Scott, you have to level with me. You were seen parked for almost two hours and at one point you were spotted in the parking lot of the...Lighthouse Manor. There have been some burglaries in that neighborhood and you are the first candidate we've seen. I know you're not up to something bad, what's going on?"

I was happy it was Paul. "I really can't say."

He smiled at my answer. "Okay, you give me no choice. I guess we're going to keep you for a lineup in the morning. We have a few witnesses to one of the break-ins and we'll get them down here to see if they can pick you out." He let that scenario sink in.

"Can I call Mike Miller?"

"Sure. Come on Scott, you can tell me what's going on. I know you're not a second-story man. Talk to me. Besides, Colleen will kill me if she knows I hassled you. It's a good thing I overheard your name and told the Captain I knew you and could vouch for you. I'm out on a limb here and you have to help me."

"I can't really say…that's why I would like to talk with Mike."

"Scott, let's play twenty questions."

I remember my ride up to Waterville with Lisa. That's the last time I played twenty questions and what followed that game was a lot of fun. "Okay, but can I ask that what I'm going to tell you be kept a secret?"

"I can't promise anything, but I'll do my best. Are you doing an investigation?" I immediately reacted to his question. "Okay, so now that we have determined that, what does it involve?"

"I'm always impressed with how you detectives quickly put pieces together." He smiled at my comment. "Mike knows I'm doing an investigation. Someone I know is being extorted. That person wants me to find out who is doing it."

"Extortion is a serious felony. Maybe we need to know more about this."

"Paul, if this gets out…well it needs to be kept under wraps. Can you help me out here, please?"

"Scott, your butt was saved twice already. Haven't you learned to focus on other things? Why do you keep getting yourself involved where you don't belong?" He closed the folder on the desk. "Do you have Mike's number?"

"Do you want it?"

"Give me the number and maybe Mike can help me where you can't."

* * *

An hour later Paul came back into the room. "Okay Mr. Tucker," he said with a wink. "You're free to go. My Captain knows Mike very well, and I shared with him that you were doing some undercover work for Mike."

I wondered what Mike had shared with him, but I was happy I could leave.

"A piece of personal advice to you. I would let Mike take over this investigation. It sounds like this could be life threatening, and unless you're a cat with nine lives, I would keep your distance."

"Thanks Paul. I appreciate the input." I stood to leave. "Can I get a ride to my car?"

"What car?"

* * *

It took Paul a few phone calls, but they located my car. I hadn't realized I parked it in a no parking after 10 PM zone and found out the car was towed.

Since Belmont contracts with private towing companies, there's an incentive for the towing companies to actively seek violators. Once they find them, they call the police and they issue a ticket and away the vehicle goes. Everyone wins, except the car owner.

It was midnight and I was tired, but glad I wasn't being held any longer, and found my car.

It cost me $75 for the tow, and the cost of the ticket another $40. I was lucky someone was at the impound lot to take my money, or I would have had to wait until 7 the next morning.

I was just leaving when I spotted Mike's car pulling into the entry area.

Chapter 28

She had no way to protect herself. When the men with hoods over their heads smashed the car window, they quickly dragged her out, covered her head with a hood, put her hands behind her back and cuffed her.

She was going to scream for help, but realized there was a gun being held against the back of her head. She was dragged a short distance and then thrown in the back of a van. Several men climbed in with her and slammed the van doors. They were talking in Spanish, laughing and pulling at her clothes. She heard her shirt rip as it was pulled off her. Then she felt someone grab her bra straps and she kicked out.

Someone up front yelled something to the men and then yelled again. Slowly the person removed his hands from her bra straps but she was being fondled. The same voice yelled out again, and the man next to her let her go. He said something in her ear, and although she didn't understand what he said, knew it couldn't be good.

Mercedes felt the cool air on her almost naked chest and realized the cool air was also on her thighs. There was no way she could pull her skirt down and just kept her legs tightly closed. *She now knew what Scott must have felt like being held a prisoner by her sister. She wondered if she would ever see Scott again.*

She could tell by the whispers the men were enjoying her condition. Periodically, one would whisper something and the others would laugh. She felt a hand slide up the inside of her thigh and a finger slide into the top of her bra cup. She knew it was dark in the back of the van and the men were being careful not to be discovered.

She was about to scream at what was happening, but felt the gun barrel press against her head again. If this was bad, she knew it would only get worse. If these were the same men who killed one woman being held, they had nothing to lose.

She was not going to let them know she was crying. *Strange she thought to herself, all my adult life my features were an asset...now, it is obvious they are a liability. There were only two ways she would get out of this alive. The police would find a way to rescue her, or Ralph might.*

She felt the hand grab the crotch of her panties and heard the sound as they ripped away. The next thing she felt was the back of a knife sliding between her breasts and then lift off her to cut her bra off. The cool air against her body told her they could now see what only Scott ever saw.

For some strange reason she was thinking of Scott going to see Maggie perform. Her mind was reeling, she remembered putting the small towel on in the cabin, which she removed to give Scott his unwrapped Christmas present.

She was trying to ignore what they were doing, but she was sobbing now. Then the vehicle came to a sudden stop, and the luxury of hands no longer touching her body. The metal click of the doors opening signaled the men to drag her from the van. She felt the only thing still covering her nakedness, what was left of her skirt, and her bra hanging in two pieces from her shoulders.

The rough wood hurt her bare feet. Despite all of the confusing banter, she heard the waves hitting the shore and then the heavy metal door clunk open, and smelled the moisture laden air. She was being taken to a building on the waterfront.

"Help me," she screamed. For a brief instant she felt something hit the back of her head, then sharp pain, and then a sense she was falling.

Chapter 29

"Mike, I didn't expect to see you here," I said.

"I could say that about you too, Scott. Are you going to give this charade up now?"

"Thanks for helping get me out."

"You, my man, are very lucky that Paul was there. You could have been locked up for quite a while."

"You're right, but can we get out of here now?"

"Let's go get a coffee and talk about some things."

I could tell it wasn't a suggestion.

We were on our second refill when Mike finally brought up what I was doing tonight. "Scott, what the hell were you doing?"

I took a deep breath before answering. "I wanted to see if I could get a look at the care facility and the people who worked there."

"Okay, so what did you discover?"

"Actually, not much." Then I remembered the license plate numbers. "I did write down two plate numbers." I reached for the paper and handed it to Mike. "One of these was a Cadillac and the other for a Pontiac."

"I see that. What do you want with these plate numbers?"

"Well, do you think you can run a plate search and find out who owns these vehicles?"

"I could, but why? What is going on?"

"One of these cars might be the guy who is blackmailing Stephen."

Mike looked at the numbers. "Okay Scott. I think it's now time for us to help you with this case...in fact, I think it is time we took over this case."

I started to open my mouth.

"Scott, you're not trained to do this shit. You're going to get in trouble, if not killed."

I thought about what he said, and part of me wanted to give up this investigation. However, it wouldn't be fair to

Stephen to drop it, and certainly not acceptable to turn it over to Mike. "How about I keep you informed about what I'm doing?"

"Scott, this whole thing is getting out of control. You have no idea what you might be getting into. Okay, let's say you continue with this…what is your next step?"

"Does that mean you will run the plates for me?"

"Regardless of who is doing the investigation, the plates are a good starting point. So, yes, I will run the plate numbers for you. What are you going to do next?"

"Well, the next money pickup is scheduled for tonight. I plan on being there."

Chapter 30

He stood at the entry to the room which was a hotbed of passion just a few hours ago. He wanted Alexis to be with him for the entire holiday weekend. However, she was complaining of cramps from her period.

All he had now were the memories and the Polaroid pictures. The pictures she took of him were missing. She took them with her. He really didn't want to see them, especially the last two shots she took.

He went through the pictures he had taken of her. She was an incredible sight. Even though the pictures were black and white, the contrast of her white body against the black sheets immediately caused his body to react. He could tell his breathing was rushed and he adjusted himself. The absence of pubic hair brought the memory of her shaving him, and his fear she could do so much more damage.

The ropes were calling to him. A few minutes later he was naked on the bed. His ankles were tied by the ropes and one wrist was. He had one free hand and was studying each photo. He recalled being totally tied up and Alexis in control.

The welts were just faint red marks now, but he remembered each strike. It was painful then, but grand now. The interesting thing was the look in her eyes when she was delivering the blows. She got very much into it, and at one point he feared she would cause some permanent damage to his special parts.

Her twin sister had kidnapped men, tortured them and killed some of them. Even though he knew Alexis for all these years, was she capable of doing those things?

Despite all of the hours of lovemaking, he was very excited now. He put the current photo down and felt the heat in his groin. He closed his eyes and remembered being blindfolded. It wasn't him doing this to his body now, it

was her. She was losing control and he loved it. He was bad
and she was punishing him.

She was amazingly bad. He soon felt drained and tired.
He slipped his free hand through the remaining loop and
pictured her taking more photos while he was defenseless.

Chapter 31

It was after midnight. He had completed all of his nightly duties and couldn't wait any longer to visit with Alexis.

He opened her bedroom door and the only light in the area was the bathroom light. She wasn't in the bathroom. He silently crept into her bedroom area. Even in the limited light he could see her pure white body lying on her back on the bed. She had the black bra and bikini panties on. She was sound asleep.

He wanted her awake, but all in good time. He was now standing beside her bed committing her image to his memory. She was gorgeous. He strained to see through the flimsy material and as his eyes adjusted could make out her nipples and areolas. The dark room and her white breasts made the dark bra disappear. He wondered if his heavy breathing would wake her.

He looked at the junction of her thighs and the small material covering her special part. Once again the material seemed to disappear and he could make out the light covering of hair beneath it. He adjusted his erection.

Her face is what he wanted to see next. However, it was hard to remove his eyes from the beauty only inches away. He wanted to reach out and feel her body. Instead he slowly traced his eyes up across her stomach, her navel, her breasts and then her face.

At the same time he noticed her eyes were staring at him, her hand grabbed him through his pants. "That was exciting for me, and I can tell it was for you too." She squeezed him hard.

It took his breath away. He was shocked she had been awake all this time.

"I've been waiting for you to come. You're late. I almost thought you might have decided not to come. However, I can tell you are glad you did." She was still holding him tightly. "Am I hurting you?"

He took a deep breath. "No, not really."

She squeezed him even harder and he yelled out.

"Shush. You will wake the neighbors." She let go of him and he took another deep breath.

"Take your clothes off," she commanded.

He hesitated. He felt the pain as she gripped him between his legs.

"Time is a wasting. Now, take your clothes off."

Less than a minute later he had his clothes off and was still standing beside the bed, and was standing at attention too.

He watched her quickly swing her legs over the side of the bed so they were on either side of his legs. "Did I hurt you?"

He looked down and saw her staring between his legs.

"Yes…a little."

"Poor baby." She kissed the end of his penis. "Did that take the pain away?"

"No, not really."

"What do you want Chris?" He didn't answer her. "Do you want to see my body?"

"Yes."

The bedside lamp went on. He felt so stark naked.

"*That,* is so much better." She reached out to him with two hands and he heard his breath escape. He felt her breath against his body. "Okay, now you can leave." She let go of him and then moved to lie on the bed.

He was crushed and just stood there.

"I said leave. Go *now* or I will scream."

"You were going to show me your body."

"I changed my mind. Now leave."

"Please. What did I do wrong?"

"You didn't do anything wrong. I made a mistake allowing you to come in my room."

"But, you wanted me too." He looked down and his erection was shrinking.

"I can see you are upset. Touch yourself."

He hesitated.

"You are making the same mistake. If I tell you to do something…you are to do it without thinking about it. Now, *touch* yourself."

He put his hand around himself.

"If I ask you something, you also have to give me an honest response without any hesitation. Do you understand?"

"Yes."

"Good. Do you like the feel of your hand?"

"Yes."

"Very good. I'll give you a reward." She reached behind her and unhooked her bra and very slowly lifted it off her breasts to expose them to him. "You like?"

"Yes."

"I can tell. You are getting more excited. Now move your hand."

He didn't hesitate.

"Take it easy. I said to move your hand, but do it slowly."

He slowed his movement down.

"You are starting to leak. *Stop.* "

He stopped, but it was hard to.

She slid over and her tongue wiped at the tip. "You like?"

He answered breathlessly, "Yes."

She slid back onto the bed again. "Good boy. You deserve another reward. Take my panties off."

He reached and started to take them off in a rush.

"No. I want you to take them off with your lips and your teeth."

He tried to remove them as instructed, but she purposely kept her legs together and her butt pressed into the sheet.

He could smell a mixture of Gardenia and womanhood.

"Yes, I have my period. Does that bother you?"

He didn't answer, and she gripped him taking his breath away. She was now totally naked. She lifted her knees and he could see the string.

"Pull it out." She touched his lips. "No, the same way as you did the panties," she said as she started stroking him.

Chapter 32

When I got to my apartment I still had a strange feeling and wanted desperately to hear from Mercedes. I think something happened, but I have no way to reach her. I said a silent prayer and truly hoped my senses were tricking me, but somehow I knew differently.

I was worried about Mercedes. She was upset with me, but it wasn't exactly Ralph I was worried about.

I had no way to contact her, and I wasn't sure she would be calling me anytime soon. She thinks I might have spent time with Maggie, and I did, but not the way she thinks.

Recalling our previous phone call, I should not have played a game with her, telling her I had bad news and bad news. I'm not at all surprised she hung up on me. Now, I wish I could hear her voice, even if she was yelling at me. *How the hell am I ever going to live with the danger she faces on some of the FBI cases?*

My phone rang and I rushed to answer it. "Hello."

"Hi Scott, it's me."

"Oh, hi Mike."

"Well, that is not the response I anticipated."

"I'm sorry Mike. I thought it might be Mercy calling back."

"I take it you still haven't heard from her?"

"No, and I'm starting to feel uncomfortable. She is in a foreign country where women are missing and turning up dead."

"She is trained and she's not alone. You might be feeling your own vulnerable situation."

"I might be, but not having a way to contact her or anyone in her group, gives me a helpless feeling."

"I understand Scott…maybe better than you do. Look, I ran the plates and have some information to share. You ready?"

"Okay. Shoot."

"Well the Cadillac is registered to a Dr. Samuel Adler who lives in Chestnut Hill. The Pontiac is registered to a Christopher Sullivan who lives in Jamaica Plain."

"Do you have addresses?"

"Yes, but I'm not giving them to you."

"Not even the Pontiac one?"

"Especially, not that one. Look Scott, I would like to help you, but you have to let me."

"I know you really want to help, and I would love the company. However, I just don't feel right betraying a confidence."

"Yes, but you already gave me enough to know it involves Stephen."

"I told you I would keep you informed. I am planning to go to the drop site tonight."

"Alright Mr. Detective, how about you tell me the location of the drop site?"

"I don't see any harm in that. It is the Dudley Street elevated train station."

"Thanks Scott. Please be careful, but if you change your mind on things, please let me know. I would be glad to assist. You know that."

"I know Mike. You are a good friend. Talk with you soon."

"Thanks, bye."

* * *

As soon as I hung up the phone, I pulled the Boston Area white page telephone directory, and looked up Christopher Sullivan. There were three, but only one listed in Jamaica Plain. I wrote the address down and decided to take a ride.

Twenty minutes later I was parked down a few doors from the address. Even though it was close to 2 AM, the street was well lit. The address was a three story duplex with six apartments. The three mailboxes on each side of

the front doors told the story. It wasn't important right now
which floor Christopher lived on. However, this address
might not be important at all, but it might come in handy.

After waiting several minutes, I decided that if a police
car were to come by and spot my car, or me, it would be
hard to explain being at this location after being picked up
at the other address.

Curiosity got the best of me, and I decided to take a ride
past the care facility. I wasn't planning on stopping, but I
wanted to see if the Pontiac was still there.

..*

Twenty minutes later I drove to the care facility in
Belmont. The only car in the parking lot was the gold
Pontiac. I went past the facility and turned at the next
intersection and came back to get a better look at the
parking lot.

The Pontiac was in the exact position it was in earlier last
night. As I cruised past the building I noticed the same light
on, in the room I assumed was Stephen's daughter's room.
It is the middle of the night, why is her light on? Maybe she
needs to sleep with the light on.

I resisted the temptation to park and walk back to the
facility to see if I could hear anything. It was too dangerous
for me to be seen in this area, let alone be parked or worse,
to be found on the grounds of the facility.

I stepped on the gas and headed back to my apartment.
However, the light on in that room reminded me of the
single light in my cell while being held captive by Melanie.
Now she had a twin sister. Could my nightmare be a sign
there is more to fear?

The lack of sleep was getting the best of me. I needed to
get a good night's sleep.

Minutes later I was in my own bed, which still felt
strange after being in Mercedes' for many nights. I thought

I could drift right off to sleep, but I was thinking about Mercedes and whether she was indeed safe. I was also wondering whether Alexis would pick up where Melanie left off. I closed my eyes and unconsciously felt the arrow scar.

Chapter 33

Ralph was still in shock. Mercedes was kidnapped right from under their noses. She should have come into the cantina with him. The driver suggested she stay in the car. He watched the driver trying to reach his superiors. Was this his plan to have Mercedes in the car alone, so she could be kidnapped?

Mercedes told him that the captain said she should not go anywhere alone, and was about to cop a feel himself. She said he suggested he come to her hotel to discuss the case of the missing women in more detail.

Jose was not making much progress getting a hold of the captain. Jose was much too calm, almost too calm. This must have been a planned kidnapping of Mercedes. He bet the captain might be involved as well. He knew he needed to get a hold of his boss, but how?

He tapped Jose on the shoulder. "Jose, if you can't reach the captain, have headquarters contact the two policemen with my boss – Max Gordon." Jose didn't seem to understand him.

He snatched the microphone from him. "This is Ralph Reynolds with the FBI. Call your policemen with my boss Max Gordon. Do it now." He did not understand the reply, but he realized they did not understand his request.

"Jose, tell them to alert the policemen who were with my FBI boss, that Mercedes Strong has been kidnapped."

Jose took the microphone back and after several exchanges Ralph could tell they understood and were going to indeed reach them. "Jose, thank you. How can we reach your captain?"

Jose just shook his head. It didn't take a genius to figure out that his earlier suspicion about the captain might be right on target. "Jose, can you take me to where the woman's body was found?"

* * *

Ralph sensed that Jose might be involved with Mercedes' kidnapping and wondered if he too had something to worry about. He was going to keep a keen eye on Jose just in case his gut was correct.

Jose put the blue light on top of the roof and rushed down side streets. This was a good sign to Ralph. Ten minutes later they arrived at the docks where the body was found.

"Mr. Ralph, there is where body found." He pointed toward the closest pier.

There was no sign of Max and the other two policemen. "Jose, contact headquarters to find out if they contacted my boss." Jose just looked at him. "Jose, call headquarters and get an update."

Ralph watched as Jose made the call and reacted to what he heard. He hung up the microphone, started the car, and pulled away in a rush. "What did you learn?"

"They have found agent."

"They found Max?"

"No, they found pretty agent."

* * *

Ralph was concerned about whether she was found murdered or found alive. He didn't want to ask and just dealt with what he would do if she was killed.

Shortly, they rounded a corner at another waterfront area. There were several police cars with their lights flashing. Two were blocking the entrance to a warehouse on a pier. "Mr. Ralph, we park here."

His heart was beating a mile a minute and he still didn't know what to expect. As they both neared the entrance to the building, a stretcher was being brought out. A man's boot was sticking out the bottom of the sheet. Ralph stopped and watched them push the gurney to a waiting vehicle.

He heard Max's voice. "You will be okay now Mercedes, but we need to take you to the hospital for treatment."

Ralph turned and saw Max guiding Mercedes through the door. She was holding her head and was wrapped in a dark blanket. She spotted Ralph and came running to his arms.

"Oh, Mercedes, I thought we might have lost you. Are you okay?"

"I'll be okay now. I thought I was never going to be found."

Ralph turned and saw the captain walking towards them. "We were very lucky. We had this building under surveillance for several days, and it paid off. You are a very lucky lady."

Mercedes turned towards him. "Captain, thank you for rescuing me. I thought I was going to be…" She started crying and turned back to Ralph.

"Like I said, you would be a prize. I thought perhaps there would be an attempt to kidnap you. We had you in our sights since you left our station. I'm sorry you had to endure what you went through before we could rescue you."

She hugged the captain. "Thank you so much." However, she had a strange feeling when he and his men burst in, that his hesitation to cover her with a blanket told a much different story.

"We have two men who we will question, and hopefully we will be able to locate the other women."

She smiled at him, but pulled the blanket tight around her. Ralph guided her to the police car they told him would take her to the hospital.

Max came up to them at the car. "Ralph, your job right now is to stay with Mercedes, and don't let her out of your sight. That is an order."

Chapter 34

As the police car headed to the hospital, Mercedes knew she was very lucky to be rescued. She doubted she would have been killed, since she was more valuable alive.

Ralph was being quiet, holding her tightly, and being respectful of her privacy. She felt herself quivering, but it wasn't because it was cold. Ralph hugged her more tightly and she couldn't control her emotions any longer and started sobbing into his chest.

"I'm so sorry Mercedes. We should never have left you alone. Thank God they rescued you."

She was sorry she hung up on Scott. He was who she needed now. He was the one she could relate what had happened to her. *Or could she?*

Her mind was playing tricks on her. Parts of what happened seem like a haze, and other parts seem so real. She played back what happened starting with her rescue.

There was a loud crash. It must have been the outside door being smashed in. There were several gunshots and yelling. She couldn't tell who was saying what, but she pictured the police confronting the men holding her.

Right after the shooting stopped, some men were handcuffed and shoved to the floor. There were three men, with their backs against each other. The captain left his men and came over to her. He just stared at her without saying a word…no, he devoured her for what seemed like an eternity. She remembered her feeling that he was not going to untie her, and her ordeal might really just be starting.

However, he left her and yelled something to his men. A minute later he came back with a blanket and covered her with it. She remembered its shocking smell, and under normal circumstances, would never have wanted it anywhere near her body.

She was glad the captain couldn't see her body any longer. The memory of his eyes slowly surveying her body, gave her a chill that he was going to pick up where the men left off. He also took too much time loosening the ropes to remove them.

She inhaled now and confirmed the blanket only had the smell of sea life, and not what she also smelled before— sweat and semen.

"Mercedes, I'm trying to comfort you, but you're shaking." She felt Ralph try to move her to look at her face, but she just pressed harder into his chest. She was happy he didn't persist.

The memory prior to her rescue was a jumble of images. She remembers when they entered the warehouse the men quickly stripped her remaining clothes, which was just her skirt and what was left of her bra. They removed her hood, and she knew she was really in trouble now since they didn't care she could identify them.

They undid the handcuffs, or maybe they did that first. They were all talking in Spanish and she was glad she didn't understand what they were saying.

She remembered being yanked over to a wooden column. She remembered seeing ropes around the column lying on the floor. One was quickly slipped up the pole and put around her neck; another was slid up her legs to her waist and both were pulled tightly. Two other ropes hanging from the top of the pole were put around each wrist.

She never felt so defenseless in all her life. She thought about the dead woman and what she had endured, and the others and then what was going to happen to her. Four of the five men just stared at her naked body while the other took numerous Polaroid pictures of her. She closed her eyes but could feel the hot flashes now against her body.

All of a sudden there were hands all over her and she must have blacked out.

She could feel her heart beating wildly now and her breathing rushed. She closed her eyes and was relieved she couldn't remember what happened.

"Mercedes, I'm so sorry we weren't there to protect you. You're going to be okay now." Ralph pulled her tightly to him and she couldn't control her sobs any longer.

The swaying of the police car was almost putting her to sleep. She considered she might be having a nightmare and remembered Scott having his. However, she is not having a nightmare—this really happened to her. She wanted to see if there was any permanent damage to her body and tried to mentally poll body parts. Nothing registered.

Then she remembered – *the pictures that were taken of her, where are they? Her nightmare is not over. The captain has her photos, and if she is not mistaken, her nightmare is only beginning. The only reason she is not his prisoner right now, is that his men were there and he wanted to have her rescue by him on record.*

Her profiling training kicked in—*his police position could provide him with the ability to deter the official investigation while making thousands on the slave-trade. Judging from his expression, the money is only a side benefit.*

She recalled his expression when he found her tied to that pole. There's no doubt in her mind that he was weighing his options and planning something for the future.

"Ralph, you need to do a better job of protecting me. Please don't leave me alone with anyone…not even with the captain."

"Do you know what you are saying?"

"I know exactly what I am saying."

"What about when we get to the hospital?"

"You can close your eyes when they examine me, but *don't* leave me alone again while we are on this investigation."

He moved her so he could see her face. "Are you sure?" He wiped her cheeks.

"I know my enemy and you are not what I have to fear. I can't exactly remember what those men did to me, but I know you would never treat me like they did."

He kissed her forehead and hugged her tightly again.

"Ralph?"

"What?"

"You could have taken advantage of me in Bermuda the night I had too much to drink, but you didn't...you've earned my trust...don't blow it."

She thought, *what will she ever tell Scott? Simply, that she is very happy to be alive.*

Chapter 35

She purposely didn't let Chris make love to her. He'll have to earn that privilege.

However, she had lost track of time, but it wasn't wasted time. When he left her bedroom, he was a happy puppy, but a sore man. The memory of their time together put a smile on her face and she was surprised she was getting excited just thinking about it.

Her bra and panties were somewhere, but it didn't matter. She would get them in the morning. She felt the cool air on her naked body. *Maybe she should ring for Chris. No, she will do that some other night.*

It was so different with Chris. Although she was attracted to the doctor, Chris was young and very handsome. His body was much more toned than the doctor's. She had burned Chris' image into her brain and would be able to recall it whenever she wanted to, including when she was with the good doctor.

She remembered his struggle trying to remove her plug with his teeth while she made it tough for him to accomplish, resisting its removal. She also made it tough for him to concentrate while she stroked him. It wasn't clear to her whether it was the removal act or what she was doing, but he was super excited.

Once he had accomplished his mission there was only his enjoyment of what she was doing to him. He was still standing by the bed, but she had repositioned herself with her thighs on either side of his. The combination of her words, hands, mouth, breath, tongue and teeth got the best of him and he sprayed her from her forehead to thighs.

She had total control of him. He looked like he was going to collapse and she made him stand there and look at what he had done. She smiled thinking about it now. She told him he had to be punished. She made him lick it all off. He was hesitant at first, but she let him linger on parts of her body and soon felt his excitement against her leg.

She had decided to test just how much control she had over him, and he passed the test. She touched herself now where he spent those many wonderful minutes. He was able to give her two incredible orgasms. One from what he was doing initially, and one more from what she made him do afterwards.

Then they showered together. Well, first she showered and made him watch her and do what he did the other night. He was more than ready. After he was done, she cleaned him in a special way before she allowed him to wash her. Then she had him wash her, and then she washed him. She made him put his hands up like she did with the doctor.

Unlike the doctor, he needed just a few strokes to get him hard again. She worked the handheld all over all his body and then changed the temperature to the cold setting. She knew all too well what the ice cold stings were like, and his body was quickly beet red and crying for release.

She told him to dry off, put his clothes on and leave.

It only took a single whack of the back of the handheld to get his attention.

She had him where she wanted him and now she had two men who would do anything she told them to do. She was starting to believe what the doctor had said about her being beautiful. She could get two men to get it up continually defying all that is natural. Maybe it wasn't her beauty, but her behavior. She will have to ask the doctor which it is.

Chris still had to be severely punished for reading her diary. What could she think up next? What would his eyes look like when she held the straight razor against him? Would he trust her? Of course he would. The doctor did.

You both have made some unfortunate mistakes.

Chapter 36

Alexis had her way with him. However, it was everything he imagined and more. He was impressed with how his body had performed, but he knew she liked it even more.

He could have left her room at any point, but he was a willing captive to what she would do next. Less than an hour since he left her room, he had indeed managed to check all of the patients to make sure they were still asleep and did not require any attention.

He looked at his name tag and realized 'Chris' was upside down. It was a good thing nobody noticed that, and he could fix it before the doctor arrived. He would have had a difficult time explaining why it was on incorrectly. He unhooked the safety catch and noticed the blood on the end of the pin. The blood would have been even harder to explain.

He recalled when his clothes were lying on Alexis' bed; she had taken his name tag off his shirt and told him he couldn't have it back. When he finally started to get dressed, he remembered she took the tag and he asked for it back. She made him close his eyes and told him he had to earn his badge back. She was going to stick him with the pin point five times.

It was her final way to say she was in control and not him. He recalled each stick. The first stick was in his navel. He flinched, and she told him if he reacted to any of the next sticks, she would double the number. She purposely made him wait minutes between each stick. She described the blood to him and then licked it away. The anticipation was exciting and he couldn't hide it from her.

Unfortunately, that just focused her attention in the wrong area for him. It was hard not to react to the pain, but he realized it wasn't so much the pain as to where she was going to stick him next and what drawing blood would mean. His body was reacting right now to the memory. She didn't have to be a rocket scientist to know where he really wanted to be stuck.

She held off until the final stick. It hurt like hell, but he tolerated it. She didn't pull the pin out and described how much blood was oozing out. He could feel the blood running down and wanted desperately to view the damage. She was testing him. He must have passed as she licked at the blood. The pin was still in him and he thought he must look like one of those little hot dogs with a toothpick in them.

He wasn't small, much to both of their delight. When she finally pulled the pin out, he could tell he was still bleeding. She even confirmed it. Her final words were, "Get dressed. That will give you something to remember me. Now we both have earned our 'red wings.'"

Chris you need to have a plan to get rid of the doctor and have Alexis all to yourself. Maybe there is a better plan.

Chapter 37

I had given some thought to going to Mercedes' apartment to get some rest. There was nothing said that I couldn't use it. However, it had been a long night and I thought I was tired enough to sleep anywhere. Boy was I wrong.

An hour into sleep and I had this terrible nightmare. It was similar to my others, but in this one it was Mercedes and I who were being held captive by her sister. It was Melanie's twin who had us captive. She wanted me to make love to her or she was going to kill Mercedes.

I refused to, but Mercedes was encouraging me to, saying that I didn't matter to her anymore. She was in love with Ralph. Mercedes was laughing at me and telling me I was a fool to believe she would love me. I had lied to her about doing investigations and now I needed to be punished. She told Melanie's twin to hurry because she was late for a date with Ralph.

We were all naked and Melanie's twin was fascinated with my arrow scar. She thought it was convenient how it pointed to my manhood. I was confused how she knew her twin had carved it, but she thought it would be very fitting to make a mirror image of it on the other side. However, she still wanted me to make love to her and was trying her best to convince my body that it was a good idea.

She set the timer on the counter and said I had until the time ran out to get in the mood. The timer was three feet tall and had white gloves for hands. Mercedes kept asking to be released because she didn't need to be here for our love making and she was late for her date with Ralph.

The timer must be broken because it was ringing before the time was up. Then it rang again, and again.

That's when I woke up. The phone was ringing. It rang again before I could answer it.

"Hello."

"Scott, I must have woken you. It's Mercedes. Something awful has happened. Scott?"

"Hi Mercy, Are you okay?"

"No, not really."

* * *

I was awake now and realized I was having a nightmare. It took a second or two for me to get my bearings. "What happened?"

"Scott, I'm okay now. But I was kidnapped earlier tonight."

Even though I was awake I was still having a problem processing what she was saying, against the nightmare I just had.

"Scott I know I just woke you, but I was kidnapped and luckily rescued."

"I'm sorry Mercy. I was just having a nightmare and I'm still trying to get my bearings. You said you're not okay. Tell me what happened."

"Well, Ralph and one of the Venezuelan police officers went into a cantina and wanted me to stay in the unmarked car. While they were in there, men busted one of the car windows and dragged me to their van."

"Jesus Mercy, I'm glad you were rescued."

"Scott, it was awful. Some of what happened is still a blur, I was knocked out. However, before that in the van they cut most of my clothes away. There were three men in the back of the van and they…well, they…never mind you can picture the scenario."

"You were knocked out?"

"Well, when the van stopped and they dragged me out, I screamed for help. That's when they knocked me out. The next thing I remember I woke up naked and tied against a pole in a warehouse. There were five men."

I heard her start to cry. "I'm so sorry Mercedes. I'm glad you were rescued."

"Scott, we believe these were the men who kidnapped the US citizens and killed one of the women."

"Did Ralph rescue you?"

She didn't immediately answer. "No, he didn't."

I could tell she was trying to control her emotions. "Thank God you're okay."

"I'm not okay. I might not be okay for a long time. I got a taste of what these women might have gone through. I never felt so vulnerable in all my life. I needed to call you to tell you what happened. Scott, I'm so sorry we argued before."

"Me too. Are you coming home?"

"No. The police force captain who rescued me wants me involved in the investigation, because I can identify all the men. Two were killed when I was rescued, one got away, and the other two are being held at the police station. This might be the break we were looking for to find the other people who went missing in Bermuda."

"Mercedes, haven't you been through enough? What if they come after you again?"

"Ralph has been given strict orders not to let me out of his sight."

I couldn't respond to that, but I had images of what that might involve.

"Don't tell me you're jealous Scott. Would you rather I was still being kept a hostage, or taken away again?"

"No. I want you safe, but I want you home."

"Now you know what it is like to worry about someone's safety…like I worry about yours."

"Have you called your father?"

"No Scott. I called you first. Just a minute—"

I heard some talk but couldn't make out the gist of it.

"Scott, Max my boss just informed me that I'm being released from the hospital now. He just told Ralph to take me to my hotel room to change and then we need to head to the police station to talk with the police captain."

"Mercy, I love you. Please be careful. I don't want anything to happen to you."

"Thanks Scott. Anything *more to happen* would be more appropriate. I have to go. I love you too."

Chapter 38

After a restless night's sleep thinking of Alexis and their time together he realized something—his career is shot. All the training to be a doctor and a psychiatrist are not important any longer. He needs Alexis all the time and not just when he brings her to his house.

He wondered if she felt the same way about him, or was it just the sex. He had enough money put away that he could cease his medical practice and take her away to an exotic island somewhere. *Would she willingly go? How could he finesse her leaving the care facility? How would he deal with Stephen?*

The only one who knows about her background is Stephen. Nobody in her family knows she even exists. If Stephen were out of the picture, that would eliminate the major obstacle. The next issue would be the care facility. He could release her to the real world and nobody would suspect anything out of the ordinary.

If Stephen was deceased, the only heirs would be his wife, and his other daughter. If they were both out of the way, Alexis would inherit the family fortune. If Alexis was his wife, they would be rich and could enjoy living anywhere in the world. He has the necessary legal papers to show the probate court she is the next of kin and entitled to the Strong estate.

He wondered if he should share Alexis' heritage with her and feel her out about spending the rest of her life with him. Even so, how would he ever do away with three people including an FBI agent? Stephen's wife has had several nervous breakdowns and a bad heart. If Stephen were killed somehow, she might just pass away with a heart attack. How the hell could he ever manage to kill Mercedes? Could he do it? Or, could he get someone else to do it? That would be a witness, who would also have to be disposed of.

My God Alexis…see what you have done to me. Maybe I should just kidnap you and run away with you.

The thoughts of having Alexis for the rest of his life caused him to become excited. He threw the sheets off and felt his hairless groin. He recalled being at her mercy and remembered at one point he felt she might just remove his manhood. There was something he detected in her eyes that gave him a concern.

He picked up her photos and very quickly all of his concerns were a distant memory while he revisited their passionate love making. He knew one thing for sure—he wasn't planning on spending the rest of his life alone.

He wasn't alone any longer and the photos had turned into a beautiful redhead intent on making his current problem history.

At this moment he had the will power to kill anyone.

Chapter 39

She was uncomfortable about meeting with her boss and Ralph. However, Max said it was urgent and wanted them both to meet with him in his hotel room.

Ralph hadn't left her alone for one minute since her rescue and he was acting like a gentleman and not an infatuated school kid.

"Ralph, before we head up to see Max I want to tell you something."

"What?"

"You know all to well that we have never gotten off to a good start. I know you want to have a relationship with me, but you know where my heart is. Your staging my apartment crossed a line and you're very lucky I'm not reporting it."

"Are we going to go into that again?"

"No, we're not. Listen to me. This is important. I'm very lucky to have been rescued from those kidnappers. I'm also lucky the captain didn't just keep me for himself. He looked like he could easily have done that. I don't trust him, and my gut says he might have been involved somehow in my kidnapping. However, this isn't about that. I want to thank you for making me feel safe. You have been a gentleman and I respect you for it. You're a good agent and I can see you have a good side. Thank you Ralph."

She realized the emotion of her trauma may have been too much for her and saying these nice things to Ralph quickly caused her eyes to water.

"Mercedes, once again I apologize for doing what I did. It was childish, but I wanted to drive a wedge between you and Scott. It wasn't the right approach to have you like me, but thanks for telling me you do in your own way."

He took a step closer to her and she couldn't resist hugging him. The emotional turmoil got the best of her, and he hugged her tighter. When the emotion passed he pushed her away from him so she could look into his eyes. She could tell he wanted to kiss her and she let him. After the short kiss she put her head on his shoulder and felt closer to him.

"Ralph, we need to get to Max's room. Will you excuse me for one minute? I have to go to the bathroom."

He nodded, but he followed her to the bathroom. "Ralph, there is nobody here…give me a moment to myself." She closed the door, but she knew he was right outside.

* * *

"Ralph thanks for taking care of Mercedes," Max said to him after they were both seated on the couch in his hotel room. "Mercedes, I know this was a significant trauma to you. We were very lucky tonight, but those aren't the right words."

"Max, I want to thank Ralph for making me feel protected. I needed to feel that right now." Mercedes looked over to Ralph and pushed on his shoulder.

"Okay, so here's the deal. Mercedes I have arranged for you to be on the first flight home tomorrow morning. Your role here is complete. It would be wrong to keep you here as you have had a significant trauma, and I don't feel you are safe any longer."

She started to object. He continued. "This is not negotiable, the decision has been made. Ralph, her flight leaves at 10 tomorrow morning. I want you to stay with her tonight, and…do I have to remind you to be on your best behavior? There is an embassy unmarked vehicle coming at 8 to take you both to the airport. You are to see that she makes it safely onto that flight. Do either of you have any questions?"

"Sir, I respect your decision, but I can be more help here than at home."

"Actually Mercedes you will take more attention away from our investigation. We would be focusing more on your safety and not fully on what we need to pursue here."

She nodded, and realized the decision was cast in stone, and it made sense to her. "Where does the investigation stand, if I might ask?"

"I met with Captain Chavez and he says the two men they have in custody will certainly shed more light on the kidnappings and what is going on related to the slave trade."

"Sir, if I may." She thought about her choice of words. "My gut says the captain might actually be more involved than we suspect."

"That is a very good observation. I have had some research done on the captain and it seems his bank account shows a heavy balance when compared to his earnings. This is where the expression comes in, 'keep your friends close and your enemies closer.'"

"Sir, bear with me on this, when he and his men rescued me, and he saw me tied to that pole…well, my feeling was he didn't want to release me. Is there any chance he is involved with the slave trade? More importantly, do you think he had anything to do with my kidnapping?"

"That my dear agent is a thought I have already considered. However, we might be able to use what he knows to find the other citizens. Hopefully we're not too late already."

"One final note Mercedes. You are to take the next week off and plan on meeting at the bureau the following Monday morning. Ralph and I will meet with you there, unless there is a reason for us to stay longer here."

He looked over at Ralph. "Do you have anything to add, and are you clear on your assignment until her plane leaves?"

"No I don't have anything to add, and I'm clear that I need to ensure she remains safe until the plane departs."

"Right. Mercedes I'm sorry you were kidnapped and put through that ordeal. This investigation is much more dangerous than we considered it to be. Please rest up when you get back home."

"What about my ticket?"

"Arrangements have been made. Go to the American Airlines ticket counter and show your ID."

* * *

She watched Ralph check out her hotel room. "Everything is okay here. Pack your bag we're going to my room."

"What?"

"You heard me. This room is too much of a target while you're still here. My room is much safer."

"Does Max know you're going to move us to your room?"

"No. But I am responsible for your safety and that makes you just that much more secure."

She wondered if it was going to be safer there. "I need to call Scott to let him know I'm coming home tomorrow."

"That's fine, but put your stuff together and you can call him from my room."

* * *

"Any luck?" Ralph asked.

"No, he still isn't picking up. He must be out." She was concerned she couldn't reach Scott.

"Mercedes, why don't you give it some time and try to reach him later."

"I have to admit, I'm exhausted."

"I'm not surprised. You had quite an ordeal. Why don't you take a nap? I'll just read through some of the case notes."

"It was nice of you to offer your room and to give up your bed for me."

"Is that what I said?"

"Ralph."

"Poor timing huh?"

"I need to take a hot bath and then I think I will take that nap. If I do fall asleep, please don't let me sleep too long this afternoon." He nodded, but when she turned to head to the bedroom he stood and started to follow her. "What are you doing?"

"I need to keep an eye on you."

"Ralph enough please. There isn't anybody in the bedroom, or the bathroom. I will be okay and I could use the privacy, okay?"

He looked like he was going to make a point, but turned and sat back down.

* * *

Her body fit nicely in the combination shower and antique tub. The hot water was very relaxing. This was basically the first real privacy she's had since she was rescued. Parts of her body were sore.

She lifted her right leg and saw the bruise on her shin, the scrape on her knee and another bruise on her thigh. It must have been when they knocked her out. She lifted the other leg, but there was no pain there and no bruises.

She didn't want to recall her ordeal, but she noticed both wrists showed signs of where her wrists were bound. Images came flooding back and she remembered her clothes being ripped and cut from her body. She remembered her bra hanging in two pieces when they were pushing her to the warehouse.

The next thing she remembered was the pain on the top of her head and watching the lights go out. When she woke she was tied to a pole with a rope around her neck and another around her waist with her wrists bound from ropes above her head. Fortunately the men's comments were foreign to her, but she could imagine what they were saying by how they were touching her body.

They took pictures of her and up close pictures of her body. So close, she remembers the heat of the flashes against her body. She looked down at her breasts and saw the red welts across her flesh. She doesn't remember how they got there, and actually doesn't remember much else of her captivity. It was only about an hour, but it felt like an eternity.

The wash cloth was hurting her skin now as she tried to get rid of the dirt and the dirty feeling she had. The only person who had ever seen her naked and touched her body was Scott. It wasn't rough and dirty, but soft and slow and sensuous.

She stood in the tub and rinsed off. She saw her image in the mirror and turned to see her back. There were marks there as well, running from her right shoulder down across her buttocks. Those must have been from the pole she was tied to, or was it from something else? Up until now there was just some tightness on her back, but standing in the air caused them to burn.

She dried her hair and dried her body and wrapped the towel around her. The memory of wrapping the small towel around her at the cabin with Scott that first night came back and she was surprised it brought a smile to her face. When she was beside the bed she removed the towel and climbed between the sheets. It hurt now to lie on her back and she rolled onto her stomach.

Ralph had been quiet in the other area and she was concerned whether he was still there or worse knocked out. She listened intently but couldn't hear anything. There was some thumping outside the bedroom door and she feared the men had come for her. She froze for several minutes trying to comprehend what she was hearing.

"Ralph? Ralph, are you okay? *Ralph, are you there?*"

Chapter 40

He had enough of his 'alone' time. He needed Alexis with him for the rest of the day and night, even if she was having cramps.

It was hard for him not to exceed the speed limit, but he knew he was rushing. The thoughts of her being back at his house for any amount of time, doing some of the things they had done, caused him to become excited. That just put a smile on his face and added a few more miles per hour to his speed.

He turned into the manor parking lot and spotted Chris' car still parked there. He was still on duty until noon today. *What is he going to use for an excuse to get her out? He shouldn't need one since he was the director, but thought he should have a reason he was picking her up. Legal issues are what he could say…or better, some legal matters which would be best to be handled in private. He remembered what she handled and he was more than ready.*

What if she doesn't want to leave the facility? She isn't going to have a choice.

He unlocked the front door and noticed Chris was not at the reception desk. That didn't surprise him though as he had rounds and other things to do. He wanted to rush into Alexis' room and hopefully catch her still in bed. *Slow down doc, don't blow it.*

He went to his office and unlocked his door and sat to compose himself. His khaki shorts still had a noticeable bulge.

"Good morning doctor, I wasn't expecting you," Chris said poking his head in the office door.

"Oh, good morning Chris. Something has come up paperwork wise and I need to review the matter with Ms. Strong. I'm hoping she is feeling better and can spend a few hours going over the legal matters with me. If she is, I will be signing her out."

"I will check on her for you."

"Thank you Chris. If she is feeling okay, please ask her to get ready to leave with me. I will be right here."

He was careful not to display his pants problem and wondered if Chris had seen anything. *I wonder if Chris is gay.* He never talks about his private life and I know he is not married. He recalled Chris' strange behavior at the desk when he was signing out Alexis. He seemed miles away.

If he wasn't gay, would Alexis' beauty have an effect on him, and should he worry about the two of them? It would be better if Chris was gay.

Chapter 41

He knocked on her door, but there wasn't any answer. He knocked a little louder, and there was still no answer. He opened the door and went into her room. The light was off in the bathroom, and he turned it on. He went over to the bed and she was nude. He looked at her face and her eyes were open.

"It took you long enough to come back." She reached and grabbed him and patted the bed for him to sit.

"I would love to spend some time with you, but the doctor just came in to cover some legal matters with you. I think he wants to take you out again."

She unzipped his pants. "I want to be with you Chris."

"Please Alexis, I can lose my job. You need to get dressed to go with him."

"Speaking of losing your job, have you forgotten our conversation?"

"No I haven't. I would love to spend all my time with you, but this is not the right time for us." He pushed her hand away and zipped back up.

She ran her hands down her body. "How can you pass up all of this?"

"We will have our time, but this is not the right time for it. Please, he's waiting in his office. I will tell him you're getting dressed."

"Then…are you going to tell him I was undressed when you found me? Are you going to tell him you had your zipper down and were going to take advantage of me?"

"That is not funny. We'll get together when you get back tomorrow."

"Promise?"

"I promise." He started to leave and she grabbed him again.

"Are you sore?"

"Yes, a little."

"Gee, only a little. You better rest up then."

He pushed her hand away and rushed to her door checking to make sure his zipper was up, but noticed his excitement showing.

"I saw that excitement too Chris."

He quickly left and stepped into the doctor's office. "She will be ready in just a few minutes."

"Thanks Chris. Oh, what took you so long?"

"I had to wake her."

"Interesting. I have a question to ask you. Have you noticed anything strange in regards to her behavior lately?"

He hesitated, wondering what the doctor was asking, and wondered if he had noticed his excitement. "In what regards?"

"Well, how do I say this? She has turned into such a beautiful woman and it is hard not to acknowledge that. I was just wondering if her behavior showed any signs that she was starting to recognize her metamorphosis and to display it in any manner."

"I would think you would be in a much better position to determine that, since you spend so many hours with her."

"Oh, I have made my professional observations and I'm getting close to releasing her from the care facility."

Alexis stuck her head around Chris' shoulder. "Interesting discussion. Is that right? If I heard that comment correctly, why haven't you told me about it?"

"Hello Alexis. If you are ready we can leave. We can discuss that progress when we are alone."

The three of them walked to the reception desk and the doctor filled out the sign out register. Chris saw Alexis lick her lips and mouth 'tomorrow.'

Chapter 42

Doctor Adler was resting uncomfortably tied to the bed. They both enjoyed their love making, but she enjoyed it more than he did. She got carried away, but even now the thoughts caused the same reaction between her legs. She would take care of that urge later, and maybe the doctor would like to watch.

Right now she had to follow up on something Chris had let slip. She wanted to know more about the details of why she was at the care facility. *Was there a world out there she was missing?*

There were parts of the doctor's house she had never been in. She was curious about what the doctor might have been hiding from her. She thought of how she could get the truth out of him, but she couldn't wait, and wanted to see if she could get some information on her own without creating a bloody scene. That put a smile on her face.

She went to his bedroom. It was on the third floor. In fact it took the entire third floor. When she reached his bedroom, the air had turned much warmer than the basement. She wiped at the beads of sweat between her breasts. She gingerly entered his bedroom.

Her feet felt the rough floor boards first. She turned on the light switch and the large bedroom had a four-poster king size bed. How appropriate doctor, and why am I not surprised? *And, why have you not brought me up here? Is it because it is too hot up here, or is it because you knew it would be much too hot with our love making?*

She walked over to the bed and put her butt on the edge. She opened the top night stand drawer and pulled out two men's magazines. *Why doctor, I'm going to have to show you these and ask why you have them. I wonder if you will tell me the truth.*

She opened the magazine and looked at the pictures of the naked women. They were beautiful and their bodies were displayed to show their best assets. She couldn't help comparing her body to those in the magazine. Her nipples were getting hard just like the blonde's, who was truly a blonde judging from the neatly trimmed pubic hair.

Part of the article caught her attention, 'yes, when I don't have a partner with me…well, I have other ways to satisfy my desires.' *I'm sure you do. Don't we all? She wondered what it would be like to be with another woman.* She felt her breast and then how hard her nipples were. She flipped thru the rest of the magazine and then picked up the other.

It was a nudist magazine. The pictures were not staged like the others and just showed people going about their routines without any clothes. She looked at the men and wondered why they were not excited. The doctor and Chris were almost always erect, even after all of the various activities.

She wondered if the nudists made love in front of the other nudists, or did they hide that activity? What did the men do when they couldn't hide their excitement? Maybe they never got erect. She felt another smile just thinking about that. She also felt the moisture between her legs, and touched herself. *Maybe I should rush down and have the doctor benefit from my current condition. Later.*

She saw the backs of some photos in the drawer and picked them up. She smiled at the thoughts of the doctor using the magazines and more importantly her pictures to masturbate. *That doesn't surprise me at all my good doctor. I wonder what you fantasize about…is it what we do, or what you wish we did? I'll have to make you tell me about that, and honesty will count heavily.*

As she flipped through the pictures, she realized that she had grown from this young girl without any hair and other assets, to this striking young lady. Even though the pictures were black and white they were still interesting, especially the positions the doctor had her in. She turned her head and tried to remember how she got in that position. She put that picture aside and would ask the doctor about that one.

Since the magazines and photos were causing such a distraction, she thought it best to put them away so she could search the rest of the room.

She stretched out on the bed and studied the room. The ceiling was coifed with a chandelier over the bed. The bed covering was an antique coverlet much like a table cloth. That is why you didn't want us up here. We would mess that up. That created another smile.

The dresser was a long cherry double drawer unit with a mirror the full length. She could see her naked body and raised a leg to contrast her pubic hair against the white of her thigh. She pulled her hair across one breast. Wow, that would create an interesting development, wouldn't it doctor? There was another tall dresser on the other wall. She thought it was strange that there was nothing on top of either piece of furniture.

She sat on the side of the bed and spotted the closet door. She walked over and once again the rough wood against her feet made her think of lying against its rugged surface. She opened the closet door and looked at the contents. Suits at one end, sports coats next, dress pants next to casual pants, white dress shirts with plastic covering them, casual shirts and finally ties.

She took a black tie and went over to the dresser mirror and tied a knot as best she could. The contrast of the black tie between her snow white breasts reminded her of one of the staged pictures in the magazine. She was getting that feeling again, and remembered the poor doctor tied in the basement. She spotted the reflection in the mirror of two boxes on the top shelf of the closet.

She went over and reached for the first box. It was heavy and she put it on the bed and opened it up. There were family photos, documents and personal things of Doctor

Adler's. It was an interesting assortment, but not really what she wanted to waste her time on.

She spotted what looked like the doctor's high school photo, and thought he looked like someone who wouldn't have turned a girl's eye. *You look so much better without any clothes on. She remembered shaving his hair off and the look in his eyes as he wondered if she was going to do some serious damage. Not yet, doc...not yet.*

She put the picture back and covered the box and returned it. She took down the other box, which was more like a legal file box, and placed it on the bed.

She uncovered the box and was shocked at its contents.

* * *

It took her over an hour to consume the contents. The first picture which greeted her was her image on the front of a newspaper. Well, she learned it wasn't her picture but it was her twin sister's. It showed her original photo and how she looked after the plastic surgery.

This box represented all of the mystery of her life. She had a twin sister who killed herself with a flare gun. She had twice tried to kill a Scott Tucker.

One of those attempts was at a warehouse on the Boston waterfront, and the other was in Bermuda. She and three other women had held young hockey players prisoner, torturing them, killing them, then throwing their dismembered bodies into the ocean, having kept some of their parts as trophies. Scott was rescued by a Mercedes Strong who was part of a task force looking for the killers. Melanie, her twin, jumped in the freezing ocean waters and was thought to have not survived.

Years later after plastic surgery and killing her surgeon, she went to Bermuda picking up where she left off. She had built a dungeon of sorts and was holding men for months against their will for sexual purposes. As a young adult, she had been in a mental institution, but was released, having supposedly been cured of her condition.

Scott was once again rescued by authorities including the same Mercedes Strong. She studied the picture of Scott and could see what her twin saw in him.

More importantly she learned that Stephen Strong was her father and had committed her to the care facility because of her deformity. She read the original letter from Stephen explaining what he wanted done and how he wanted her residency to be kept a secret even from his wife.

She learned her father was a very rich real estate developer who also had a prestigious real estate firm. She saw the picture of her mother and saw the resemblance. Her own mother knew nothing about her and her father gave her up.

He also paid money each year for her care and a separate amount to the doctor to maintain her personal care and to keep things a secret. Her father was a very attractive man, but the two pictures she kept going back to were the one of Scott Tucker and the one of her sister Mercedes Strong. She was very attractive even in the newspaper shots.

However, the one of Scott and the knowledge of what her sister put him through caused her body to react. *This was the other life she was deprived of. This was the man her sister lusted for, and to be more exact, both of her sisters lusted for. She couldn't explain exactly why she was so drawn to his picture, but now there were three of us that lust for you Mr. Tucker.*

She didn't want to put the material back, but realized she needed to. *The thoughts of what her twin was able to do with multiple simultaneous prisoners, including one woman, brought her recent memories back of what she felt when she put the doctor and Chris through their paces. She was now certain she had those genes, but uncertain as to what she was going to do with that knowledge.*

Now I'm going to go spend some pointed time with the good doctor to see if he is going to be honest with me. However, it will be much more fun if he is not.

Chapter 43

He heard Mercedes calling to him and thought she might be in danger. He rushed over and opened the door to the bedroom area. "Are you okay?" he asked, standing in the doorway.

"I heard some noises outside the bedroom door and wondered if there was a problem."

"Oh that. I was just moving a chair against the door."

"I'm sorry I bothered you Ralph."

She looked very relieved, but also very attractive holding the sheet against her. "It's okay. You had a significant trauma and I understand." He started to return to the sitting area.

"Ralph."

"What?"

"Do you mind sitting over there until I fall asleep?"

"Sure, just let me get the files I was reviewing. Okay?"

"Thanks."

When he returned she was laying face down way over in the bed with her face facing the far wall. He sat down and resumed his case review. Several minutes later he looked over and she must have fallen asleep. He noticed her uncovered shoulders rising and falling in a slow rhythm.

The sight of her long red hair and uncovered shoulders reminded him of the time she was naked in her hotel room.

They, actually she, had too much to drink that night. She was going to be sick and had to leave the dining room. He guided her to her hotel room. After being sick in the bathroom, she came into the bedroom and started undressing. Realizing he was watching her, she got pissed at him and pushed him out of the bedroom as she unhooked her bra. She had an incredible body and he could have taken advantage of her, but didn't and left.

His thoughts were interrupted now by her crying out 'no.'

The sheet had slipped down and exposed the side of her breast. He went over and took a mental picture of how she looked. He reached down and pulled the sheet up to her neck. Then he reclined on the near side of the bed. It was all he could do not to take his clothes off and get under the sheets with her. He wondered what she had endured and knew this was not the right time for him.

Being close to her like this made him realize that he was indeed protecting her. He had failed once this weekend, and was not going to fail her again. He took a deep breath and smelled the fragrance of Gardenia. He remembered holding her close and dancing with her. His thoughts were soon replaced by images of what must have happened to her.

He looked over at her shoulder and saw the red welts. *I'm so sorry Mercedes; I let you down once...it will never happen again.* He took another deep breath and wished she felt the same way about him.

He thought he heard something in the other room. He listened intently and seconds later thought he heard the chair sliding across the floor.

Chapter 44

"Lighthouse Manor, how can I help you?" Chris
answered the phone.

"I'm glad I caught you."

"Alexis?"

"Surprise, surprise, yes it's me."

"Aren't you with the doctor?"

"Yes, I am. However, he is tied up at the moment. Do
you know where he lives?"

"Yes, I've been to his house. Why?"

"How would you like to keep me company for a few
days?"

"What?"

"Consider this a call from Doctor Adler. He is going to
take next week off."

"I'm not sure I totally understand."

"Chris, listen to me. I don't want to go over this on the
phone with you. I would like to talk to you in person. I
have learned some things and I'm not sure I'm going to go
back to the facility. In fact, I know I'm not going back. I
need your help. Doesn't your shift end at noon? Can you
come to his house when you get off?"

"Yes it does. I guess I can."

"Good. The next question is whether you can take any
days off next week, or better the whole week?"

"I have several days of vacation, but I don't think I can
arrange coverage on such short notice."

"Work it out any way you can. Think of it this way. How
would you like to have *me* for hours and hours, or more
appropriately, days and days? Doesn't that give you some
thoughts?"

"What about Doctor Adler?"

"He won't be an issue."

"What?"

He heard the click in his ear followed by the dial tone.

He replayed parts of their conversation. The doctor is tied up and he won't be an issue. She has learned some things. More importantly his mind quickly went to being with Alexis for days.

He quickly pulled the reserve schedule list from the file and called Maureen Doyle.

"Hello."

"Maureen, this is Christopher Sullivan over at the Lighthouse Manor. I'm sorry for the short notice, but an emergency has come up and I have been called away. Do you have any days available this week where you could cover my shift?"

"As a matter of fact I have all week."

"Well, I might need all week. Can you cover this week for me starting tomorrow afternoon?"

"Yes, I can. Why isn't Doctor Adler calling to cover your shift?"

"Well, he is taking this week off as well and has signed out Alexis Strong also."

"That's interesting. He's never done that before."

"He said his time off has to do with Alexis getting back into society. I'm not sure exactly what that means."

"Okay, I'll cover your shift. What about the weekend?"

"I should be back to work by then."

"If you are not going to be, just give me a call and let me know. I can cover that if you need me to. Oh, what is your emergency?"

He realized he should have thought about that before he called. "I just got a call from relatives in Arizona that my uncle and aunt went missing and they haven't been heard from in over a week."

"Oh, I'm sorry to hear that."

"Thanks, I better go. Thanks again for covering for me on such short notice. I'll leave details for you on each of the patients, but if you need more information, you can talk to either Betty or Pam."

"Good luck…I hope you locate your relatives and they are safe."

"Maureen thanks again, you are a life saver." He hung up the phone and made some mental notes about what he used for an excuse.

He wondered what Alexis had learned and what she could possibly do with the doctor for the entire week. Those thoughts were quickly replaced with the memory of their last time together.

Then he remembered the money pickup was later tonight. He could do both. Should he take this opportunity to share her family information with her? That gave him some thoughts.

Chapter 45

She thought about Chris coming. That could have two
meanings. She was going to have both. Thank goodness the
good doctor had the number of the care home in his address
book. There were many things she needed to consider, but
the idea she might have a week to work them all out gave
her a comfortable feeling.

Speaking of comfortable feelings—I wonder how the
good doctor is dealing with his loneliness. She slid the
black tie knot tight up against her throat. It was hard to
breathe and it hurt. Her image in the mirror shocked her.
Her face was beet red, but her body looked sensuous in the
bedroom light. She loosened the tie and headed quickly
down to the basement.

In her bare feet she was able to sneak up on the doctor.
She moved slowly and stole a look at him. His eyes were
closed and he was obviously missing her. She hadn't seen
him limp like that in all the time they had been together.
*Maybe I'm not giving myself enough credit for what I do to
men.*

There were many things to think about. Right now she
was thinking about her twin sister and what she had done.
*Could she be like her? She kept men captive for sexual
purposes, and isn't that what she is doing right now?
Melanie we should have met. In fact, we should have grown
up together. Maybe things would have been different.
Maybe we could have been double trouble to these men.
Just maybe we would not have been stopped.*

Her thoughts drifted to her other sister. Mercedes is an
FBI agent who managed to save her boyfriend from her
twin. Yesss, he is definitely worth saving. The doctor is
good, and Chris is much better, but there was something
about Scott Tucker's picture that she was drawn to.

She could feel her plan developing. There was a way to have many things. However, right now she needed to test the good doctor.

* * *

She leapt into the bedroom, her feet pounded on the floor. The doctor's eyes opened and he focused on her image. She could see his eyes move down to take in the black tie hanging between her naked breasts. She pulled her long red hair across the front of her body and he smiled at her. His eyes traveled the length of her and he was showing signs of liking what he was looking at.

There were beads of sweat on her body from the warm temp in the upstairs bedroom. She could see her body glistening in the soft light of the lamp on the nightstand. The urge she had was still there, but it was much stronger. She wanted the doctor's body now, but knew she needed to wait.

"You like what you see?"

"Yes indeed."

"I can see you're telling the truth based on your reaction." She looked at his semi-erect penis. "Did you miss me?"

"Yes. You were gone a long time."

"I wanted you to miss me." She looked at him tied to the bed and helpless. His wrists were tied, and he wasn't just holding onto the ropes. "Is there anything you need?" She climbed onto the bed and sat down on his thighs.

"More of what we did earlier would be nice."

"You like what we did?"

He nodded. She felt the coolness of his legs against her warm rear end. She touched him briefly, and his body jerked.

"I have to go to the bathroom."

She smiled. "No."

"Alexis, please. I have to go."

"You remember what we did the last time you needed to go. However, since you didn't like that treatment you will just have to wait."

He tested the ropes at his wrists, but he was securely fastened.

She ran her finger down between her breasts and gathered some sweat on her finger. She put her finger against his lips. "Shush."

She could tell by his expression he was distraught and by his body's reaction excited.

"Where were you?"

"That is no way to talk to me. You are not in a position of authority any longer. I am your master. If you want to ask me a question, you better phrase it with some respect." She blew a long breath down from his nose to his groin. She smiled. "That's the kind of respect I was hoping for."

"You were gone so long, I really missed you my lady."

"That is much better. You never told me about my family. Do you know who they are?"

"You were dropped off at the facility as a little girl."

"I know that. I can only remember being here. So, you don't know anything about my real family?"

"No, not really."

She nodded to him, and briefly touched his penis again. "Do you play with yourself?"

"What do you mean?"

"You know exactly what I mean."

"No."

"You don't...what did you call it the other day— masturbate?"

"No."

"Interesting."

"Do you ever have fantasies?"

"I guess. Where is this going? I need to go to the bathroom."

"Tell me about some of your fantasies."

"Alexis, please."

"Please what?"

"Why are you doing this?"

"Once again you fail to respect your position and me."
She directed a slap that caused him to yell out.

He took a deep breath. "I'm sorry…master."

"If you want some of your fantasies fulfilled you need to
tell me what some of them are. Now, do you ever
masturbate?"

"No, not really."

"You know for a studied doctor, you sure are being
oppositional."

"Why do you have those magazines in your nightstand?"

"You were not supposed to go in my bedroom."

He wasn't getting it at all. She slapped him again twice
between his legs.

"Why do you have my pictures in your nightstand?"

He didn't answer her. "Close your eyes." He hesitated.
"*Close* your eyes." He did cautiously. She licked once at
his pain. "Does that make you feel any better?"

"Yes."

"Good. We're getting somewhere. Now do you use those
books and pictures to play with yourself?"

"Yes."

She rewarded him with her lips. She noticed he was
getting even bigger. "Didn't you tell me once that everyone
played with their body? That it was natural to have those
feelings and to enjoy your own body? Did you forget what
you had me do, when I was younger? You watched me, and
I watched what happened to your body. You hypnotized me
at that point, but we know now that I never was."

"I should have been truthful with you, I'm sorry. You
remembered your lessons well."

"I should have. You have been taking advantage of me
for years now. But, we both know you like things reversed.
Isn't that correct?"

"Yes...yes I do."

"You need to be rewarded for your honesty." She formed her lips over his swollen member, and then lightly bit him.

"You like that don't you?"

"Yes. I need you."

"Which is it...you need to go to the bathroom, or you need me?"

"I need both...master."

"If you're truthful with me, we will get to your fantasies and your immediate needs." She slid her chest up his body and across his face.

He lunged at one of her breasts.

"Not yet my love." She looked at his lower body bobbing. She smiled. "I guess you really did miss me."

"Master, I need you. Please. I'll do anything."

"Finally we have reached the point of truth." She teased him some more with some light breaths on his erection. Then she grabbed him roughly between his legs. "You lied to me about not knowing my family." She grimaced and squeezed him tightly. She let go and leapt off the bed.

"You could have had everything, and all your fantasies fulfilled."

She watched his eyes bulge when he saw the straight razor. "That's right doctor. You lied about several things, but you lied about the most important one. You need to be reminded of the penalty for lying. One last question and think carefully and truthfully about your answer."

His head and eyes followed her and the knife as she climbed back on his legs.

"Do you think you should be punished for not telling me the truth about my family?"

Chapter 46

I was entering my apartment when I heard the phone ringing. *Maybe that is Mercedes.*

"Hello."

"Scott, its Stephen. You need to come over to my office right away."

"Is this about the money drop?"

"*No.* Drop everything you are doing and come over right away. Something terrible has happened."

I heard the click and then the dial tone. *I hope he hasn't done anything drastic. He said he wasn't going to take much more of this shit.*

I quickly put the things which would go bad into the fridge and headed to his office. Unfortunately, the drive is not that long, but long enough to think about several scenarios that were not pleasant at all. *Maybe I should have called Mike. No, that didn't make any sense as I didn't know what I could tell him.*

My car bottomed out as I entered his parking lot much too fast. I wondered what damage I might have caused, but would worry about that later.

I took the stairs two at a time and went into Stephen's office. He was sitting with a half empty glass in his hand looking out his window at the Charles River. He turned around and gestured toward the liquor area. "Get yourself a drink; you're going to need it."

I went over and poured double the amount of bourbon I normally take.

"Scott thanks for coming so quickly." He got up and went over to the liquor area and refilled his drink. He sat down in the sitting area and took a long hit on it. I sat down across from him and took a small taste of my drink.

"About an hour ago I got a call from Max Gordon who is Mercedes' director. He was calling from Venezuela. He said he wanted to let me know what happened before it got reported by the news agencies."

Oh no. I don't like the sound of this at all. Please God don't let this be—

"Scott, Mercedes and another FBI agent Ralph Reynolds, were kidnapped just a short while ago. They were forcibly taken from their hotel room. I also learned she was kidnapped and rescued earlier in the day. Mercedes was being sent home on the first flight tomorrow."

I heard what he said, but it wasn't making any sense.

He continued talking. "Director Gordon didn't have too many details, but given the situation, they wouldn't be able to keep it under wraps. He wanted me to be aware of what was going on in case I heard anything, or someone contacted me for any ransom demand. He gave me two numbers where I could reach him." Stephen downed the rest of his drink and headed over to the bar.

"Stephen, maybe you should slow down in case something develops, or someone calls." *I felt uncomfortable advising him that, but I had no idea how many drinks he had consumed.*

"Perhaps you're right. I should be home waiting for another call, or –"

"Thanks for calling me to come over. I'm glad you didn't tell me about this while we were on the phone."

"Scott this is one of the worst things that could happen. Not just that she has been kidnapped, but because my wife will not be able to cope with this new development. If she hears this on the news, well...her condition might get worse. I don't know if I should tell her, but my gut says to keep her from hearing anything about this."

"What about the money drop?"

He went over to his desk, unlocked his middle drawer and pulled out a brown paper bag. "Here it is. You'll have to make the drop."

Chapter 47

I could feel the room spinning. Maybe I drank too much too quickly. If Stephen was talking I couldn't hear him any longer. Mercedes was kidnapped twice. I felt so helpless at the moment. There wasn't anything I could do to rescue her. I tried to play back our last conversation but I couldn't recall it. I tried to consider that this was a dream, but I could feel the glass in my hand.

Stephen took the glass from me. "Scott…Scott close your eyes."

I closed them but I could still feel the room spinning. I got this strange taste in my mouth and went running for his office bathroom. I was sorry that I hadn't eaten anything, and glad I hadn't. I felt my insides coming out and couldn't control my reflex. I kicked the door closed to the bathroom. Hugging the toilet didn't seem to stop the feeling. I tried taking deep breaths, and realized I needed to flush the toilet.

When I finally came out there wasn't any sign of our drink glasses. I took a seat in the sitting area and waited to make sure I had truly passed the danger point.

"Do you feel better now?"

"To be honest, I'm not really sure."

"This was a shock to me, and I can tell this was for you too. I should have been more delicate relating the news."

"You did fine. I just can't believe this happened, and happened twice in the same day. Did Gordon give any indication of whether they knew where they took them?"

"He did say they were working closely with the local police there, but there were some issues. He didn't elaborate. There's nothing we can do. Look Scott, you can understand I really need to be home in case the people make a call for money."

"I understand. Do you really want me to make this drop tonight?"

"Yes I do, or you could just *kill* the son of a bitch. I really can't deal with this situation any longer. I've lost one daughter already; I don't need to lose another."

I wondered why he wasn't thinking about his other daughter. I thought about Melanie and noticed I was rubbing my scar through my clothes.

Chapter 48

There was something powerful having the doctor tied to the bed with his fate resting in her hands. Right now something else was in her hand, and the other hand could easily remove it from his body. She ran the back of the straight razor down his chest, across his stomach and then in a circle around what she was holding. She felt him flinch.

"Close your eyes." He resisted. "You are in a very precarious position and need to trust me. Getting me upset is not in your best interest. Now, do as I say. Remember, I am your master." She watched him close his eyes, but he wasn't smiling at all. She ran the back of the blade under his testicles. He flinched. "Careful doc, one false move by either of us, and you might need to use the ladies room in the future.

"Why are you doing this?"

"Did I hear you correctly?" She squeezed him and he started to get harder.

"My lady, please don't hurt me."

"That's much better, but I thought you liked it when I hurt you. You do don't you?"

"Yes...but you could cause some real damage with that razor."

"Are you saying I'm not careful?"

"No. I know you are trying to make me excited."

"Is that right?" She looked at how clean shaven he was. "There's no hair here to cut any longer. Open your eyes for a moment." When she saw his eyes open, she reached down and felt for one of her pubic hairs and cut it. She took the razor and sliced it to make two. "I wasn't expecting it to be that sharp." She jumped off him quickly and he gasped.

She went over to the drawer where she found the razor. There was a leather strap in the drawer. "You must have been a Boy Scout. Always prepared. Were you?"

"Yes, I was."

"Open your mouth and keep your eyes open." He hesitated, but then responded.

"Once again I am not going to ask twice. Don't think about things, just do them. Understand?"

He nodded. She put the end of the leather strap in his mouth. "Bite this and hold it tightly." She pulled on the strap from the other end and his head rose slightly. "Hold still." She took the razor and started to sharpen it on the strap. His eyes were bulging seeing the razor flash back and forth in front of his nose. "Good boy." The razor sounded like a firecracker as she worked it back and forth.

"You can let go now." She took the strap out of his mouth and studied the razor, moving off him to stand by the bed. She held the leather strap in one hand and the razor in the other. She looked at him and noticed he was getting more excited. "Did you like the taste of the leather?"

"It did have an interesting taste."

"Interesting taste huh?" She brought it to her mouth. "It does have a flavor. She held it and licked it. She noticed his body's reaction but didn't say anything. The end was quite wet now. She ran the leather strap down across his mouth and down his body.

When she got to his penis she dangled the strap back and forth so it would bump him there. She saw him lick his lips and swallow. "Soon doctor, very soon." She put the razor on the small nightstand and climbed back on him and resumed the bumping. He was moving in anticipation of the strap's bumps. Then she brought the motion against his testicles. She saw him exhale.

"Close your eyes." He closed them immediately. She dangled the strap letting it touch his skin in different places. It was a game and she was playing him like a fish. When he was getting comfortable with the game and liking what she was doing, especially when she touched him in his special places, she snapped the strap and hit him across the chest.

"Owe. That hurt."

"Silence." She struck him two times on his upper body. His eyes were still closed but he was grimacing. She couldn't resist any longer and resumed the previous dangle. She could hear his breath escaping periodically. Then she wrapped the strap in half and put both halves against his penis. He must have know what was going to happen next as he flinched.

She pulled both ends and both halves of the strap crashed into his penis with an awful noise that even made her grimace. His head rolled to one side, but he didn't utter a sound. "Did that hurt?"

He exploded a *"yes."*

"You have a choice doc." She didn't say anything more and just waited.

"What is it master?"

"I can continue that or I can move it to your balls." He didn't respond other than scrunching up his face. "Would you like to have a comparison?"

"No...no thank you master."

"So, you have made your decision, is that correct?"

He didn't immediately answer, but when she moved slightly he answered, "Yes."

"To make things more pleasurable, I will kiss each place I strike you." She leaned down and kissed the three areas where the strap hit his chest. "You like? Do we have a contract?"

"Yes master."

"She kissed the last place and she knew he no longer was in control.

* * *

It was about fifteen minutes of pain and pleasure. She didn't know what she liked more, pulling the strap to cause him almost intolerable pain, or kissing his pain away. He eventually got what he wanted and he confessed he did masturbate often to her pictures. He was sticky, but she took care of that too.

"Master, I still have to go to the bathroom."

"Not yet. You haven't earned that yet. I have some questions to ask you. And this time, you better not lie once or I will take the razor and make you regret you're a man."

He quickly nodded.

"I want to know about my family."

He didn't say anything or nod.

"I can ask you questions, but in your condition there could be a risk in that. Or better, you can tell me what I should know."

"I will tell you, master. Will you reward me?"

"We'll see." She moved up to sit on his hips instead of his thighs. He took a deep breath. "Show time, doc."

She listened to him for a very long time and he related everything she knew from the file upstairs and some new things. Of course with every tidbit of information she moved against him. He couldn't get the story about her and her family out fast enough.

"Is that it?"

"Yes, master that is everything I know."

"What is going to happen to me next?"

He didn't respond not knowing how to.

"You must have some thoughts about where I stand. Share them."

"Master, I have fallen in love with you." She inserted him and she almost had an orgasm with the feeling.

"You are no longer the ugly little girl who came to the facility. You are extremely beautiful and I want to spend the rest of my life with you."

She studied him and when he opened his eyes she didn't penalize him, but she started moving her body against him. His eyes closed. She thought of Chris, and if it wasn't for him she might just consent to being with the doctor for the rest of her life. She was quickly lost in the feelings, but her fantasy right now was the picture of Scott Tucker. That's who she wanted and who she was going to have. Chris was coming soon, but the two of them were coming now.

Chapter 49

This kidnapping was very different from her last one. There were no men molesting her in the back of a van. They were not tied up nor covered with hoods and she was not stripped. She tried to remember exactly what happened, but she was asleep when they were confronted.

Ralph had said he heard something in the sitting area and told her to stay put. There was a confrontation in that area and Ralph yelled to her to get dressed. By the time she realized what was happening three men were already in the bedroom area. They pointed their guns at her and she thought they were going to shoot her right there. They yanked the sheet away from her and were surprised she was naked. They yelled, "Clothes."

There was no way to hide her body from them as they encircled her. There were some words spoken in Spanish, but this was not like the other abduction. She started to move to her suitcase to get clean clothes and one man pointed his gun at her head. Unfortunately, she never put out clean clothes to wear and had to explain by waving her hands in front of her that she needed some clothes.

He smiled, said something to one of the other men and studied her body, then felt her hair and then laughed. He held the gun continually near her head still focused on her body as she found her underwear and put them on, and then she put on black slacks and a white sweater.

She started to head to the bathroom and the man stepped in front of her. She motioned toward her feet and he shook his head. He waved his gun toward the bedroom door and she knew he was telling her to leave.

When she came out of the bedroom, Ralph was lying in a heap on the floor. One of the men put his gun behind him into his pants and sat Ralph up. A second man came over and did the same thing. They lifted him up. Once Ralph had his bearings they were quickly ushered to the housekeeping staff elevator. As they descended, Ralph was checking out the men in the elevator. One of the men let go of him, pulled his gun and put it to Ralph's head.

When the elevator doors opened they were in the hotel's housekeeping main work area. She noticed women working in the area, but they stopped what they were doing to watch what was happening. One of the men waved his gun at the people and they froze. Once outside they were both pushed into a van and two men got in the van with them.

Ralph was bleeding on the back of his head and when she tried to help him, one of the men pushed her away from him. She pushed him back and looked at his wound. His hair was matted and when she looked at the bleeding it looked like it was stopping, or had already stopped.

Twenty minutes or so later, the van stopped, and then seconds later entered through an automatic door, which immediately closed. Hoods were put over their heads and they were pushed and pulled out of the van. A strong hand grabbed her wrist and she was guided through the building.

They made a couple of turns inside the building and when the hoods were removed they were in a small 8x10 room with just two chairs in the center of the room. Nothing was said to them and the men closed the door and left.

"Mercedes, are these the men who took you earlier?"

"No. These are not the same men, and seemed much more disciplined. They seem like they could be police, or have that background. Let me see your head."

"I'm sorry Mercedes."

"What?"

"I promised I would protect you, but obviously I didn't follow through."

"We're both alive, which is the important part."

"They could have easily killed me. One of the men had a silencer on his gun. They came prepared to do that if they needed to. I'm glad it didn't come to that."

"Ralph, I'm sorry they struck you. Obviously, they want me and you came along unfortunately for the ride. Misery loves company."

"Mercedes I don't want anything to happen to you. It doesn't look good."

"Thanks for being honest with me, but our priority is to stay alive and see if we can learn anything about the other missing people." She remembered some of her captivity, and didn't want to experience it again.

"Are you worried?"

"Yes, I have to admit I am. If this is who I think it is, I'm not sure we will be rescued this time."

Chapter 50

For once she could no longer get the doctor to respond to her urgings. In fact, he was exhausted and falling asleep. That was fine for her because Chris should be here at any minute. She went to the front door and watched for a car approaching. She wondered if she should get dressed or just greet him this way. Her mind was busy mapping out her plan and she decided this was her best strategy. Finally, she saw headlights enter the driveway.

She wondered if Chris was going to come to the front door or the back. She felt her heart beating. What if this is not Chris. *Who else would visit? Her mind quickly went to the hairdresser. She has seen the hairdresser, and she was very attractive. I should ask the doctor if he taps her. Regardless, if it is her she looks like she could be fun.*

She heard the sound of somebody on the front porch and too bad it was only Chris. She unlocked the door and opened it, but stood out of sight. Chris entered the hall apprehensively. Once he was inside the front door, she pushed her hip against it and put her hands around his eyes. He almost collapsed. "Surprise."

"Thank God it is you."

"Are you sure?"

He put his hands behind him and she felt his hands roaming over her naked body. "Oh yeah, I'm sure."

She reciprocated and touched his groin which was showing some signs of excitement. He started to turn around. "No, just stay where you are." She unzipped his pants and reached inside to touch him.

"What about the doctor?"

"Would you rather see him?" She grabbed his belt and unbuckled it and slid it out of his pants. Then she unbuttoned his pants and let them fall to the floor. She slid his briefs down next. She heard his rushed breathing. His right hand had found the junction of her thighs. With one hand under his balls and another around his erection they stood there and enjoyed their renewed touching.

"Stop," she said abruptly. He continued touching her. "Stop, I said." She squeezed him with both hands and his knees started to give out. He stopped and she heard him catch his breath. "Now listen to me. On the third floor I have a surprise for you. There's only one room on the third floor and it has a king size bed in it."

"Okay."

"Go up there and take off all of your clothes. Get on the bed and put your ankles in the ropes at the bottom and put one wrist in a rope at the top of the bed. I'll give you five minutes to do that. When you are done, close your eyes and wait for me."

"I don't know about that Alexis."

She reached, moved her hand and could tell his words were hesitant, but his body was saying something entirely different. "I want you to remember why you're here. We have hours and days to be together. You are going to love it as much as I will. Now go before I send you away."

Without saying anything he stepped out of his pants and headed up the stairs. "Chris?"

"What?"

"You also have a very nice butt."

* * *

When she came in the room, the only light was the afternoon sunlight coming in the windows. She avoided looking at him and went to each window and pulled down the shades. Then she turned the light on.

Chris had done exactly as she had commanded and had his eyes closed. She was sure he peaked, but that was his secret. She came over to the bed and ignored what she really wanted to look at. She slid the slip knot tight to one ankle and then the other. Then she slid the slip knot tight to the one wrist he had put in that rope. She headed to the other side of the bed, but leaned down and blew on him causing him to bounce.

"More bounce to the ounce. You look excited to see me, or better said, you look excited not to see me. You will soon." She continued to the other side of the bed and slipped his wrist into the remaining loop and cinched it up tight. She could see the beads of sweat already forming on his torso. "Warm up here huh?"

"Yes," he responded and pulled on the ropes.

"They aren't too tight are they?"

"Just a little."

"Good. Well Chris, here we are. Or, better said, there you are." She studied his body. He was much better built than the doctor. "Did you open your eyes?"

"No."

She knew he was telling the truth or he would have reacted to the belt over her shoulder. "Keep your eyes closed, I'm doing a study."

"What?"

"I'll tell you later." She climbed onto the bed and sat down on his thighs. "Why are you so excited?" She could see moisture forming on his tip.

"Anticipation, I guess."

"What are you anticipating?"

"I felt how excited you were downstairs. You're up to something."

"Yes, and so are you." She leaned down and blew on his erection. She heard his sigh. She wanted to do more than that, but needed to pace herself. She lifted the belt off her shoulder and dangled it. She touched the tip of the belt to his ears, nose, lips, chin, neck and then watched as his body reacted to touching it to where she knew he would enjoy it the most. "You like?"

"Incredible."

"You're easy." She could see how he was enjoying the light touching. "Open your mouth." He did as instructed and she guided the leather tip of the belt into his mouth. "Suck on it." He obeyed and she couldn't help smiling. She fed more of the belt into his willing mouth, and finally caused him to gag. "If you want me to do this to you, show me what you want me to do."

She could see his tongue moving against the leather, and soon he was almost pulling the belt out of her hand. He started humming and then biting. "Is that what you really want?"

He nodded and started chewing the belt. His erection was straining at its limit and the veins were popping. She lowered her head and licked the salty tip. His middle body lifted off the bed. "Stop."

She slowly pulled the belt out of his mouth. The light brown color had changed to a dark brown from the moisture. He was straining to keep his eyes closed. She dangled the belt over his chest.

"Open your eyes." He did, and his eyes got huge. "That's right Chris…it is so much better with a wet belt." She leaned back and brought the belt down across his chest. He took the blow without showing a sign of pain other than his eyes getting even larger. She slid back down his thighs and struck him again across his chest. He yelled at that one. "I'll do my best not to hurt you." She struck him even harder.

His eyes questioned what she said.

"I lied." She dragged the belt down his chest and across his stomach and then his erection, then very slowly down one thigh and up the other and finally across his most sensitive pair. Then she dangled it against his penis, bumping it from one side and then the other.

His eyes must have known what was next as she slowly bumped him and then picked up the pace. She knew where this was going to end, but he didn't. The sound the belt made striking his body, just increased her focus. He was crying out, but she didn't hear him.

"Alexis, stop…please stop. You're hurting me."

She stopped. "Finally. I thought the study was going to go on for ever. I have to admit, I learned some things about myself, but I also learned some things about you. Now, close your eyes you need to be rewarded."

She leaned down and put her lips around him for just a couple of seconds and then looked up at him. "Open your eyes and watch." His eyes opened. "Good. Now if I understand your treatment of the belt…is that what you really want?"

He nodded.

"But you have to be very sore." She kissed him there. "Are you sure?"

He nodded again.

"I can't hear you."

"*YES*, that's what I want…I can take it." He felt her long red hair against his body. As much as he must have wanted to watch, she noticed his closed eyes blocking out the wonderful pain.

Two men in the same house at the same time in the same condition, but neither of them was who she really wanted. They were just practice for when she would have who her twin had lusted for. Maybe she is more like her twin than she realized. She thought it was Chris, but it was truly Scott. Wouldn't he be surprised when Melanie showed up once more? He would do anything she demanded if Mercedes was threatened. Her plan was indeed forming.

She liked this way too much, and knew the study was over…she could indeed keep men and even better be able to kill them. However, only after she sucked out their life.

Her father deserved a much different treatment.

Chapter 51

It was bitter sweet, but he realized he needed to share some things with Alexis. He wondered if he would be able to walk after what she did to him. He had studied psychology in college, but realized there wasn't really a future in it. However, he knew enough about her behavior to know he was on dangerous ground.

He was still tied up; make that, in a dangerous bed in a very dangerous position. She was cuddled up against his body, and he wasn't surprised he wasn't having any reaction to it. He could tell she had fun doing all those things to him, and he enjoyed most of them. He knew she wasn't going to do anything life threatening to him, or she wouldn't have the new toy to play with anymore. *A part of him wondered if she would get tired of all of these games, and then what?*

She had finally let him make love to her. Well, it was more she made love to his body. It wasn't about his need, it was more about how to satisfy her craving. She was the beautiful, sensuous, but wicked witch. He was glad she didn't have a broom or she might have used that too. However, he soon would have a problem.

He was going to have to leave to pick up the drop money. How was he going to explain that situation? He looked at his wrists and he was going to have to wear long sleeves to hide the rope abrasions. *Was she going to untie him? She did ask him to take the week off. He knew what he needed to do.*

* * *

"Alexis." She didn't respond. He kissed her on the ear and whispered, "Alexis."

She stirred and opened her eyes and looked at his, and then down to where her thigh was across his body. "Don't tell me you're ready again." She moved her thigh. "No, from the looks of it, you won't be ready for hours, if not days."

"Alexis, we need to talk."

"That is something we haven't tried."

"Alexis, I need to tell you some things." He pulled on the ropes. "Please Alexis, untie me. I need to talk to you."

"No Chris, I like things just the way they are. Have you ever been this sore?"

He sighed. "No, this is definitely a first. If you won't untie me, I still have to tell you some things you need to know."

"I think I already know them."

"This is about your father."

"Okay, you have my attention. What do you know about my father and family?"

"Please don't get upset with me, but I think you need to know some things and maybe we can team up to get you what you deserve."

"You have my interest, but you've had everything else."

"I feel at risk being tied up and about to tell you these things."

"Do you think I *really could hurt* you?"

"It crossed my mind somewhere recently."

"Good. I'm not untying you yet. I have some other plans for our time together. Start talking or I will start hitting." She reached for the belt, but stopped short of picking it up.

"Okay, but I want you to promise that you will untie me if you appreciate what I'm telling you."

"I thought contracts were made with free men...you're not really in a position to negotiate."

"Your life is going to change in the next few minutes."

* * *

It took over an hour to convey the details as he knew them. She was quite interested and didn't interrupt him once. As time went on he felt more at ease telling her the details. He started with her arrival at the facility within days of her birth, why she was sent to the facility and what her father knew and what her mother didn't. He told her who her father was and what he has contributed each year to keep her at the care facility. He also told her about the doctor's role in her care since she arrived at the facility.

"Alexis here is what is most important. I hope you are ready for this." He studied her, and she seemed interested. "Alexis you had a twin sister. She was a beautiful child and turned into a very beautiful woman. You have that same beauty…you're strikingly gorgeous. However, as you know, you were covered with hair as a child. What nobody really knew is that it was not permanent. Your beauty today shows that you should really be in the world you were denied."

He continued. "Your father pays for your care each year and pays the doctor separately to maintain his secret. He also has been paying an extra amount recently to keep his secret."

He felt her reaction as she pushed herself up on her elbow and stared directly into his eyes.

"Alexis I have been blackmailing him for weeks now. There is supposed to be another money drop tonight, which I need to pick up around midnight. The money your father is paying to keep you at the care facility, along with the payment to the doctor to maintain the secrecy is really your money. The extra money I'm getting from him is really your money too."

"How did you learn about my father?"

"Good question. I came here once for Doctor Adler and discovered his hidden files. I made copies of them and when I finally reviewed the copies, I learned about everything I told you."

"What else?"

He took a deep breath. "Your twin sister was committed to a mental institution. When she was finally released her behavior got worse. She and some other young women took revenge on some young men. They were kidnapped, tortured and dismembered while still alive. One of those captives was rescued by your other sister, Mercedes."

"What was my twin's name?"

"Melanie. Here's an interesting twist. When Mercedes and some others rescued the young man, Melanie jumped into Boston Harbor. She was thought to have died in the ice cold water as it was the middle of winter. However, she survived somehow and resurfaced months later."

"I'm confused."

"Resurfaced was a bad choice of words. She underwent plastic surgery in England. She killed her surgeon and managed to get to Bermuda. There she built a dungeon like facility and eventually lured several men and held them captive. Some of those men were found murdered. However, a number of them were rescued. The same young man your sister Mercedes rescued was one of the remaining prisoners and was rescued."

"What was that person's name?"

"Scott Tucker."

"I don't understand why she was holding the men prisoners. Was she asking for ransom money?"

"No, she was holding them it appears for sexual services." He felt her thigh move and her fingers touch him.

"So, that is kind of what I have here...right?"

He realized the impact of what she asked. "Alexis, we're just mutually agreeing to this arrangement...right?"

"I don't remember any real agreement. You just did as I instructed you to do. I didn't put you into these bindings. You put yourself into them. Well, other than the last one."

"Yes, but that made me unable to get untied."

"That Chris is a very brilliant observation, but a very stupid predicament." He felt her hand teasing him, but worse he felt his body reacting to it.

"Alexis please."

"Please what?"

"Please let me explain my thoughts." He was being distracted and knew he needed to get this out quickly. "Alexis, we can have all of your father's money. He's rich and you should be entitled to all of it."

"How do you figure that?"

"The only family you have left are your mother, your father, and one sibling, Mercedes. If they were out of the way, you are the next of kin and would inherit all of the family money. You could go anywhere you want and do anything you ever wanted to do."

"Are you saying to kill them?"

"You're the one who has been punished for all of these years. You've missed out on a childhood, school, family fun, boy friends, holiday adventures, and other things. Aren't you kind of pissed off about being basically held a prisoner all of your life?"

"Well, you're in a fine position to be talking about being a prisoner. I see you're starting to enjoy my attention."

"Alexis, what I'm trying to tell you is that I can help you get what you deserve. Then we can have each other for the rest of our lives, and we can live in luxury."

"What about the good doctor?"

"Funny you call him the good doctor…isn't he one of the worst of the bunch? Hasn't he kept you from having your own pleasure and keeping you for his?"

"Are you suggesting something?"

"Maybe he needs to be the first to regret what he has done. Don't you feel violated?"

"I don't think I can kill him."

"Well, your sister didn't have a problem keeping men for her sexual pleasures and then disposing some of them.

You're half way there." Her lips found his body. "Owe, that hurts. Alexis, please stop."

She said something against his body, but he wasn't sure what he heard. It sounded like 'shot.' His mind wasn't on the money pick up any longer.

Chapter 52

"Hello."

"Hello, this is Scott Tucker. Is Mike available?"

"Hi Scott. How have you been?"

"I was doing pretty well until just recently, which is why I need to talk with Mike."

"I'm sorry to hear that. Let me get him."

"Hi Scott. I understand things aren't going well. What's up?"

"Mike, I guess you are the only one I could call. Mercedes has been kidnapped in Venezuela."

"I'm glad you called me. Do you want to get together to talk about this?"

"I guess that makes sense. Mike, I'm really worried about her. She was kidnapped twice. They rescued her the first time, but both she and another agent with her were kidnapped this time."

"Look Scott, I have one thing to take care of and then I can leave to meet with you. Let's plan on meeting at the office in say…an hour."

"Thanks Mike. I'm sorry I'm taking you away from your family."

"Scott, come on, you are family. I'll see you in an hour."

* * *

I pulled into the office parking lot behind the Brattle office. There wasn't much going on for a Sunday afternoon. I knew Mike wouldn't be there as it was only a half hour since I talked with him.

I unlocked the office and turned on the lights and headed to my office. I felt like hitting something. *How could this be happening? I can't lose her too. Losing Lisa was bad enough. I lost my cousin to the strangler, Lisa to a bad car accident and now I could lose Mercedes to people connected to the slave trade in a foreign country.*

I had to do something other than look at my office walls. Coffee sounds like a plan.

They say a pot never boils if you're watching it. I was staring at the coffee pot and could feel my heart keeping beat with the tempo of the pot. I heard a car door and shortly Mike entered.

"I'm making coffee, would you like a cup Mike?"

"Do you have anything stronger?"

"No, coffee will have to do."

"Okay then. Let's meet in the conference room."

I carried two cups to the conference room next to my office and put them down on the mahogany table.

"Judging from your hands shaking I would say you also need something stronger."

"Mike this is like a bad dream. Mercedes' boss called Stephen and told him the news about her kidnapping. Ralph, the other agent, was with her guarding her." *When I said those words I hadn't thought about their being close together. However, there were bigger problems.*

"What can you tell me about her kidnapping?"

"She was rescued from her first kidnapping by the police. She was taken at gunpoint from the car while waiting for her partner and an undercover policeman to check out what could be described as a club. Mercedes told me she was taken to a van and eventually stripped and tied to a pole. She doesn't remember much of the details."

I could tell I was losing my voice and drank some coffee. "When she was rescued, there was a gun fight and I guess one or two kidnappers were killed, one escaped and the other two captured. The police captain rescued her as they had the building under surveillance and saw her being taken into a warehouse on the coast. The latest kidnapping was from the other agent's hotel room. She was being sent home tomorrow because they were concerned more effort would be spent protecting her."

"She will be okay."

"Thanks Mike, but how can you be sure of that?"

"I guess I can't. On another subject, are you still involved with that other investigation?"

"Yes, but right now I'm more concerned with her kidnapping. In fact—"

"In fact what?"

"In fact I am supposed to drop off the money for Stephen tonight. He's at home waiting in case there's a call from the kidnappers."

"Scott, you have to distance yourself from that activity. You're going to get yourself killed."

"I'm not sure I care anymore."

"Well, others around you do."

"Mike, those people there are going to do some awful things to her. She's so beautiful, which is going to work against finding her."

"Scott regarding the missing people from Bermuda."

"Yes, what about them, that's why the FBI is in Venezuela?"

"Right. Do you remember the fellow's name that was missing?"

"Do you mean Ralph Reynolds?"

"No, I'm talking about Richard Damelio."

"I remember his name. What about him?"

"Well his older brother Robert is a private investigator. We have been working closely with him on his investigation of his brother's disappearance. He's in Venezuela and has been for a few weeks. He thinks he knows where his brother and the two other women are."

"That might help in locating Mercedes and her partner. I'll call Paddy to let him know what happened to Mercedes and have him put a call into where Robert is staying."

"That sounds like very good news. How can I help?"

"You have enough problems. Once again this is our forte and not yours. I'm going with you to the money drop."

I started to object, but Mike held up both hands and I knew he was right.

"What time are you dropping the money off?"

"Around ten o'clock."

"Well, then we have some time to get something stronger to drink. Let's go to the pub."

"Yeah, why not add Maggie to my problem list."

"That my friend is your issue, not mine."

We started to turn things off in the office. *I thought of Maggie's dance routine and the pole, and then thought of Mercedes being held against her will and what might be happening right this minute to her.*

Chapter 53

Fortunately for Scott, Maggie was not working at the Harvard Pub today. He has enough problems without going down that path. He was going to meet Scott later to make the money drop. After two beers, Scott was going back to his apartment, and he went back to the office to call Paddy at home.

"Hello."

"Paddy, its Mike. I need to let you know what has happened and get your thoughts of what our next action should be."

"I'm going to put you on hold and take this in my office. Hi Mike, I'm back. What's up?"

"I just met with Scott for a couple of beers. He's all upset. Mercedes, as you know, is in Venezuela. She and another agent were kidnapped today. In fact, she was kidnapped and rescued earlier."

"Oh my God. It looks like she might have been a target."

"Somehow she got separated from her partner and was kidnapped the first time from that team's unmarked vehicle. The police fortunately had a building staked out and saw the kidnappers bring her into the building."

"I know where this discussion is going," Paddy said.

"You most likely do. She was going to be sent home as she experienced quite the trauma, but while she and the other agent were together in his hotel room, they were kidnapped. All this happened just a little while ago."

"Do you want me to call Robert Damelio to see if he knows anything?"

"Yes, and something else."

"What is it?"

"Scott is still doing that investigation and is actually doing the money drop tonight."

"He shared that with you?"

"Yes, I think he's really shook about Mercedes' kidnapping."

"Mike you have to do something. Scott is getting in way over his head."

"I already took care of that. I'm going with him tonight for the drop, and to see if we can catch this guy before he leaves the area."

"I better call Robert right now. Where can I reach you?"

"I'm in our Harvard Square office, and I will stay here."

"Call you as soon as I have something to report."

* * *

"Hello."

"Mike its Paddy. I spoke with Robert and brought him up to speed. Here's the status of things there. He has a resource that used to be on the police force there. Between the two of them they believe they have located where his brother was taken, and he is still alive. He also believes he knows where the sister of the murdered woman is being kept. However, he is still trying to find out where the other woman is."

"What is his plan?"

"Well, he thinks his brother is not in any immediate danger. His plan was to continue to investigate to see if they could locate the other missing woman. However, our timing was excellent."

"Why's that?"

"He saw some activity during their stakeout and wondered if that had something to do with the other woman. Now he thinks that activity had to do with the two FBI agents being taken to that building."

"Is he going to get the police involved?"

"Well, here's where it gets dicey. They have enough evidence to show that the police captain, Chavez, is involved with the slave-trade operation. He might even be the ring leader. Regardless, the former policeman with him doesn't trust the captain."

"So, where does that leave us?"

"He wants to contact a high-ranking friend in the military for his advice."

"Paddy, time is of the essence."

"I know, but think of how far we are compared to where we would have been. I'm going to tell Robert to have his associate contact that person and tell him we can get our government agencies involved if need be."

"Paddy, would you please ask Robert if he feels comfortable trying to rescue Mercedes and the other agent?"

"I already have. He says there's too much at stake to risk it."

"Paddy, you know what that means for Mercedes don't you?"

"She's a smart lady. I think she will be okay until she can be rescued."

"She's also too beautiful a lady…if you know what I mean."

Chapter 54

"Would you like to see the doctor?" Alexis asked.

"No, not really. Why?"

"I thought you might be getting tired of being tied up, and would enjoy someone else's situation."

"Sounds to me like, you would enjoy my watching."

"It had crossed my mind. You could even watch him pee in a bottle."

"You've got to be kidding."

"No. He needed to go, and that was the best method I could think of. In fact, I just remembered he wanted to go hours ago. Are you sure you don't want to watch?"

"I'm sure."

"Maybe I should keep you tied up until you're in the same predicament. I even took pictures of him while he was going. However, they're in my room. It would be nice to have some of you and some when you are going to the bathroom. Do you need to go?" She tickled his stomach.

"Alexis, let me go. We need to talk about where we're going from here."

"Good. Then I'll wait for when you need to go."

"That's not what I meant and you know it."

"I'm going to go get the camera."

"Alexis please untie me."

"I will give you a choice…I can untie you and you can do what I tell you to do to the doctor. Or, I can untie him and bring him up here and let him see who is in his bed, and let him do what I tell him to do to you. I think he will be pissed, no pun intended, and it won't take much effort on my part to have him punish you."

"You wouldn't."

"Do I detect a dare? Chris, think about the situation carefully. I would much rather be with you than the doctor. Besides, if I were to untie him…I don't think he would let me restrain him again. You on the other hand, I think enjoyed things. As a matter of fact, I think I detect junior raising his head."

"Alexis please stop. We need to make some plans as to what we are going to do."

"In another minute or so, you will change your mind."

"I promise after I pick up the money you can do whatever you want with me, but I have to get the money."

"Will you allow me to tie you up?"

"If that is what you need. Alexis, the doctor has a lot of money, and your father is rich. Our priority needs to be on those two people and not on each other."

"Wouldn't you rather be with a younger man for the rest of your life? I can help you to get what you deserve. The doctor should pay for how he has treated you all these years. Your father is even worse. He should have checked on you, or your condition, at least once in all these years. You have been screwed by them."

"Are you any different?"

"Yes, I came because you asked me to."

"I think you came because I made you come. In fact, I would like to see you do that once more and then I will let you go. I promise." She started running her fingers along him to get him excited. "Would you like to see his surprise if I brought you downstairs naked, and showed him what your body is capable of doing?"

"No. Owe, that hurts."

"Yes, but you love it and we both know it."

* * *

Chris had drifted off to sleep. She got up without disturbing him and headed downstairs. She wasn't going to try to sneak up on the doctor. She found him asleep as well.

"Good evening Doctor Adler," she said as she sat on his bed.

"Alexis you have been gone a very long time. Where have you been and what have you been doing?"

"I would have thought you would remember your training. But no, you are right back where you were when you first came here. I better get the belt."

"I'm sorry master. I missed you and wondered why you left me so long."

"Nice try, but that doesn't sound very genuine to me." She slipped off the bed and stood right beside where his head was. She watched his eyes scanning her body. After his eyes had made the rounds a few times she started touching her breasts, and then pinched her nipples. She closed her eyes and thought of what it would be like to have Scott doing these things to her."

She didn't know how long she had been playing with her body, but when she opened her eyes it was long enough to get the doctor very excited. It wasn't the doctor who was tied up, it was Scott. She had him right where she wanted and she had control of his body. She climbed on the bed and across the doctor with her buttocks near his chin and closed her lips around his erection.

He bit for the bait and she did the same. He was doing a great job of hitting the right spot and when she finally screamed, she felt him pulse and pulse and pulse. *Both her sisters had tasted Scott, and now she had too. Then she realized the doctor had tricked her. Chris was right. The doctor would be the first to pay for how he has treated her.*

She thought of her sister Melanie and the other women keeping body parts as trophies. It was as plain as the nose on her face, what parts she was going to keep. She wrapped the fingers of one hand around his parts and with her index finger ran it from one side to the other. Practice makes perfect.

He said something but she didn't hear what he said.

She ran her tongue over her teeth and thought that would be a better method. *Would she have enough control over*

Chris to have him take Polaroids of that moment? Which would make a better picture, his face or elsewhere, or even both? Chris, I now have some input to the plan. A picture of the doctor's surprised expression would have to do.

* * *

She left the doctor resting and headed back to the upstairs bedroom. When she entered the bedroom, Chris was awake and his eyes followed her from the doorway over to the bed.

Alexis started to untie Chris, but wasn't saying anything to him. Chris wasn't saying anything, and might have feared if he did she might not finish untying him.

When he was all untied she watched him rub his wrists. "Sore?"

"Yeah, some."

"I wasn't talking about your wrists."

"Yeah there too."

"Good. How does it feel to be free again?"

"I like it. Would you like to be tied up now?"

"No thanks. Maybe some other time. Would you like that?"

"Yes, I really think I would."

"Me thinks you might like it too much. We'll see. What do you want to talk about?"

"You were gone longer than I thought you would be. Did the doctor get to go?"

"Not exactly."

"What does that mean?"

"Would you like to find out?"

"I don't think so."

"Too bad, you would have really enjoyed it. I know I would have."

"Alexis, let's talk about what happens next."

She reached for him.

"No, let's focus on what we need to plan."

"I've given that some thought already. What do you suggest?"

"I've had some time to think. We need to take all the doctor's money, somehow. Then we need to have you get all of your parents' fortune. You really are next in line to inherit the estate, but if your sister was out of the picture it would make it neater."

"Are you planning on killing the doctor, and my family?"

"Yes, but I haven't figured out how to eliminate the members of your family yet."

"Then you figured out how to kill the doctor?"

"Yes."

"I have my own plan there, but you have to promise me you will take some pictures."

"You mean you're going to kill him yourself?"

"The thought had crossed my mind."

"You couldn't do it."

"Remember, if I do it, you have to consent to take pictures."

"No problem."

She looked at him and smiled. *Would she kill Chris the same way and keep their remnants as her trophies?* She looked down between Chris' legs. *She wondered what Scott looked like. She was definitely determined to discover the answer, and Mercedes was going to be her bait.*

Chapter 55

He had time to think now that Alexis left him again. She was up to something, but he didn't know what it was. She was spending much more time elsewhere, and although was visiting and giving him pleasure, he had the feeling she was capable of really hurting him. He has to get free.

He pulled on the ropes and they cut into his wrists. If he pulled real hard would the rope pull free from the headboard? He pulled, but there was no sign the rope would pull free. He spotted the straight razor on the nightstand only a few feet from his right hand. He rolled his body and reached but he was still a foot away from it. The pressure on his bladder reminded him he really needed to go.

It was all he could do when Alexis was playing with his body, not to present her with a different kind of a present. Without any question, if he had let his bladder go, she would have punished him for it. *What is she doing? Why is she leaving him like this? If she ever let him tie her up again, she was going to really regret what she has done to him.*

He reached for the razor again, but it was still too far away. He realized the end table was a few inches away from the bed. His fingers were just inches away from it. He pushed his arm as far as he could and extended his fingers. No luck. His other hand was close to the wall on the other side. He stretched his hand and his fingers touched the wall. He pushed with all his strength and the bed moved slightly.

He reached for the nightstand, but his fingers couldn't reach it. He repeated the process and the bed moved just an inch at best. He could feel his heart beating a mile a minute. *Was the noise he heard Alexis returning? He remembered her finger simulating cutting his precious parts. If she were to catch him trying to reach the razor, would she indeed remove them?*

She was turning into her crazy sister right in front of his eyes, and there was no room to speculate as to her capacities…it was too risky. If she read those articles on what her twin did, it might give her thoughts about keeping body parts. She would be lost if I wasn't her resource. He remembered the look in Chris' eyes when he was signing her out…has she secured him as her other resource? Shit!

Chapter 56

She said a silent prayer for her own safety and for
Ralph's. *Without any question she knew she was more
valuable alive than dead. That is her bargaining chip, but
she wondered if she could make it last.*

"Mercedes, I'm sorry." Ralph broke the silence.

"We're both alive. There wasn't anything you could have
done given the situation. Right now we just have to focus
on staying alive and hoping somehow the police or Max
will find a way to find us and rescue us."

"Mercy, I'm worried more about you."

"I know how to take care of myself. I did it once, I can do
it again." She thought of Scott and how she wanted to be
with him now. By now, he must know they have both been
kidnapped. *Maybe he doesn't know. Why would Max have
called him? He doesn't even know how to reach Scott.
Maybe Max called my father. If he did, surely my dad
would have called Scott.* Her thoughts were interrupted by
the sound of the door being unlocked.

* * *

The door opened and two men came into the room. One
of them pointed at the chairs. "Sit." They went over to the
chairs and sat down.

"You FBI pigs." The same man hit Ralph across the side
of his head with his pistol. Ralph was knocked out and fell
off the chair, landing in a heap on the floor. The two men
looked at her. "Take off your clothes."

"In your dreams," she yelled.

Both men looked at each other and smiled. "We have
ways." One man came over and knelt down and looked into
her eyes. "You will. Take him." They both went over to
Ralph and dragged him out of the room. She started to get
up, but one of them pointed his gun at her. She watched the

two men drag his unconscious body out of the room. The sound the lock made echoed in her head.

A half hour later she heard some yelling and then Ralph's screams. They were beating him up from the sounds of it. She looked at her watch and it was almost 11 pm. They had been doing this for only minutes, but it seemed like hours. Ralph was barely screaming now and sounded like he didn't have the strength any longer.

The key turned in the lock and the door slowly opened. She wasn't surprised when she saw who was standing there.

Chapter 57

They took Mike's car to the Dudley Street station. Mike watched from his car while Scott made the drop an hour ago. There was some activity around the station, maybe because it was the end of the holiday weekend. He had been lecturing Scott on staying away from any new investigations and it looked like he was making progress.

It was now 11 pm and he pulled out his 45 and caulked it.

"Is that necessary?" Scott asked.

"Maybe not, but it might even the score if we happen to have a crowd who don't just want to ask us how we enjoyed the holiday weekend."

"I suppose you're right. Mike, have you given any thought about how close we are to the gang that kidnapped those men?"

"The thought had passed my mind. They do have a score to settle, and if they recognized you, we might not have enough bullets."

"How many do you have?"

"Don't ask."

"So, you feel you might not have enough?"

"Let's just say that my handgun might not be enough fire power to even the score. Isn't this fun? Are you thinking about not involving yourself in any more investigations?"

"Yes. I didn't want to get involved in this one. However, I felt compelled to help Stephen out. Right now, I'm more concerned with Mercedes' safety than ours."

"Well, that is about to change real quickly," he said as he looked in the rear view mirror.

Scott turned to see five men in dark clothes, two on the sidewalk and three coming down beside the cars parked behind them.

"Hold on," Mike yelled as he started the car. He floored the accelerator just as the men reached the car. One of the men looked familiar. Mike was anticipating gun shots, but none came.

* * *

They were several blocks away when Mike pulled the car over. "I don't think they were going to ask us about the weekend, do you?" He looked over, smiled and shut the car off.

"I'm glad I wasn't alone."

"If you were alone, I'm not sure we would see you alive again. I thought one of those men looked like one of the gang members from the shootout in Lowell."

"Thanks Mike."

"Alright here's the deal Scott. I can bring you to your apartment and this is the end of your involvement in this investigation, or we can go back to the drop point to see if we can get a fix on the guy who picks up the money."

"Tough choice."

"Scott, this isn't funny any longer. You are in way over your head and *you* can't continue this investigation *alone* any longer."

Scott didn't immediately respond. "Okay Mike, you win. I agree that this has gone too far. I'm not equipped to handle this alone any longer. I'll do whatever you say."

"That my fine friend is the first sensible thing you've said tonight." He pushed on Scott's shoulder. "Now, do you want me to drop you off at your apartment, or do you want to risk your ass again?"

"Since you put it that way, I'd be a fool to go back there."

"Yes, you would. However, I know despite your Harvard education, where we're both headed." He reached under the seat and pulled out a small revolver. "This might just save your life or mine. The safety is next to the trigger on the right side and you just point it and pull the trigger. If you need to use it, don't be afraid to…we'll deal with the consequences, but we at least will be alive. Hopefully. I don't suppose in all of your investigations you have ever shot a pistol before?"

Chapter 58

"Chris, why are you in such a rush to get dressed?" Alexis asked.

"If I don't get dressed now, I might miss picking up the money from your father."

"So, you would rather have the green stuff instead of this white and red stuff?" She ran her hands down her still naked body.

"Alexis I'm already sore. I'll be ready again when I return and I will spread all those hundred dollar bills across your naked body."

"Am I going to be tied up?"

"That is up to you."

"What do you want?"

"It would be nice to have you tied up instead of me."

"And what would you do to me?"

"What would you like?"

"If I'm tied up, it's not really up to me, is it?" She jumped onto the bed and grabbed the ropes with her hands. "How do I look?"

"Good enough to eat."

"Doesn't it bother you that I have my friend?" She looked over to his briefs. "I can see you're getting excited again." She hooked a toe into the top of his briefs and tried to pull them down. That wasn't working too well, so she just put her toes on his bulge and wiggled her foot. He backed up.

She let go of the ropes and sat up putting each ankle into the ropes at the foot of the bed. Then she grabbed the ropes again. She slid her body back and forth across the sheets. "Oh Chris, stop doing that. Oh Chris, stop."

He wasn't doing anything but it was obvious his body was reacting to her display.

"Come on Chris, play out your fantasy. Make me want to make love to you. I've made you do things for me. Now make me regret what I've done. From the looks of your tent, it won't take you too long." She let go of the rope with one hand and slipped the rope tight onto the other wrist and then grabbed the other rope. "Chris, I'm only one rope away from being your prisoner. Surely, you've thought of me this way since you saw what the doctor was doing to me that first night."

He pulled off his briefs and jumped on her. He tried to put her remaining wrist into the last rope, but she let go of the rope and grabbed him between his legs. "Nice try, but this will give you something to think about."

He moved quickly to her side and felt between her legs. "You don't want me to leave. You want me as much as I want you." He watched her head move from side to side.

"You're wrong Chris. I want you even more than you want me. Tell me what a bad girl I've been and punish me like you saw the doctor punishing me." He resisted and knew he needed to leave.

"Do it Chris, or so help me, I will get you tied up and you will regret having appendages." She removed her hand and grabbed the remaining rope.

He went over to the dresser and brought the belt back. He dragged it down her body and then back up. He saw her eyes as big as saucers. "Close those eyes and open your mouth." He slid the belt into her mouth. "Lick it." She did as he told her. "Bite it." She did as he told her. She opened her eyes and winked at him.

"You're bad. You are very very bad." He remembered his pain.

He heard the whack, whack whack and his breathing was rushed. The belt's noise wasn't painful any longer.

"Stop. Owe. Chris stop. *Chris stop, that hurts. Stop, I said.*"

He felt her hitting his body with her now free hand, but he didn't stop...he couldn't.

He wondered if the doctor could hear the whack, whack whack.

He heard her sobbing. She was a bad girl because she was turning him into a monster. He threw the belt away and started kissing all of the body parts he had abused. He heard a deep sound coming from her throat. Her warmth soon engulfed him and she was no longer crying. He felt her nails dig the flesh of his shoulder. It hurt but he was punishing her in a different fashion.

* * *

When he left he was sore, but she must have been as well. Her body was covered in red welts. He could have easily slipped her remaining wrist into the rope, but for some reason he didn't. He just consumed the image of her lying on the bed.

Was he afraid of what she might do to him later? He guessed that was part of it. He remembered her scream when she tightened on him and felt her orgasm followed quickly by her second one.

He wondered if the doctor heard her scream, and if he did, what he thought might have been happening. He's not a dummy and might know by now she has another distraction.

It was obvious he was never going back to the care facility and it was time for major changes. Having Alexis for the rest of their lives was going to be a very interesting time. One of them might not survive the other. He was going to be sure after she got her father's money that it wasn't going to be him. He thought about how he could make it look like a murder suicide. That meant the doctor had to be kept alive for an extended period of time.

He thought about watching her torture the doctor. She would be even more excited than she was a few minutes ago. That gave him some ideas.

He pulled his car into one of the many parking spaces out of sight of the Dudley Street station, but where he could

easily get away. The last rushed escape was an ugly
memory.

Chapter 59

"Hello Mercedes, are you surprised to see me?"

"No, not really."

"From the time I last rescued you, I've pictured you being here with me."

"You know captain…I had a feeling you were involved in some manner with these kidnappings."

"It's not such an ugly business and it has its side benefits. The women are all attractive and eventually realize that it is better not to resist."

"So, are the other missing citizens alive?"

"You are really in no position to be asking the questions."

Ralph's weak scream caused them both to listen.

"What are you doing to him?"

"My dear Mercedes, I am not doing anything to him."

"Those men are then."

"No my dear Mercedes. They are not doing anything to him. Would you like to see him? You can stop his pain you know."

She was surprised he hadn't approached her or threatened her in any fashion. However, she remembered how he looked at her body when he found her tied to that column in the warehouse. She felt her body crawling. He came over to her side and she smelled the same smell from before; a combination of sweat and semen.

He put a hand on her arm and she shook it off. "Fine, have it your way. Come. Let's see why your agent friend wasn't killed when we kidnapped you."

* * *

As they left the room, he was following her. She felt his eyes consuming the back of her body. She didn't see Ralph anywhere. The captain pointed down a hallway and she hesitantly headed in that direction. There was an open door and the light was shining into the hallway. She headed to the doorway.

The room was an L-shaped. In it she saw a bed with a bare mattress and a grey blanket. There was also a long table. She expected to see Ralph, but he wasn't in the room. There were a number of instruments on the table, none of which looked that comforting. The captain held out his hand in the direction of where the room turned. She went in hesitantly.

She saw the two men standing at the corner, but the rest of the sight made her double over.

Ralph was blindfolded and stretched naked to this suspended apparatus. He was covered in blood. Next to him was an attractive and nearly naked woman. She was clad only in her bikini bathing suit, which looked like it had seen better days.

Mercedes saw the captain nod to the woman and she struck Ralph across his chest with something resembling a small whip with multiple leather tendrils. Ralph let out a weak yell. Mercedes turned to the captain. "Stop this. She's killing him."

"No she's not yet. This can go on for hours. Don't ask us how we know."

Mercedes looked over at the young woman who was holding the whip with her head bowed. "Mercedes I would like you to meet Ms. Scott. This is Helen Scott. Her sister Paula was the one found murdered. Ms. Scott here has learned that it is better to do as directed than to be stubborn and be tortured herself. Isn't that right Helen?" She didn't answer, and he took a quick step towards her.

"Yes."

"That is better Ms. Scott. Now strike him again and this time show Agent Strong how adept you have become."

She hesitated. "My two associates would just love to satisfy their pent up desire and teach you your lessons again. Do I need to do that?"

Tears were running down her cheeks.

"Agent Strong and her fellow agent Mr. Reynolds are here to rescue you. So, if you think you are about to be rescued you can think again. Now *hit him*."

She started to move her arm, but Mercedes intervened. "Wait. Please don't hit him any more." He obviously had lost a considerable amount of blood.

"That is up to you Ms. Strong." She looked at Ralph, then the poor young girl and then at the captain. She had a question on her face.

"Take your clothes off." She hesitated. "As you insist...hit him." She didn't make any move. The captain took the whip and struck her across her shoulder, and then took a step toward Ralph.

"Wait." Ralph was here to protect her and now she needed to protect him. She knew it was going to come to this anyway, so she needed to save him from being punished anymore. She lifted off her white sweater and noticed Helen bowing her head. She was undoing her pants and could see the bulge in the captain's pants.

"Jose, take her away and make sure she learns her lessons better the next time." Mercedes stopped and watched her being led by both men out of the room. "Close the door."

She heard the door slam and the woman scream.

The captain motioned to her to go over to the bed. She stood there in her underwear. The captain went back to Ralph and picked up the whip.

"Wait."

He watched her turn away from him and then she unhooked her bra.

"Remember my sweet agent...I am not making you do this...you are doing this to save your friend from being punished. Now turn around and act your part, or plan on seeing your friend torn to pieces."

She reluctantly turned and finally dropped the bra.

"You are even more beautiful than I remembered." He walked over to the bed and stood with the mattress separating them. He had his uniform shirt off and had unzipped and stepped out of his trousers. "Come over here and show me the rest."

Scott I'm so sorry. Please forgive me, but I have no choice.

Chapter 60

He wasn't going to be asking Stephen for any more money. His plans were focused on getting all of the Strong fortune and Alexis was the means to that end.

That reminded him of how sore his end was since Alexis was so mean to his body. I'll remember all those things you did to me, and return the favor. Despite all of his body pains the memory of her beautiful body made it worthwhile.

Right now he wished he had never asked for this additional money. Chris you are smarter than this. If you get yourself killed you won't have the opportunity to enjoy all the money and more importantly Alexis.

It was now midnight. He hadn't seen any activity in this area for over fifteen minutes. Double checking around his car and the station there wasn't anyone around. He pulled the bulb out of his overhead light and opened the car door. He walked across Columbus Avenue and headed quickly toward the station building.

There were some cars parked on Tremont Street, but nothing that caused him any concern. Once inside the station he jumped up on the bench and felt for the money bag. His fingers hit on the bag and he quickly pulled it out and jumped down from the bench. He wanted to get away from this area as fast as he could. That is when he saw them.

Two white men were headed across Tremont and were focused on him. They were surely out of place in this area of the city and at this hour of the night, he wasn't going to chance that they had other business. They could also be plain clothes cops and he didn't want to answer any questions. He stepped out of the building and hustled around the corner. They changed direction as well, and he knew they were after him.

There was no traffic to speak of on Columbus Avenue and he made a dash for his car. He looked over his shoulder and they were running across the street about fifty feet behind him. He quickly unlocked the car, started it and put it in gear. The older of the two men stepped right in front of his car but dove out of the way as he accelerated. If they were cops, they wouldn't have a cause to shoot, but he hunched himself down just in case.

He was speeding down Columbus headed into downtown Boston, but wanted to be headed in the opposite direction. He had the money, the men were not following him and Alexis was most likely waiting for him.

Well, actually to put it more accurately, she was anticipating his body's return. The fact that his head was attached was incidental. What if the doctor got free and he is waiting? What if they are both waiting? He wondered if he could really pull off killing the Strong family.

He reduced his speed to just over the speed limit and was finally headed to the doctor's house. *It occurred to him that he had never examined the bag to see if the contents were really money. He wasn't going to stop to see and if the money wasn't there…there was nothing he could do about it.*

Chapter 61

The gold Pontiac nearly ran Mike down, but he dove out of the way. It all happened so fast I couldn't believe what Mike was trying to do. *Did he actually think the driver was going to stop?* I ran over and helped Mike up.

"Mike, my God that was close. I thought he was going to run right over you. Are you okay?"

He brushed off his pants. "I'm okay, but my pride is a little tarnished. I had no idea he would actually try to run me down. He's more desperate than I thought. I got a good look at him, despite the headlights. You must have gotten a good look at him too. Would you recognize him again?"

"Mike, I recognized the car. That's the same '63 Pontiac that was at the care facility. He must be one of the staff. I doubt he's headed back there."

"You're right there."

"Mike, I know where he lives. It was one of the addresses you gave me. Do you want to check that out?"

"What do we have to lose?"

* * *

Twenty minutes later we had made two passes of that address with no signs of the gold Pontiac.

"Well Scott, do you have any other ideas? Pretend I'm not here. What would you do next?"

"I say we wait here another few minutes to give him time to get here. He might have taken extra time to lose us if he thought he was being followed."

"Okay." Mike pulled into a parking space and turned off the car and the lights. "And if he doesn't show up, then what?"

I thought of Mercedes' kidnapping and wondered if I would ever see her again. "We can catch the next plane and head to Venezuela."

"Worried about Mercedes?"

"Mike I know what it's like to be held a prisoner. Being held as a sex slave for Melanie's pleasure is not a pleasant memory. Mercedes is a much more valuable commodity than I was, and I'm really concerned that I may never see her again, or worse."

"I understand, I really do. However, there's no way we can be any help down there. We need to hope our connection, or the FBI, will be able to find her before too much time goes by."

"Mike, I was worried she was going to get too close to Ralph, the other agent, but now I wish he was even closer. Does that make any sense?"

"My money is on Mercedes."

"Mike, would there be any chance that she could come to work for our office and support our investigations?"

"That, Scott, is a very interesting scenario. I'll have to talk to Paddy about that."

"That's assuming she survives."

"Scott she will."

Surviving is one thing, but being able to love again might be more difficult. I realized I was fingering my arrow scar. *What kind of emotional and/or physical scars was Mercedes going to have after this? Somehow, I had to make this a heads' up kind of day. It could only improve, right?*

"Mike, you had a second address for the manager of the care facility. Maybe we should check that address…these guys could be both involved in the extortion."

"Much as I hate to say it…have you thought of doing investigations in the future?"

"Not any more Mike."

"Progress was made. I have the address in my notebook. Scott, will you open the glove box and read me the address under Adler."

Chapter 62

"Agent Strong you are one of the most beautiful women I
have ever seen. Please sit on the bed." She didn't move.
"Do I have to remind you of how vulnerable your agent
friend is? Good girl."

He had seen her naked before and she didn't like his
devouring gaze, and she liked it even less now. He still had
his boxers on, but it was obvious he was enjoying himself.
"I take it captain that you are the leader of the slave trade
here in Venezuela?"

"My dear Mercedes, you give me much too much credit. I
am only connected with the business here in Maracaibo. I
would not be physically able to sample the wares in all of
Venezuela. However, I do enjoy the benefits connected
with teaching these young ladies how to respect their care
takers. You saw for yourself how Ms. Helen learned how to
duplicate the punishment she received."

"Why did you kill her sister?"

"I'm not a killer, I'm a lover."

"Okay, then why did you have her killed?"

"She was not learning her lessons well at all. She was
creating too much, how do you say, chaos within the girls.
Although she was tortured, she still was resisting our
instructions. More was to be gained by setting an example
for the others. It worked, but it was a waste of a fine body.
However, yours is many degrees more exciting than hers.
The contrast of your red hair and your fair skin is
intoxicating."

It was obvious that his boxers were the only thing
separating them. She knew she had to keep him talking.

"Close your eyes Agent Strong." She did not. "Please
close your eyes Agent Strong, I would hate to mar your
pretty body." Her eyes closed but she jumped when his
fingers felt the consistency of her pubic hair. "Your country

is foolish to let you come to a country like ours. You my lovely lady are worth a king's ransom."

"How many other American women do you have captive?"

"Would you like to trade answers for services?"

She didn't answer him.

"I thought not. However, we have almost twenty women from your country and another fifty or so, from other European countries. They have all signed contracts." His hands left her body and she heard him remove his boxers.

"What do you mean contracts?"

"I see what you are doing. You are trying to keep me talking to prevent me from getting you excited. However, the longer I take the more excited I will be." His hands returned to her body. "Okay. The women were all 'rescued from their captors.' The fee for their rescue varies, but a value is put on it. A contract is established between them and our organization…a business contract, which they sign willingly, and they earn money for services to pay off their rescue amount."

"So, Paula Scott wouldn't sign the contract. Is that correct?"

"You have beauty and brains, what a lovely combination. However, I can't fuck your brain. You are going to sign a contract too. In fact, your contract will set a new record. You will be an old lady before you earn enough to pay it in full. I am making an exception for you, and the contract will be between you and me. You will be working at my ranch."

"Where is Mr. Damelio?"

"He is working on my ranch. He is a skilled accountant and he keeps the books for the ladies."

"Now for all this information you owe me something in return. I'm sure you don't want me to go to your agent friend and remind you of how much pain he was enduring."

She looked down her body and saw Ralph in the other area, but he looked like he had passed out possibly from blood loss. She knew what the captain wanted and it was only a matter of time until she couldn't delay him any longer. "You don't need to punish him any more, he's suffered enough."

"You sound like you have more than a working relationship with him. Has he seen your lovely body? Has he made love to you?"

"That is none of your business."

"Then he has. Yes it does have something to do with my business. If you are pure, then your rescue amount should be worth more. If you are, let's say experienced, your rescue amount would not be worth that much. You certainly look very preserved to me."

She smelled what she smelled before, a combination of sweat and semen. It was turning her stomach. Other than looking over to Ralph she had kept her eyes closed.

"You have a scent of Gardenia. It is very intoxicating. I think we have talked long enough."

She felt his hands on her breasts.

There was a crash against the door to the room.

"Captain…I'm very sorry to disturb you, but there are military vehicles at the entrance. We need to leave." He started to run out of the room.

"Wait. We need to take the women with us," Captain Chavez said.

"There's no time. We need to escape through the tunnel. They are ready to break the door in." He ran out and left the captain, who was fumbling with his clothes.

"You are a very lucky lady. Two days in a row you have been rescued. I could kill you right now, but mark my words, I will find a way to get you again…and next time I won't waste time talking." He was semi-dressed and heading out the door. "You need to make sure you are never alone again."

She heard the loud banging and hurried to get dressed. She heard loud yelling, but she was trying her best to get Ralph untied from his restraints.

Three men ran into the room with rifles drawn, saw her and pointed their guns down to the floor. One of the men spoke. "You must be Agent Strong judging from your red hair, and this must be Agent Reynolds. Is that correct?"

"Yes." But she was shocked he knew their names. "How did you find us?"

"You and I have friends in this country. Do you know where his clothes are?"

"No." She went over to the bed and took the grey blanket and covered him. "This will have to do for now. He needs to go to the hospital."

"Do you?"

"I'll go with him, but I don't need medical attention. Do you know where Agent Max Gordon is?"

"Who is he?"

She felt the hair on the back of her neck stand up...who was her friend that got the military involved?

Chapter 63

He pulled his Pontiac into the doctor's driveway. The concern over whether there was money in the bag was put to rest. There were hundred dollar bills in five neat stacks. He wouldn't have expected anything less from Stephen, but none the less he was glad the money was there.

He walked up the driveway to the front door and realized he had no way to enter. He contemplated ringing the doorbell, but the door opened suddenly.

"Welcome home Chris," Alexis said as she moved away from the door. "Don't you just love to come home to a naked woman?"

He looked at her body and smiled without answering.

"I see you brought a present. Did you happen to bring anything to eat?" she said as she closed the door.

He remembered their last sex session. "Not exactly."

She ran up the stairs without saying anything more.

He wondered what she had been doing while he was picking up the money. When he got to the third floor bedroom she was on the bed and had resumed her tied position. "It is even nicer to come home to someone who is ready for sex."

"You know that because?"

"I bet you're wet."

"You know that how?"

He went over to the bed and looked at her body. He thought he had it already burned into his brain, but it was obvious this was better than any memory. She had the ropes at her ankles pulled tight around them, and one wrist was also tied tightly. He went around to the far side of the bed. He put the bag down between her thighs and saw her smile. He took his shirt off and undid his belt. "Close your eyes, I want to surprise you."

Her eyes went to the bulge in his pants. "Somehow I'm not surprised by how excited you look." Then she closed her eyes and smiled.

He quickly grabbed her wrist and pulled the rope around it and tightened it. "Now are you surprised?"

She pulled on all the ropes and yelled, "Untie me now."

"You're the one who is not in control any longer. I asked you if you were surprised."

"Not only am I surprised, but I'm pissed. Now untie me."

He slipped his remaining clothes off. Then he climbed onto the bed sitting on her thighs.

"Well at least you look more than happy to see me tied up."

"Yes, you can say I have been thinking about finally getting you in this position. How does it feel to really be a prisoner?"

She bounced her body on the bed pulling on the ropes.

"It's very hot up here. I can see you're starting to sweat." He ran the back of his middle finger down between her breasts and confirmed she was indeed sweating. His fingers continued down past her navel and rested against her opening. He could see her rushed breathing.

Neither of them moved at all for well over a minute. He saw her nipples confessing her excitement. He loved her beauty and wondered if he would ever risk letting her go. He felt the heat against his fingers, but had not moved them. Her eyes were tightly closed. He lightly blew on one nipple and then the other. Her body lifted up off the mattress putting pressure on his fingers.

He wanted her to want him as much as he wanted her. He was learning how to play her body like it was a puppet. He saw her lick her lips and beads of perspiration were very evident between her breasts. He flicked his tongue at the beads and her head moved from side to side.

One nipple was rubbing against his ear and he turned to put it in his mouth. A deep rush of air escaped her mouth.

His teeth closed on it gently, but enough to let her know where they were. Then he bit harder. Another rush of air escaped. Her rushed breathing was causing her chest to rise and fall, and she was pressing harder against his fingers.

He bit quickly at the other neglected nipple and they both could hear her breathing. He blew on the pink bud and then across to the other. His breath went down to her navel and his tongue tasted the sweat forming there. He resumed his blowing down past her navel and across his fingers. He could smell Gardenia mixed with the scent of her excitement.

His fingers left her body and her head rolled from side to side. He blew on her lips and her body rose towards his lips. A quick flick of his tongue and he confirmed she was fully excited. "What do you want Alexis?"

She didn't answer, but he knew the answer. She was breathing heavily and if her eyes were open she could plainly see how much he wanted her.

"You're not going to tell me, are you?" She didn't answer him and he just watched her breathing and movement without touching her at all. Minutes passed and he felt he couldn't resist her any longer. Every pore of her body was hot for him and he loved that he could control her.

He opened the bag resting in front of both their crotches. He took one of the bundles and fanned it near her nose. Then he fanned it against her chin. He paused and let her think about where next. To his surprise both her nipples were even larger and redder than before. He fanned the bills and she let out a sigh followed quickly by, "Oh yes."

He repeated the fanning against her other breast.

"Alexis, tell me what you want."

No response, but she moved her upper body to what he was doing. He knew if she had a free hand she would be bringing herself to a climax. He whipped the wad of bills across her face, lightly on one side, then the other. Her mouth closed tightly with a slight grimace. "What do you want Alexis?"

No response but she lifted her back off the mattress. He lightly touched the wad against her nipple just holding it there. Seconds later she rolled her body back and forth against the money. She's not talking, but she's certainly telling him what she wants. He obliged with two light hits against one and then the other. Soon the sound of the money hitting her breasts resembled the sound of the belt.

He stopped abruptly. "What do you want Alexis?" Still she didn't answer him. He dragged the money down her side and up the other and across her breasts. Each time the money was getting lower and lower. He could feel the moisture on his manhood, and saw the glistening forming between her legs.

He wanted to put more than his fingers into her body, but he wanted her ready to explode. He resumed hitting her breasts with the money and her breasts were now pink rather than milky white.

"Alexis talk to me and tell me what you want. I know you love this, but I also know what you want next. *Tell me.*"

Still no answer, but her breathing was rushed and she wasn't trying to hide it any longer. Her body was rising and falling and rocking from side to side. Her arms and legs were pulling against the restraints.

He threw the money on the floor followed by the bag of money. He got off her thighs and stood beside the bed. "Pleasant dreams Alexis. I have to go count the money now."

She quickly shook her head back and forth. Against his better judgment he untied her right wrist. Then he watched for a minute and then it turned to two. Her body was covered in sweat, but everything about it showed how super excited she was.

"Alexis, I changed my mind. What do you want?"

She took a deep breath and moved her free hand between her legs and her fingers disappeared. Then she brought them to her mouth and sucked on them and replaced them. Her hand was moving quickly and he watched to learn how best to bring her to a climax. One finger was working a special area and her head was rolling from side to side.

"Alexis stop. *Stop.*" However, she didn't and her movement increased. He grabbed her hand and quickly tied it to the rope.

"You bastard," she finally yelled. She closed her eyes and he saw her rubbing her thighs together.

"Alexis, it's okay. Tell me what you want." She didn't answer, but she looked like she was in pain.

He put his fingers where hers had been, but didn't move them. She was incredibly wet. He looked at his fingers and saw some blood on them, and reinserted two and then three. "Is this what you want?" She still didn't answer him, but her lower body did. He found the little nub and swirled a finger around it, and then two.

"You bastard."

"I can stop if you would like me to."

"You bastard." She was raising her groin to his finger. "No, I don't want you to stop…please don't stop. Oh yeah. You bastard. I'm going to cum, but I want you inside me to feel it."

He climbed onto her, but just placed himself at her entrance. "Alexis, are you sure?"

Her body seemed to grab him and the hot wet feel along with her rushed motion was quickly too much for him to hold back and he could feel her climax at the same time.

He wondered if he could ever trust her to tie him up again. He considered whether it was more fulfilling teasing her, or finally giving in to what his body needed. He thought about all the things he had done, and his body was starting to show his excitement.

"Chris, that was incredible. Now untie me, it's my turn."

Chapter 64

She left Ralph in the Emergency Room where he was still being treated by a doctor and two nurses. He was conscious and thankful they were both rescued. He could obviously tell what had happened to his body, but she didn't share the details of her short captivity with him.

She wanted to take a nice hot bath and get rid of the clammy feeling she had. The thoughts of what the captain had done to her were nothing compared to what he was going to do. She was thankful for her rescue once again, but was still confused about who was behind it. Max Gordon was on his way to the hospital to see both of them.

However, right now she needed to talk with Scott. She was glad she was safe and hopefully would still be leaving on a plane later this morning. She was told where the pay phones were and contacted an operator. It was difficult to deal with the original operator who did not speak English, but she passed her to another one who did. She gave the operator the number to call and her name to make a 'collect' call.

She could hear the phone ringing and ringing but there was no answer. "I'm very sorry Ms. Strong, but no answer. Would you like another number?"

She thought of calling her father, but decided against it. "Would you try it again? It's 1 am. Maybe he's still asleep."

The phone rang and rang once again. "I'm very sorry," the operator said.

"Thank you very much for trying." *So, where are you Scott? It's very early in the morning and you're not in your apartment. Are you by any chance with Maggie? Scott I really need to talk with you. Maybe he is staying at my apartment since he was expecting me home later tonight.*

She was headed back to the phone booth to place the call. "Mercedes."

She looked over and it was Max Gordon. She went running to him and he caught her and hugged her. "I'm so sorry you were kidnapped again, but thrilled you were rescued. How is Ralph doing?"

"He's pretty beaten up and lost quite a bit of blood. They might have killed him if they continued beating him."

"Let's go see him," Max said.

"They are still working on patching him up. Can we talk first?"

"Sure. I'm interested in knowing how you were rescued so quickly."

"You mean you don't know?"

"No. I was trying to make some contacts when I learned you had been rescued."

"Max, I mean sir, am I still going home on that flight this morning?"

"You certainly are. If I could get Ralph to go with you, I would."

"I don't think he's in any condition right now to make that flight. We have a lot to talk about."

* * *

They were seated in the corner of the hospital cafeteria and she could feel the coffee cup shaking. "I'm sorry sir."

"It is okay Agent Strong. You've had more than one trauma recently. Would you like to tell me about what happened?"

She remembered the ugly part of her captivity and decided to tell him what he really needed to know. "Max, once we were brought into that building they blindfolded both of us and took us to a room. When the blindfolds were removed all that was in the room were two chairs. It was different from my other abduction because these three men

239

were disciplined enough to respect my…well, respect my body."

"Then they didn't molest you?"

"They didn't but Captain Chavez did. Well, he started to but the military arrived before it got carried away."

"I guess your gut was right about the captain."

"Yes, it was. He is the leader of the gang operating in Maracaibo, but they are not the only gang operating in Venezuela. Here's what else I learned. The two missing citizens, Helen Scott and Marie Quinlan, are both still alive. Richard Damelio is alive as well. The women are indeed being held for sexual purposes, and there are about twenty women from the US and another fifty from other countries."

"Why haven't we known about all of those citizens?"

"I can't answer that. The way they work their captivity is they make the women sign a contract stating that they owe a considerable amount for their rescue. Their services, and obviously it relates to sex, earns them money which is applied to their debt. In a fashion, it looks legal, but was indeed coerced. The captain was going to have me sign a contract for his earlier rescue, but he was going to keep me at his ranch for his pleasure."

She watched Max nod.

"Richard Damelio is being kept at his ranch also. He is keeping the books on the women and most likely knows where they are being kept. Helen Scott was the person who was beating on Ralph. They obviously make them do the punishing instead of being punished themselves. She looked like she had been through hell, but she was at least alive."

"Is that it?"

"We were very lucky to be rescued when we were. Captain Chavez was going to use the threat of more punishment to Ralph to get me to have sex with him."

"I have to ask this…did he have sex with you."

"Not really. He had his hands on me, but it worked to my advantage because it slowed him down enough to provide some of the details I told you about."

"You did extremely well. I have a contact in the military, and I'm going to try to find out how they knew where to find you. More importantly, I'm going to ask for their assistance to capture Captain Chavez and his men. We need to pursue him quickly to prevent people from being killed. His ranch sounds like the place to go next."

"Sir, I'll be okay, and Ralph isn't going anywhere soon. Make your calls and do what you need to do. If we can get back our citizens and many others, that is what we came here to do and they are more important right now."

"Thank you Agent Str...thanks Mercedes. Are you sure you're okay?"

"I have some things to consider going forward, but I will be okay. I'll say goodbye to Ralph in a while, and pick up my things at the hotel."

"Forget going to the hotel. We will take care of your belongings. I have arranged a military guard until you are on that plane." He hugged her and left.

Scott might not be okay, unless he has a very good excuse why he wasn't home.

Chapter 65

I was only hearing some of what Mike was saying. My mind was trying to deal with Mercedes' kidnapping. The recurring dream kept coming to mind. Melanie's torturing me and cutting the arrow into my body caused me to relive the pain. Deep down, I couldn't shake the feeling that Mercedes might be suffering the same consequences or worse.

"Scott, did you hear what I said?"

"No, I'm sorry Mike."

"I said the doctor's house is right down the street. Let's go check it out."

I was glad Mike was with me, but I wanted to be with Mercedes. I needed to save her life like she did mine.

This is your investigation remember? So, is that what you want to do next?"

"It sounds like the right plan. Shouldn't we call the police first?"

"You, who wanted to do this entire investigation all by yourself, now want to get the police involved."

"Stupid, huh?"

"Earlier no, now, yes. Let's go. Take the revolver with you."

"Do I really need to do that?"

"No, not really. You can let this guy, whoever he is, stick his gun in your mouth and blow your brains out. Asking him not to do that might be a little out of the question. Take the gun and remember how I told you to use it."

I reached under the seat and picked the gun up. "Got it."

"Good, stick it in your pants and don't blow your balls off with it."

"Tell me that doesn't happen."

"Okay, it doesn't happen."

"Really."

"It certainly changes the perspective on life. Come on Scott let's go see if our investigation…correction…let's go see if your investigation is making any progress."

"Mike, I'm worried about Mercedes."

"That is tomorrow's problem. Right now I'm worried about your focus. Wait. Before you open that door."

"What?"

"Promise me this is the last investigation you are going to get yourself involved with."

I looked at the revolver in my hand. "I think you're right Mike. I promise."

"That makes some real progress for such an early Monday morning."

I opened the car door and wondered if Mercedes, and even Ralph, were doing as well.

Chapter 66

He had mixed emotions about seeing Alexis. Seeing her beautiful face and body was a dream come true, but seeing what she was carrying was a different kind of a dream.

"Doctor Adler you don't look pleased to see me. Don't you have to empty your bladder?" She started to tickle him.

"Please don't do that. Where have you been? I've really needed to go for hours."

"Why doctor, you have forgotten all those lessons you learned?"

He started to rephrase the statement, but she had her finger pressed against his lips. "Maybe more time will change your focus, or maybe my fingers will help you."

"Please don't do that. I'm sorry. Will you please allow me to go to the bathroom...master?"

"Are you questioning whether I am your master, or whether I will allow you to go to the bathroom?"

He could feel his anger building. "No master I have no question about that, I was asking if you would please let me go to the bathroom."

"That is much better. I'm sure since you're not excited to see me, you will have a much better chance of going in the bottle." She put the bottle on his stomach and he felt her fingers insert him into it. A moment or two later, "Well?"

"I'm having a problem going while you're watching."

She climbed onto the bed and sat on his thighs with her knees on either side of him. "That must be an interesting picture. Junior in the bottle and my counterpart just inches away." She ran her fingernails of both hands down his waist. "Did I detect some reaction?" She bent down and he felt her lick him. "If I keep that up you will have some real problems going. *Do it." She slapped him where she just kissed.*

He felt himself going and going.

"Oh shit, we have a problem," she announced.

He felt her slide the bottle to his hip, but it was impossible to stop at this point. He felt the moisture running down his hip.

She lifted the bottle and they both looked at it. "Wow, you really did need to go. Feel better now?"

"Yes, much better."

"You were a bad boy and wet the bed. I'll be right back."

He was worried now as to what she might be up to. He heard the water running in the bathroom and then she came back in. He noticed how comfortable she seemed to be walking around without clothes.

She climbed back on him and had a wash cloth with her. "Problem solved." He felt her wiping his hip and just under him and then she came back and washed his penis. She was doing it very gently and his body was reacting to her attention. He felt the cloth now raking at his body and at all the appendages there and he cried out. "Was I not doing it correctly?"

He thought about the correct answer. "No, you were doing it okay."

She quickly resumed the treatment.

"Owe, that hurts."

"Not good my dear doctor." She took the wet face cloth and struck him across the face and then back again. Then she was striking him across his chest and then she stopped suddenly.

He gave thanks she stopped hitting him knowing where she was headed and the pain it would cause.

"You can open your eyes now. I stopped." He opened his eyes and regretted it. She had managed to pick up the belt and had the end right in front of his eyes. She touched his nose lightly from one side, and then hit the other. He felt her pick up speed and with every hit it hurt more. She was now hitting the side of his face, lightly at first and then with more force.

His eyes were closed and he felt her body lean down onto his. She kissed his nose and then his cheeks. "Pain and pleasure doctor. You must know the difference by now."

He knew where this was going and felt her sit up.

"Well, what a surprise. You wouldn't have thought that junior would be sticking his head up to see what the noise was. However, he's more than looking around, he looks pretty focused." She leaned down and kissed his erection, which bounced. "I just love how it has a mind of its own."

He felt the pain from her nip. It was a mixed blessing.

"Do you want me to stop?"

He didn't answer and he quickly regretted it. She hit him hard twice with the belt. Then quickly put her lips and mouth against him. "Do you want me to stop?"

He didn't answer her and felt the pain followed by a soothing kiss.

"Do you want me to stop?"

He realized the pain was getting more severe and the kisses more focused. He could hear her asking him questions but he was not answering—he couldn't.

When the pain was almost to the point he couldn't hold back yelling any longer, he felt the warmth of her body engulfing him. He realized she was more excited than he was. The flow against his erection and body caused him to let go.

He looked up at the window and saw two men looking at them, and another standing naked in the doorway. It was Chris, but he had no idea who the other men were.

"We have company Alexis."

"I know, he's been here for a long time."

"No, not him. Look up at the window."

Chapter 67

Heads turned in our direction and they obviously looked shocked to be discovered.

"Scott this is not what I expected to see. Two naked people having sex and one tied to the bed," Mike said.

"Make that three people. There's another standing at the doorway," I responded.

We already knew one of them was the blackmailer since the gold Pontiac was parked in the driveway. Now we knew it wasn't the older man tied to the bed. I had no idea what our next action was. "Mike what do we do now?"

"Well, if we call the police to have the blackmailer questioned, it will become public knowledge about what he was doing and what Stephen's secret was."

I watched the woman climb off the man and stare at the window. *It was Melanie. I knew that couldn't be, but her face and definitely her body were what I remember from my captivity in Boston. The naked man tied to the bed brought visions of my own captivity.*

Mike was saying something, but it sounded like he was far away. I had no idea what he was saying. I had an urge to get to my feet and run. I watched the woman grab the straight razor and point it right at me, and remember Melanie cutting the arrow in my body.

Mike said something, but I was frozen in place.

The man tied to the bed must be Doctor Adler and she must be Alexis, Melanie's twin. I couldn't hear what he was yelling, but he was pulling against his ropes.

She lowered the razor and turned to the man on the bed. She stepped over to the bed and waved the razor in front of his face and then grabbed him between the legs. The panicked look on his face was replaced by pain and I looked to see her remove his manhood. She held the bloody parts in front of his face and then turned and held the parts up to us.

I felt Mike move and he was running to the front of the house. She turned back to the man whose groin was covered in blood and leaned towards him. She paused and must have said something to him. I saw her hand with the razor move from one side of his neck to the other. She sliced his throat. Blood was spurting everywhere.

The other man, who was holding the bag of money from the drop-off, came running over to her and yanked her away from him, and then pulled her out of the room. *All I could think of was that could have been what I looked like when Melanie had me captive. I thought of Mercedes and her being kidnapped and wondered if she was suffering at this very moment.*

I knew I should be moving, but I couldn't move. I watched the helpless man losing his grasp on life. One minute he was satisfying Alexis' needs, and the next he was being killed for some reason.

There was some noise behind me and when I turned I briefly caught the image of a rock being swung at my head. I heard the sound it made and then the lights went out.

Chapter 68

He came running out the back door to see the Pontiac barreling backwards out the driveway. He could see a man driving and the woman in the passenger seat. He ran around the back of the house and Scott was not at the window. In less than a minute he realized they had taken Scott.

He looked in the cellar window and realized the man was beyond any help. He considered running to his car to give pursuit but it was parked too far away. He quickly ran in the house. *He thought about the new 911 system and wished it was implemented, but no such luck.* He dialed Paddy's number instead.

"Hello."

"Paddy, its Mike. We have a big problem."

..*

Paul Brosque was one of the early police officers to arrive. He had called and specifically asked for Paul to explain what happened. Ten minutes after his conversation with Paul the area was swarming with police cars and officers.

He spotted Paddy flashing his identification and went over to him.

"Paddy this is not a pretty scene. Like I said we have Doctor Adler dead downstairs and Scott kidnapped."

"Any word on the vehicle they took off in?" Paddy asked.

"No there's no sign of the car. They have the full description along with the plate number. The police have gone to the care facility in Belmont and have Chris Sullivan's apartment in Jamaica Plain under surveillance. However, they don't think he will be stupid enough to go to either location. Alexis Strong attacked Doctor Adler with a straight razor and then sliced him ear to ear."

"What about Scott?"

"The doctor's house was searched as a precaution, but they took him with them when they left."

"What else can you tell me Mike?"

"Well, Scott and I staked out Dudley Street Station after Scott left the money for the blackmailer. After the guy, Chris Sullivan, picked up the money, we lost him, but came here on a possibility he would come here. When we checked out the property we witnessed Alexis Strong and Doctor Adler having sex while he was tied up. They spotted us and that's when all hell broke loose and the doctor was subsequently killed."

"Any other concerns?"

"You bet. Scott has a revolver with him and there's no sign of the murder weapon. Paddy, this is Melanie Strong's twin and we know how Melanie was hell bent on keeping Scott prisoner and almost killing him twice. This is the worst possible scenario for Scott."

"This has certainly gotten out of hand."

"Paddy, before she killed Dr. Adler, Alexis took his manhood and held it up for us to see."

"Maybe, but maybe she was holding it up for Scott to see." He watched Paddy thinking about things. "Mike, have you called Stephen Strong?"

"No."

"You better call him and tell him what has happened and what he can expect the newspapers will do with this. His secret is no longer going to be under wraps, but will surely be front page fodder. You might want to tell him to make his twin daughter public information before it comes out another way." Paddy looked at Mike. "Is something bothering you about calling him?"

"No, that's not what is concerning me. I saw what Alexis did to the doctor. Her twin sister was Melanie and we know how focused she was on Scott...I just hope she doesn't have the same infatuation."

"Well, she has the other guy Sullivan with her."

"Sure she does, and she had the doctor with her too. Did you hear anything about the status of Mercedes' kidnapping?"

"Good question. I better try to reach Robert Damelio. He might have been trying to reach me. I think we better say a prayer for both of them."

Chapter 69

I could feel my body being tossed around. I took stock of my senses. My head hurt something fierce. The last memory I had was the rock being swung at my head. I opened my eyes and realized I was lying on the back seat of a car. It hurt to open my eyes but I saw the long red hair hanging over the passenger seat and the blackmailer driving the car very fast on a highway.

I reached for the gun in the front of my pants and it was missing. I could smell the scent of Gardenia and without any question it was Melanie's twin Alexis. Then I remembered what I witnessed and my thoughts quickly went to my own captivity. It's happening again.

"Slow down Chris. The last thing we need is to attract attention." She turned and looked at me. "Our guest is awake. She kneeled in the seat and waved the razor near my nose. "Don't try anything funny or it will be the last thing you do. Now stay down and don't stick your head up."

I noticed they were both dressed. My head continued to throb.

"Do you have a headache Scott?"

I didn't answer and I was surprised she knew my name.

"Yes Mr. Tucker I know who you are, who you love, and what my sister did to you…not once, but twice. Welcome."

"Alexis we have to decide where we're going. They will obviously be looking for this car."

"You know what is around. I don't even know how to drive. You pick it."

"We need to get this car into a parking garage with a hotel nearby. I know where we can go."

"Chris, don't go too far from the city. I need to pay my parents a visit and you're going to have to drive me."

I heard what she said and wondered what they were going to do with me. *I didn't like those thoughts.*

Chapter 70

She had the operator try to reach Scott at his apartment, but there still wasn't any answer. It was 2 am and Scott was still not home. She had the operator try her apartment without any answer. *Where are you Scott? More importantly what are you doing? She thought of their conversation and if he is with Maggie, she is going to kill him.*

Despite her better judgment, she needed to have the operator try another number.

"Hello."

"Mr. Strong, your daughter Mercedes Strong is calling from Maracaibo, Venezuela. Will you accept her collect call?"

"Yes I will."

"Go Ms. Strong. Your father has accepted the call."

"Dad, its Mercy."

"My God, are you okay? You never call in the middle of the night like this."

"I'm still in Venezuela and there have been some...complications. I'm headed home later this morning. However, we have made some progress on finding the missing people. Look, do you have any idea where Scott is? I have tried him at his apartment, and at mine, but I can't reach him."

There was dead silence on the other end of the line. "Dad, do you know where he is?"

"No, not exactly."

"What does that mean?"

"I can't elaborate. Just a minute. Go back to sleep honey, it's Mercedes. She's calling to tell me she's coming home from her Venezuela trip. Now, go back to sleep. I'm back. Where were we?"

"You were in the midst of what sounded like you knew where Scott was, but you were covering for him."

"You don't stop being an investigator, do you?"

"Please dad, I'm concerned about him. This isn't like him at all. I need to talk with him."

"I understand. Let me try to track him down and have him call you."

"You can't reach me here. Why do you think you can track him down? What aren't you telling me?"

"Mercy I will explain everything when you get home. In the meantime I will try to track him down. Call me before your flight leaves and I'll either have him here, or I will let you know where he is."

She was trying her best to hold her emotions back. "Dad, I've had a very trying day here, and I really need to talk with Scott. If you could get him there when I call back around 9 before my plane leaves that would be great."

"I'll do my best."

"Thanks Dad. I'm sorry I was so short with you. How is mom doing?"

"The same. Things are very fragile here. We'll talk when you get home. There's much we have to talk about."

They said their goodbyes but she knew her dad well enough that he wasn't telling her the whole story. She never told him she had discovered who he was having an affair with and wondered now if that was what he was going to share with her.

She thought about her mom. She hasn't been the same for several years and when the news came out about Melanie and the other women keeping and killing men in Boston, well she had a nervous breakdown. When Melanie's exploits were reported in Bermuda and then when she killed herself, that caused her to have a heart attack. If she knew what her father was doing, it might just cause another. She knew she could never tell her mother she was kidnapped and molested twice, but knew she could share it with her father.

Could she ever share that with Scott?

Chapter 71

"Hello Mercy?"

"No, Stephen its Mike Miller, Scott's work associate. You were expecting a call from Mercedes?"

"Well she just called a minute ago to tell me she was coming home later this morning. However, the real reason she was calling was she couldn't reach Scott, and wondered if I knew where to reach him."

"That's why I'm calling Stephen."

"About Scott?"

"Yes. Look, I know that Scott was doing an investigation for you to find out who was blackmailing you." There was dead silence on the other end. "Here's what has happened. Scott has been abducted. We know it was the guy who was blackmailing you. His name is Chris Sullivan and he works at the Lighthouse Manor where you have hidden your daughter."

"Please hold for a minute, I need to pick this up in my office. No honey, its Mercedes calling back and I need to talk with her in my office. Go back to sleep."

"What time is it?"

"It's very early, so please go back to sleep. Everything is okay." There was a pause on the phone. "Mike, I'm back. So, Scott has told you what he was doing?"

"He only told me about the blackmailing. I went with him for the money drop tonight and Chris picked up the money but we lost him. We located him at Doctor Adler's house."

"Why was he there?"

"It gets more complicated. Here's the bottom line...I'm calling to give you a heads up. The press will be reporting what I'm about to tell you and I want you to do what you need to do ahead of them. Your daughter Alexis was torturing the doctor who was tied up in his basement. After they both discovered Scott and I observing what she was doing, she killed the doctor. Before she did that she said something to him and took his manly parts with a razor."

"You have to be mistaken."

"I wish, but I witnessed it first hand. She held up what she cut off before she sliced his throat. All three of them were naked."

"Three?"

"Chris was there watching her have sex with the doctor before she took his parts and slit his throat. Chris and Alexis took Scott before they left in a car."

"That's why Mercedes couldn't reach Scott."

"Look Stephen, I know Scott was trying to help you find out who was blackmailing you, but now we know and it has gotten a lot more serious. This was a courtesy call to tell you some of what you might hear."

"Thanks for the call Mike. I hope Scott is going to be okay."

"You know Stephen, if Melanie tried to kill Scott twice, and did some other horrible things while he was in captivity, her twin might just pick up where she left off. You better pray for his safety. Do you have any idea where she or Chris might go?"

He heard a click. "Did you hang up the phone in the bedroom?"

"Shit," Stephen answered.

He heard the dial tone next.

Chapter 72

He slowed the car down realizing Alexis was right about drawing attention. It was hard to believe what Alexis did to the doctor. Not the part about torturing him and then making love to him. It was cutting his manhood off and then slitting his throat. All while she knew he was watching her and while she knew there were others outside the window.

He stole a glance at Alexis who was sitting back in the passenger seat. She seemed to be in a trance and very quiet. She was staring at the straight razor blade which he noticed was still covered in blood. He looked back at the road and then saw something out of the corner of his eye. It couldn't have been what he saw. He confirmed what he saw—she actually licked the blade.

"What?" Alexis asked.

"Are you okay?"

"Why…because I wanted to taste his blood?"

"Yeah. Don't you feel bad about what you just did?"

"Should I? He treated me like a slave for years. It was a good thing I enjoyed what he was doing, but that doesn't forgive him for how he took advantage of me. Speaking of what I did…you didn't take pictures did you?"

He didn't like where this was going. "No, you did everything so fast I never had a chance."

"Are you sorry about what I did to the doctor?" He didn't respond. "Be thankful it wasn't you." He saw her turn to look in the backseat. When she turned back around she turned the razor over and licked the other side.

He thought about how casually she took killing the doctor. He wasn't a stranger to her at all, but she doesn't seem to be regretting what she did. He remembered being tied up and it could have been him that she parted. He was glad they had company who she might focus her attention on. He remembered she wants to go to her father's house.

That doesn't sound good, but the good news is that she needs him to drive her there. He had planned to kill her parents at some point. Maybe she was going to do it for him. That would leave her other sister Mercedes...what about her?

* * *

He pulled into the Burlington mall covered parking area. He noticed a few cars parked on the third level and backed his up against the wall.

"Nicely done Chris. This is just what you were looking for."

"There's a hotel right next door. We just need to get Scott into a room without attracting attention. It is early in the morning and checkout time is in just a few hours."

"Just tell them you're from out of state and staying more than one night. You need to check in, you know I can't."

"Are you going to be okay alone with him?"

"You have got to be kidding. I have a razor that is still very sharp despite its recent use, and I have his gun. He wouldn't dare try anything...would you Scott?"

There wasn't any response.

"Cat got your tongue?"

Still no response.

"That gives me an interesting idea. I wonder what he values more, his tongue or his..."

"Should I go now?" Chris asked.

"Yes, and Chris...relax a little. You look like you were the one who would be using the ladies room today."

"What name should I give them?"

"If you were with a girlfriend, or somebody's wife, what name would you use? Oh, and Chris...we need two double beds, one for our guest. In your travels see if you can find something to tie him up with."

"At least he doesn't have a door to get out since this is a two door."

"That gives me another idea." He watched her climb over the seat still with the razor blade exposed. "We'll be getting acquainted while you're gone. There are some things I'm curious about."

He looked in the rear view mirror. She was seated way over on his side of the car, and Scott was still lying down on the seat. He could feel a tinge of jealousy.

"Well, the quicker you get us a room, the quicker we can get settled in. Hi Scott, we haven't been properly introduced yet, I'm Alexis. You've seen me before, but I had a different name. Aren't you going to welcome me back? Didn't you miss my attention, or was Mercedes satisfying all your needs?"

"Alexis, don't kill him in my car."

"Tsk tsk tsk, giving orders again are we? Scott won't be much use to me dead. You can leave now. I have some research to do."

The light came on in the car as he opened the door. He heard her ask, "So when you were watching the good doctor and me, what part did you like most?"

There was no answer.

"Cat still got your tongue, huh? Fine, stick out your tongue."

He was still standing by the car and saw her hit him in the groin, fortunately with the hand without the razor. He heard Scott yell.

"Okay Chris, the shows postponed for you. You were going to get us a room." He watched her turn back to Scott. "Now stick out your tongue."

He walked away from the car, but wondered even more what she was capable of. He could also feel some jealousy forming, but knew he shouldn't show it to her.

Chapter 73

He wasn't feeling any pain now, since he was on some heavy duty pain killers. His injuries could have been much more serious. He knows they were rescued relatively soon after their abduction, but he still wondered what Mercedes had suffered. If he asked she probably wouldn't tell him. He still felt bad about not protecting her like he planned.

"Feeling some better now Ralph?" Mercedes asked as she came over to his side.

"Yeah, I could use a handful of whatever they gave me for some future time," he replied.

"Ralph, I'm so sorry they beat you so badly."

"It could have been much worse. I'll be okay. I'm sure you did your part to limit my injuries."

"Actually it was getting to that point."

"Mercy, are you okay?"

"I'm okay. We were both lucky we were rescued when we were. We still do not have any idea who called the military and told them where we were. There's an angel out there and I could give him a big hug."

"Speaking of hugs…I'm sorry I didn't protect you like I planned."

"Ralph, you did as much as you could. You weren't even armed. Fortunately, they didn't kill you."

"No they wanted me there so they could get you to give your body up. I need to ask you this." He tried to think of the best way to ask it. "You seem to be in good spirits considering what we went through…did any of them take advantage of you?"

"If you mean did they rape me? No they didn't. Captain Chavez was the only one who came near me, and fortunately I kept him talking long enough to avoid any real issues."

"Then he did do something to you."

"Ralph, all he did was put his hands on my body. I suffered worse than that when I was kidnapped the first time."

"I'm very sorry."

"Please don't give it another thought. I'm okay and I learned some information that will help us find the people we were looking for. Other than Paula Scott, the people who went missing in Bermuda are all alive, but there are more than sixty other people, many from the US and the balance from Europe, who still have not been found."

"Mercy, I know I apologized for what I did to your apartment. It was childish of me and you didn't deserve that treatment. I hope I haven't caused a problem with Scott."

"Thanks for telling me you're sorry. I know you like me and I think we can be friends. Scott at the moment is in some hot water of his own."

"Why, what has he done?"

"I'm not sure. I've tried to reach him, but he isn't at his apartment or mine. There's a slight chance my earlier words might have sent him to someone else."

"He would be a fool."

"Thanks. He told me he had some bad news and some bad news. I asked him what the first bad news was and he said he went to see an exotic dancer do her stuff."

"Well he told you."

"Yes that is Scott. He doesn't lie. However, he wouldn't tell me what the other bad news was. I hung up on him and haven't talked to him since."

He saw her tears forming. He put his arms out and she bent over. He could smell a hint of Gardenia. It hurt to hug her but they both needed it. He realized how lucky they both were, but Scott was luckier than he was.

"Ralph, that was nice of you. I needed a hug. I'm going to share something with you and it has nothing to do with you."

He saw her tears running down her cheeks and realized she wasn't as tough as she seemed. He tried to wipe them, but the IV prevented him from reaching her cheek. "Once again I seem to be just a little too far away."

She wiped the tears. "Ralph, when I get back to the states, I'm giving my notice. I've had two close calls and there are more important things to do with my life. I can't take the chance the next time I won't be this lucky."

"I'm going to miss working with you partner. For all the dumb things I've done, I'm sorry."

"You're a good agent and will do even better without my distraction."

"Yes, but you were such a nice distraction."

She bent down and surprised the hell out of him kissing his lips briefly but with some obvious feeling. He could feel his own emotions and his eyes started to water.

"Hello you two," Max said as he entered the treatment room. "Is everything okay here?" Max looked at Mercedes for an answer.

"Everything is just fine here and couldn't be better," Mercedes said as she kissed him again, but this time on the forehead. She left the room without saying anything else.

"Ralph, she looked like she was crying. Are you sure everything is okay?"

"We both patched some things up. I'll be fine and she will be even better."

"I've found out who we have to thank for both of your rescues. Richard Damelio's brother Robert is here and is working with a former military person. Robert got a call from the states that alerted them that you and Mercedes were abducted. They got to the right people in the military to make a timely rescue.

"I guess we all have our angels when we need them most."

"Should I be worried about you and Mercedes working together?"

"No, that won't be a problem at all."

"Good. I arranged for you to return to the states in two days. Do you think you are going to be ready to travel by then?"

"Thanks Max. Sounds good to me, and I'll miss these pain killers, but I will be ready."

Chapter 74

She left Ralph's room and went to the ladies room. Several things surprised her. The first was that she told him she was giving her notice. She had only thought about that, but while she was with Ralph she solidified her decision.

Her two close calls were weighing heavily on her and she was very lucky she wasn't more seriously damaged by either of those two abductions.

The other surprise was that she felt very close to Ralph. Not as a lover, but as a friend. She was glad he was alive, and she was glad he made her feel like she had value. He obviously has deep feelings for her, and she was sorry she couldn't reciprocate his feelings. They would be friends for sure after she leaves the FBI.

She was surprised she was crying back there and now. She rarely does that, but for some reason all the emotions were too much to handle. They had both been rescued. He from being more seriously hurt, and her from being raped and having to live with those scars for the rest of her life. Her beauty was an asset in many ways, but she realized it was a definite liability when dealing with the scum of the earth.

She was also concerned about Scott and sorry they had words. She was wrong hanging up on him and should have been more tolerant. Not being able to reach him and talk to him, along with not knowing if he was okay, was also a major concern. If he had actually spent some time with Maggie, she was going to forgive him. He must have needed her. That was her fault, not his.

All her adult life she had worked to become an FBI profiler. She had managed to reach that, but it wasn't what she really needed. She wanted Scott and she wanted a family. Having children would be risky if she were still with the force. It wouldn't be fair to them if something were to happen to her. It obviously could have already happened. Her angel saved her and this was a wake up call.

She asked Scott not to do any more investigations, but realized she was asking him to give up something she should be giving up. They both need to do something less risky and more conducive for family life. They had skills and would be able to use them.

She looked at her image in the mirror and noticed how white her face looked. She looked sickly and suddenly felt her stomach turning and an awful taste in her mouth. She made it to the toilet just in time. Maybe she should have eaten something. She felt the same thing and leaned over the toilet once again.

She was trying to concentrate on getting her stomach to relax, but thought of Scott's scar. He was so lucky to be alive. Her sister could have killed him twice. Then she thought of what she had forced him to do. He has never really told her what she made him do, but can imagine what her sister had made all the men do. Since she was keeping them for that purpose, why would she think that her sister wasn't successful?

She then thought of Ralph being tortured and the pain Scott must have endured when Melanie cut the arrow into his abdomen. She felt her stomach turning again, but this time it was just bile coming up.

Once she had some composure back, her thoughts went to her dad. He was keeping something from her, she could tell, and she wondered if it was the affair he had had. Maybe he's still having one. Her mom hasn't been right for years since Melanie's first rampage in Boston with those other women. Prior to that, her mom had shared that her relationship with her father was just for show and to keep the business on an even keel.

She missed the simple times before she attended Harvard. Sailing with her grandfather and her sister was a special time. Why is everything so complicated now?

Scott losing his wife Lisa in that car accident was a tough pill for him to swallow. However, it took her call to him two years later to get him off the dime and for him to realize he needed to get on with his life. From the time she first met him at Harvard and they did that exercise to identify the classmate's description with the class member, she felt her body react to Scott. Then in the cabin, when she wanted him so badly, even with both of them naked, he was faithful to Lisa.

She knew now Scott couldn't have spent any private time with Maggie. He had shown her many times how much he loves her, and although he saw Maggie dance, that doesn't convict him of making love to her. There was something else Scott was hiding from her.

Her father was hiding something too. That's got to be it…he's doing an investigation, which is the 'other bad news' he wouldn't tell me about. So, he must be doing an investigation for my father, which is the only person he would take that risk for. That explains why my dad was acting strangely about contacting Scott.

She thought she was done being sick, but it was just dry heaves this time. She stood and went to the sink to wash her mouth out. She did her best to make herself presentable and knew she needed to find Max to solidify her travel arrangements.

So where are you? What kind of investigation would you get involved in for my father? She had a strange feeling that Scott was in trouble. *Unfortunately I can't help you this time Scott…I'm hundreds of miles away. You need a guardian angel, and it isn't me this time.*

She knew Scott was going to ask her to marry him and she already had her answer prepared. She said a silent prayer and hoped it would be enough.

Chapter 75

Scott finally had his tongue out. "Progress at last. You can put your tongue back in your mouth. We only have a few minutes until Chris comes back. You know very well what I want to see."

"Alexis don't you feel bad about what you did to the doctor?"

She couldn't hold the smile back. "Okay Scott, here's the deal. The good doctor has been caring for me since I was a baby. I was sent to that facility by my uncaring father because I had hair on my face and elsewhere…basically I looked like a werewolf. He took advantage of me from the time I was twelve. He thought he hypnotized me and took pictures of me in various positions. That's not the worst part."

She saw him watching the razor as she waved it back and forth. "He made me do things to him while he thought I was under a trance. To be honest, once I failed to tell him he hadn't hypnotized me, I had to play along with what he instructed me to do. He made me do some things to his body, which I learned to like. I think I was doing a good job of learning how to make him really happy." Her free hand was trying to undo his belt.

"Once my body started to lose the hair covering it, he told me I got more beautiful. It took me years to finally understand that I had indeed developed into a butterfly instead of an ugly moth." She needed to put the razor into her mouth while she used two hands on his belt.

"At the same time, he showed how excited he got when I was naked. He liked to play with my body and I tried not to show him how much I liked it too. However, I learned my dad was paying for my care at the facility and paying him separately to keep my presence a secret. He never once came to visit me. So for years, Doctor Adler took me to his home and, in effect, trained me how to make us happy."

She undid his pants and slid his zipper down. "You thought I wouldn't get to this point by having me talk. Right?" He didn't answer and she made him regret it. "Right?"

"Okay, you're right."

She lifted his shirt and slid his briefs down slightly.

"Well look at what we have here. Looks like an arrow. How did this happen?"

"Your twin cut me when she had me prisoner."

"Were you worried she was going to cut something else?"

"It had crossed my mind."

"Okay enough banter. Let's see what the arrow is pointing at."

The interior lights came on when the driver's door opened.

"I got us a room. What the hell are you doing?"

"Mind your own business."

"Alexis, we have two queen beds. I suggest you wait until we get in the room and then do what you want?"

"Will you watch?"

"Do I have a choice?"

"See how well he has learned his lessons. You will have your opportunity too. Besides, the suspense of what you really look like down here will make me even more excited." She tapped against him. "Save me the effort of getting you back together. When we go through the hotel, don't do anything to call attention to us. I have nothing to lose in killing you. Besides, anyone there should be focused on my entry not yours."

She closed the razor but kept it in her hand. They started towards the hotel.

She wondered if she should do a twin arrow on Scott. Wouldn't that be a fitting memorial?

Chapter 76

There was only the desk clerk in the hotel lobby as we passed through. I tried my best to give the impression I wasn't happy being with the two of them, but had no idea if he picked up on it. Two men with one woman should have given him something to think about.

If I made a break for it, I might make it, but they might kill the desk clerk, because he could have identified them. I was hoping I would have another opportunity later. Once inside the elevator, Alexis put her hand on my crotch and was licking my lips.

"Alexis, can't you wait until we're in the room. The elevator might have a camera."

"Mind your own business Chris. I won't forget you're in the room with us. You might even like not being on the receiving end of my focus. Did you find a rope?"

"No. As a matter of fact, I didn't even look. I came back to the car as fast as I could."

"I thought you were back pretty quickly. Are you jealous?" She reached over with her other hand and grabbed his crotch. "Once again I find myself with two attractive men with more than a handful."

"That hurts," Chris yelled.

"Gee, Scott didn't complain."

"I thought we were going to be alone."

"Then you are jealous. That gives me some ideas." She let go of Chris' pants but then started to reach down mine.

The bell sounded and the elevator doors opened and she stopped. "Scott you were saved by the bell. That will be the last time."

Chris led the way and I noticed Alexis was focused on his rear end. "Wait Chris." Alexis went over to a door that read 'Maintenance' which wasn't shut completely. We were all standing in the doorway. The room was filled with furniture and some small appliances. "Chris, take this razor and cut the cords off these vertical lamps."

"What?"

"Never mind. Watch Scott for a minute." She went in the room and quickly cut the cords off all three of the lamps standing in the corner. "These will do very nicely." She closed the door and we continued down to the end of the hall to room 369. We entered the room and Alexis whispered in my ear, "Interesting number."

The room was a typical hotel room. Bathroom on the left as you enter, a closet next and then two queen sized beds with a common night stand. The television was sitting on top of the long dresser on the other wall. I watched Alexis go over to the windows and look through the white curtains. She pulled the heavy drapes closed. "That bed is yours Scott." She pointed to the far bed. "Chris, go see if you can get us something out of the machines to eat and drink."

"Will you be safe with him?"

"The key question is whether he will be safe with me." She opened the straight razor and then pulled the gun out of the back of Chris' pants. "Don't forget to take the room key."

I watched Chris processing things and he grumbled something but did as commanded. Once the door closed she pointed the razor at my nose, with the gun in her other hand. "Just you and I for a couple of minutes, now pull the bed covers down."

I leaned over and pulled them down exposing the bottom sheet. I knew what was coming next.

"Okay Mr. Tucker, strip. I want to see what my sisters are so interested in." I hesitated and she swung the gun but missed. "It would be a shame to waste you so soon, but I will...now, do it."

I did my best to take my time, but when I was down just to my pants I hesitated again. She quickly put the back of the razor between my legs and I saw my chance. I lunged at her but she stepped to the side and brought the gun down across the side of my head. The lights went out in the room.

..*

My head was hurting worse than before. It even hurt to open my eyes. When I did, I wished I hadn't. I noticed Chris lifting the end of the bed to slip the electric cord under each corner of the footboard. The other ends were tied tightly around my ankles. Alexis was watching what he was doing. I felt the cool air on my chest and waist and realized I was naked. Alexis turned back to my face and saw my surprised look

"You are everything I expected and a little more. Isn't he a cute one Chris?" There was no response. "I didn't expect an answer. Chris I thought you were in good shape, but Scott looks like he works out. Do you?"

She had something in her hand, but I didn't see what it was. It wasn't the straight razor thankfully. I didn't answer her. I pulled on my arms, but my wrists were tied the same way with another electrical cord.

Now that the cords had me secured, Chris was standing at the foot of the bed. Alexis turned to him. "Are you going to stand there and watch, or would you like to give us a few minutes alone?" He didn't say anything and didn't move. "Okay, why don't you get on the other bed and I can conduct some research on both of you." He shook his head and headed toward the bathroom. I heard the door close.

She smiled and looked at my eyes and then slowly down my body and then back up. "I like, but I didn't like that I asked you a question and you didn't answer me. If I ask you a question you need to give me a fast and honest answer."

That brought back some ugly memories. I looked at her and she was focused on my groin. I should have remembered the other electrical cord, but realized she had the end of the cord showing two separate pigtails. She pulled the cord and separated the ends, smiled and touched it between my legs. I felt the electricity cycle several times through my body as I rose off the bed.

"Now that I have your attention, do you work out and did that hurt?"

My breath escaped. "Yes."

"I haven't tried this before, but I can see this might be very motivational." She started towards me with the end of the cord and I moved away as best as I could. "Just remember what that pain was like and do as I tell you." She started to undress.

I knew what Melanie's body looked like and the memories were starting to reappear. I tried my best to think of other things, including worrying about what was happening to Mercedes, but Alexis' naked body was identical to Melanie's.

Alexis climbed onto my thighs and sat there. "You might not want to react to what you see, but your body does. You would think I had rank the way you're starting to salute me. I have quite a bit of time, and I'm going to get what I want in the end. Room 369, what an interesting number." She got up and turned around and sat on my chest. "Chris you can join us now." She was holding the electrical cord up in the air with her left hand. I knew she wouldn't be afraid to use it again, but I have to admit I was.

Chapter 77

He had thought it would be different with the doctor out of the way, but he had new competition. Scott had similar features to his, and it concerned him as to how Alexis was going to focus her interest. Having a younger and more handsome man wasn't what he originally bargained for.

He heard Scott yell out and it was soon followed by Alexis asking him to join them. He would much rather have Alexis to himself even if it was in the bathroom. That brought back images of Alexis showering and her focus on his body.

"Chris, don't be bashful. Come join us, you might just like how excited I am."

He reached for the bathroom doorknob and noticed his fully dressed reflection in the mirror. He knew Scott was naked and tied up, and wondered if Alexis had her clothes off. He remembered the third electrical cord and wondered if Alexis had plugged it in and shocked Scott with it.

If she had, he was sure he knew where she would have placed the live end of the cord. There was a big risk not having Scott gagged. If someone heard him yell they might call hotel management or the police.

He came around the corner and it was an erotic sight seeing both of them on the bed. Alexis was sitting with her butt almost on Scott's face and her mouth was occupied and her hand was busy. Other than being tied up and at her mercy, Scott could have been a lucky man.

Alexis looked up but didn't stop what she was doing. He saw her mouth curl into a smile. Scott had his head turned toward the wall, and it was obvious he was trying to avoid her anatomy which was only inches away. Her other hand held the cord with the live ends separated. "Chris, take off your clothes and join us."

He was reluctant to give in to her but he definitely wanted her attention as his body started to react to the scene.

Her mouth left Scott, but her hand still had him captured. "Chris if you don't take off your clothes I'm going to shock him again."

She might have wanted him to take off his clothes, but she really wanted to torture Scott again. She let go of Scott and brought the cord to his groin. She had both hands on the opposite ends of the cord.

Scott yelled, "No."

However, it was too late. She touched both ends to the sides of his penis and his body shook under her. "Scott I can only imagine how that must have hurt. I'm going to do it again." She held the cord ends next to his erect penis but didn't touch him. "Unless you want to be shocked again, you have right in front of you a way to avoid it. Do it, or I will." She slid her body up further and then started to move the cord.

He watched Scott close his eyes and then stick out his tongue. He touched her finally.

"Good boy. Oh yes. Now Chris, take off your clothes or I will shock him again."

He wondered why he was hesitant as he wanted Alexis and could tell she must be extremely horny at this point. He started to take his clothes off and she smiled at him. Then she moved the cord and grabbed Scott's penis again and ran her tongue around the end of it.

The more he watched what she was doing the more he could feel his erection growing. He realized Scott wasn't going to tell anyone about this party and he wanted Alexis' mouth. She moved her long hair away from her face and turned to watch him strip.

When he removed his briefs she took Scott totally into her mouth and motioned with her free hand to come to the side of the bed. He stepped to the side of the bed and her hand grabbed him. Alexis was moving her lower body to get the most from Scott's attention, while moving her head up and down and her hand stroking him. He reached out and grabbed her closest breast. Her hard nipple pressed into his palm.

All three of them were soon trying to reach a needed climax. He saw her lift her head and move her hand from him back to Scott. Then her hot mouth engulfed his penis and he could soon feel his climax starting from deep inside. He felt his ejaculation at the same time as he felt the electrical current enter his balls. She quickly removed the cord, and her mouth and tongue cleaned him thoroughly. *How could she tolerate the shock which must have touched her lips?*

Then her mouth went back to Scott and he soon watched her climax against Scott's face, followed by Scott's body lift off the bed, obviously succumbing to her attention.

He went to the other bed and tried to catch his breath. Alexis came over and arranged herself on top of him. She kissed him and started to move her body against him. He could taste the salty taste of what she had done to both of them.

He was surprised he was getting excited again, but he knew she wasn't surprised.

"That was exciting for me, and somehow I know it was for you too. Room 369, we will always remember what happened in this room," Alexis said smiling.

She moved to sit on his lap facing him and in one other motion helped him enter her. He felt her hot and moist. She gave him a few kegels, squeezing him intimately with her vaginal muscles. He didn't know why he was so hesitant a few short minutes before.

She pushed herself up and down, "Are you going to kill Scott, or do I have to? Regardless, I think I've earned a souvenir to show my sister when I finally meet her. She can have what's left of him, but I will have gotten his best part."

Chapter 78

I was ashamed of what Alexis was able to get my body to do. She definitely reminded me of her sister, and not because her body was identical. It was how she loved to torture her mates, and get them to do what she wanted.

I heard her ask Chris just now if he was going to kill me, or did she have to do it. She also said loud enough for me to hear that she was going to take my best part to show Mercedes. I couldn't reach my scar and she didn't say this time that she was going to cut a duplicate on the other side. What she did say was bad enough.

Unfortunately, the thoughts of Mercedes being tortured possibly at this very moment made me want to give myself up if it meant she wouldn't be harmed or maimed. I could hear them making love in the next bed and wondered just how much time I had left. They had said they were going to go to Stephen's house. That doesn't sound good at all.

I pulled on my right wrist and the electric cord was tight without any give at all. I pulled on my left wrist and there was some play in the knot. I looked over to make sure neither one of them was looking at what I was doing. They were in a sixty-nine position and much too engrossed.

I turned my left wrist back and forth and felt the knot slipping up my hand. I couldn't tell whether the knot was loosening, or just not tied tightly. I felt the electric cord lying on top of my thigh and wondered where the live ends were. I pulled on my wrist trying not to move my body in any manner. The knot was sliding up my hand even more. Maybe they will leave me here when they go to Stephen's.

I looked down and could see the ends of the live electric cord only a fraction of an inch away from my body. It was much too close for comfort.

"I'll give you a big reward if you whip him. Chris, will you do that for me? Will you do it using the live cord?"

I wish I hadn't heard her say that. I recalled what I saw when I looked in the window, and my end, or worse, could be right around the corner.

They were engaged again and not focused on me at the moment. I didn't hear Chris' answer, but hearing what they were doing now, if the answer was no, it was going to be yes for sure when they were done.

I couldn't believe I got myself into another life threatening situation. I remembered the naked dream I had when I woke up in Mercedes' bed. That was the last time we were together. The visions of my last captivity came to mind. Melanie had me for an extended period of time and I had learned it was useless to delay the inevitable…she got what she wanted and why not avoid the pain associated with resisting.

She almost killed me twice and now her sister was going to pick up where she left off. The fact she knows about Mercedes is not good for either of us. Now she's going to her father's house and without any doubt she's planning on killing him, if not both of her parents. What if Mercedes happens to go there while they are there? Oh shit. All three of them might die. My only hope is to be there and maybe I can save her, and her parents.

I heard the bathroom door close and then the water sound of the spray. I looked up and saw Alexis smiling and headed towards the bed.

"Well now Mr. Tucker, you look all tuckered out. Did I overdue it before? Chris is good, but there is something about seeing you defenseless that excites me." She came over to the foot of the bed and just stood there.

I didn't need her anywhere near my bed or my body. I saw her eyes move to the cord and wish I could have done something to distract her. She moved and sat on the bed next to my hip. Her hand moved and she picked up the cord.

"After our shower Chris said he would do as I asked him to do. He is going to whip you with this live electric cord. That will give you two things to cause you pain, the cord itself and the ends of the cord if they touch you at the same time. I know I could keep him from doing that if you give me what I need."

I watched her dangle the cord over my body and closer and closer to my arrow scar.

"There's only so far you can push your body into the bed. At some point you're going to have to let up. I should join Chris. He's probably playing with himself by now."

"Do you?"

I didn't answer and cried out from the electricity entering my body. It stopped but I was breathing fast and could feel my heart beating a mile a minute.

"That looked like it really hurt." She put the cord against her body and jumped from the shock. "Shit. That does hurt like a bastard."

"I asked you a question...do you?"

"Yes."

"That's my Scott. Honest Indian. I'm going to share this with you. I'm going to kill Chris at some point and if you are still alive and a man...you and I can really have some fun." She put the cord down on my body, but it wasn't close enough yet to shock me. "I have to tend to Chris' needs, but I think he's jealous of you. So, he might really want to hurt you, or even kill you. You have only me to save you...think of that."

She put her fingers to her mouth and then touched me between my legs. "I want you to miss me and to think about how you're going to stay alive."

Chapter 79

It was 9 o'clock back in Boston. She had just checked in at the airport and picked up her boarding pass. She would be home in less than ten hours and it couldn't be fast enough. She was concerned about Scott since she just tried his apartment and hers and there was still no answer. She knew this wasn't like him, and she feared the worst.

She knew the process to make a collect call and this time she was calling her dad. He accepted the charges.

"Hi Dad, it's me."

"Mercedes I can't tell you how great it is to hear your voice. Are you at the airport?"

"Yes, I'm about to board the plane. Have you heard from Scott?"

"Honey something bad has happened, but the authorities are involved."

"What? What has happened?"

"Scott has been abducted."

"When did this happen and where was he…and what the hell was he doing?"

"There are many things we need to talk about and this is not how I want to tell you about them."

"Jesus, Dad, my concern right now is Scott. You can tell me the other things later, but I want to know what has happened to him. This is like déjà vu and I'm not there this time to help." She was attracting attention. "I need to get on the plane, but tell me what you know about his abduction."

"Mike Miller called me this morning very early. Scott and he were doing an investigation and they both witnessed someone being attacked and then killed. Mike said he went to help the person, but the attackers escaped and in the process took Scott."

"I'm going to kill him."

"Mercy I'm so sorry. You might want to kill me first."

"Oh Dad, don't tell me he was involved in something for you. I think I knew this earlier when you wouldn't elaborate why you knew how to reach Scott. Dad, I'm really worried about him. This is his third abduction and it might be his last. You said 'attackers.' Who the hell were they and why did they take Scott?"

"This is too involved to go into on the phone."

"*Jesus, Dad, that g*ives me something to consider on the plane. This is the man I want to marry and you're not telling me what I need to know.

"Okay, you're right. Just give me a second to gather my thoughts."

"Dad the final boarding call has just been announced. Why can't you just tell me? It can't be that bad?"

"It is Mercy…it really is. You have another sister. Worse, Melanie had a twin sister. She was one of the abductors and Mike said she is the one who killed their original captive."

"*Oh my God, no! This can't be happening again.*" She beat the receiver against the payphone. This was just too much to hear especially after her rescue. She heard the dial tone and her name.

'Would passenger Mercedes Strong please report to gate twelve for final boarding? Once again, would passenger Mercedes Strong please report to gate twelve immediately? The plane is about to depart from the gate.'

"Ms. Strong?"

"Yes."

"This is for you."

She opened the white paper and read the note.

'Proceed immediately onto the plane.
Do not talk to anyone. We have eyes everywhere.
I have your associate, Ralph Reynolds.
Enjoy your flight.
I am looking forward to *seeing* you soon in Boston.
You will be greeted when you arrive.

Captain Chavez'

It was a bad day and it just got worse. As she entered the gate she turned to see the man who gave her the note smiling at her.

She had just a few hours to plan what she was going to do to make it a 'heads-up' kind of day.

Chapter 80

I heard them in the shower and this was my chance. I knew I couldn't break the power cord, but I might be able to slip it off my wrist.

This time there was nobody watching me and from the sounds in the bathroom it might be a few more minutes until they might check on me. I wrapped my fingers together into the tightest ball I could and pulled. The loop of the cord slipped up my hand just a little as it did before. I twisted my hand and pulled as hard as I could. The loop slipped a fraction of an inch more. I looked over to see how much progress I had made and it had just about an inch to go and it would be over my knuckles.

I twisted and pulled again with all my might and the loop was almost there. I did it again and this time I tried to move my body. The pain was excruciating.

I bit my tongue as the electricity coursed through my body. I shot my hips up almost as a reaction to the shock but it was enough to move the cord away from my skin. I looked down and the cord was still dangerously close to shocking my body again. I lifted my right knee slightly and the cord slid towards the wall. I lifted my left knee and saw the cord hang even closer to my body.

I heard them laughing in the bathroom and wondered just how much time I had left. I realized I was either going to be shocked again, or the cord was going to slide to the wall some more. I jerked my right knee and the cord slid some more. With only a small amount of freedom to move it was like watching a snail move. The thoughts of being whipped with a live cord gave me some additional strength.

I moved everything I could and did a slight bounce on the bed. I lifted both knees quickly and the cord slid off me down beside the bed. I pulled my left wrist again and withstood the pain of the cord. Repetitive twists and one final pull and I had freed my left wrist.

I rolled my upper body to my right side and started to work on the knot Chris had tied. I realized I no longer heard the water running. I frantically pulled on the knot and tried to work it loose, but it was not in the right place to get leverage on it. I don't know why I didn't realize it before but with my left wrist out of the loop my right arm could pull the cord from under the bed.

In two seconds, I was sitting up in bed with the length of the cord laying on me while I tried to undo one of the knots holding my ankles. I heard the bathroom door open and saw a blur out of the corner of my eye. It was Chris running naked at me and he was reaching for the revolver.

"Alexis he's trying to get loose."

I heard the loud crack and felt the pain on the side of my head and everything went dark.

* * *

I don't know how long I was knocked out. My head hurt in two places and every beat of my heart made it sound like the ocean waves were washing over my head. I kept my eyes closed and heard the television. My mouth was very dry and I wanted to lick my lips, but didn't dare. I didn't feel cool like before, and I realized I had clothes on. There was a strong scent of Gardenia and I knew Alexis was close at hand.

'...police are looking for the two suspects seen to be driving a 1963 gold Pontiac Tempest. They were last seen in the Chestnut Hill area of Boston. They are described as a male, Chris Sullivan, about six feet tall with blonde hair. The woman, Alexis Strong, is about five nine with long red hair. There is no description about what they were wearing. Police caution the public not to approach these individuals and to call your local police department should you spot them or their vehicle. They are armed and considered dangerous. Once again, these suspects are wanted in the death and mutilation of a Doctor Samuel Adler who was found murdered in his basement early this morning. We resume our regular broadcast.'

"Well we're famous now. I wonder why they didn't mention Scott's name." I could feel her eyes on me. "I think our guest is awake and might have a serious headache."

If I wasn't awake the slap to my groin would have woken me.

"It's nice to see those bright blue eyes of yours. Sorry you're dressed Scott, but we need to be on the move. It was fun dressing you, but Chris wasn't happy about what I did before I dressed you." She looked down and I could see the blood stain on the left side of my pants. "It would have been more fun if you were awake and watching me. In case you're wondering I duplicated the arrow design. Mercedes might enjoy the stereo road signs, but she's not going to have that luxury."

I wasn't tied up and they looked ready to leave the room.

"The good news is you avoided the punishment we had planned for you, but the bad news is you will still have the joy of it later. Better said, we will. Chris is very upset with your attempted escape and if he doesn't kill you, I might enjoy watching Mercedes squirm as I cut you piece by wonderful piece. I'll even let Chris have my sister. I owe him some reward for his help."

"Chris she plans to kill you too," I yelled.

The straight razor appeared right between my eyes from some place. It was a good thing she stopped its movement before it sliced my nose off. "That's right Scott, that's your blood on the razor." Her face distorted. "Lick the blood off." She didn't like my hesitation. "Do it, or I will slice your tongue instead...or, maybe you would like an amateur circumcision?"

"Alexis we have to get out of here."

"Scott, I'm not going to ask you again."

I licked the razor and wondered if she was going to cut my tongue anyway. I tasted my own blood and there was a metallic taste to it. At least I was alive. She turned the razor over and I knew what she wanted and obliged.

"Something you should know. Scott doesn't lie. Behave yourself Chris, but be very careful."

Chapter 81

"Mike, I wanted to give you an update on where we are in locating the people who took Scott," Paul Brosque said.

"Paul, thanks for calling. Any progress?"

"None yet. We have an APB out for Sullivan's Pontiac, but have not had any reports of any sightings. I think that's strange and I feel they may have ditched the car, or parked it completely out of sight."

"You're probably right on that score. One other thought is that they made it out of state by now."

"That's a possibility, but I'm betting they got off the road pretty quickly. Mike do you have any idea why they abducted Scott?"

"I have one thought on that. If Alexis knew about her twin and what she did and attempted to do...well, she might just pick up where her sister left off."

"We have a problem then. When we searched Doctor Adler's house we found an extensive collection of material including news clippings on Melanie Strong's two rampages, one in Boston and the other in Bermuda."

"Paul, I was afraid of something like this. What else can you tell me?"

"Well the straight razor used to kill Adler was not found at his house and looks like they took it with them when they left. You already reported Scott had a revolver with him. We also found a file box of material on Alexis Strong which the doctor kept hidden. He kept a very detailed account of her progress, but it was obvious he was using her as a sex toy. The pictures he took were not meant to be seen by anyone."

"I think Scott might just have walked into a very unfortunate situation."

"Mike...we also located Ms. Strong's diary. Although the doctor thought he was doing things while she was hypnotized, it was obvious by her notes that she was just playing along with him. That may have been the reason she mutilated him before she killed him."

"Do you anticipate they might go to either Scott's apartment or Sullivan's?"

"I hardly think they would go to either location, or to Stephen Strong's house or office building. However, we have all four under surveillance."

"Thanks Paul. I'm waiting here at the Brattle office for Paddy. When he arrives, we're going to get involved in some manner. If something breaks, try us here. We'll also be monitoring the primary channel for any developments."

"Mike, what's the story on Mercedes?"

"The last word I had was she was headed back on an earlier flight from Venezuela."

"Scott's abduction by Melanie's twin sister is going to devastate her."

"I think you're right about Scott's abduction, but I don't think she knows anything about her sister's twin yet. We're going to pick Mercedes up at the airport and let her know what has happened."

"I'll try my best to keep you informed of how things are progressing. If you don't hear from me, call me. If you can't reach me at the precinct, have dispatch reach me on the radio."

"Thanks again Paul."

Chapter 82

She needed to stop worrying about Scott for a minute and take some positive action to ensure her own safety. The thoughts of being in Captain Chavez's hands again, or even worse, in the hands of the men who abducted her the first time, made her stomach turn. She knew the next time she was abducted it would be her last time.

She took a piece of paper and a pen from her leather satchel and wrote a note.

'My name is Mercedes Strong. I am an FBI agent.
Before boarding the plane, I was given a note.
My fellow agent Ralph Reynolds has been abducted in Venezuela. I was warned, I will be abducted myself when we land.
I have been given instructions to contact nobody.
Please call FBI headquarters in Boston to alert them.
Do not say anything to me because they could be watching me on this plane.
This is not a joke. My life could be in serious jeopardy.'

She folded the paper and put it in her purse. She tried to assess the surrounding passengers to see if any might be watching her. There was only one man who was back three rows on the other side of the aircraft who looked like he was staring at her. *Maybe I'm not as attractive as I thought I was.*

She got up and headed up to the wait station. A stewardess was preparing some coffee. She tapped her on the shoulder and opened her purse and handed her the note. She put her finger to her lips with her back blocking the gesture. She closed her purse, took a bag of peanuts and headed back to her seat.

Her heart was beating rapidly as she took her seat. The man she spotted earlier was smiling at her, but she ignored him. Her mind was going a mile a minute. Scott and Ralph were abducted. It was hard to believe but she could smell Captain Chavez just like he was sitting beside her. She turned and the man was still looking in her direction, but got up and walked to the same stewardess.

He came down the aisle a minute later and sat in the seat beside her. She tried to ignore him, but he tapped her on the arm. She looked at him and he handed her back her note.

There was a commotion up front and she saw two other stewardesses running to the coffee area.

"You were warned once. You will not be warned again. You caused one death already, don't cause any more. Ralph didn't send his best wishes, but unless you want his best parts sent to you...stay in your seat."

She watched him get up and thought he was leaving. He opened an overhead bin and then another. He came back and sat down and put the small blanket over both their laps.

"Your attention please. Is there a doctor onboard? Please, if there is a doctor on board we have a medical emergency. Passengers, if at all possible please remain in your seats for the balance of the flight."

They both watched a man near the front of the aircraft come back to where the stewardesses were. One of them closed the curtain.

She felt the man's hand sliding up her thigh.

"Captain Chavez told me he would be joining you very shortly, and told me you were well worth my life. You forced my hand a few minutes ago, but he told me I could amuse myself with you until he arrived in Boston."

She felt his hand between her legs.

"I'm glad it's a long flight," he said with a smile. "Aren't you glad we have hours to enjoy...the flight?"

I could kill him with one quick elbow. But would killing him be risking Ralph's life if he didn't check in?

"Ms. Strong, do you remember Jose? I'm his brother and the captain's cousin. My name is Hector. Please forgive my inability to shake your hand as it's rather busy at the moment. Will you please unbutton your slacks, or do I have to create a scene and do it myself?"

She wished someone was sitting in the third seat, but no such luck. *She was glad she was going to give her notice, but wondered if she would actually have the luxury any longer.* She felt his hand slip inside her panties and grip her flesh. She was very dry and he was hurting her.

He pulled her hand under the blanket to him and she wondered when he had exposed himself. She felt his fingers lessen the pressure on her sex, and realized what the contract was.

"Ms. Strong this is nothing compared to what you are in store for. You will make my cousin a very rich man indeed. You are not only beautiful but you have other nice assets including your fingers. Use them please."

She saw them covering the stewardess' body. "Why did you have to kill that young girl?"

"You are so wrong. You were given specific instructions and you didn't follow them…your actions got her killed. Don't make another mistake."

She felt a second finger enter her. She squeezed his penis hard and she quickly regretted it.

"My dear lady, we have hours to enjoy the flight. Let's take our time to enjoy it. I have some toys in my pocket that will cause you considerable pain. I would much rather please you than hurt you, and I expect the same in return."

She wasn't stupid and knew what Hector wanted. *She wondered if Ralph was still alive. Without her with him, what did they have to lose in killing him? Maybe her being with Hector would give him a few more hours. This time I'm sorry Ralph. Her thoughts went to Scott and she wondered what her crazy sister had done to him, was doing now, or would eventually do.*

"You're crying. I'm sorry if I hurt you too much."

"We regret to inform you that we will be making an emergency landing in Miami. Once we land, no one will be allowed to leave the aircraft. Officials will investigate the death of one of our staff. We expect to resume our scheduled flight to Boston once officials have completed their investigation. We appreciate your patience and there will be complimentary drinks and cocktails."

They both listened to the message replay a second time.

She wondered if Hector failed to check in at the scheduled arrival time in Boston…would Chavez assume something went wrong and kill Ralph.

At the present time he was paying only a slight attention to her body and was obviously ready to pop his cork.

"Excuse me. We're very sorry for the unexpected stop. Would you two care for something to drink…maybe a cocktail?" She looked down at Hector whose eyes were closed. "Is he okay?"

She responded by nodding towards the tented and moving blanket.

"Oh my," the stewardess responded.

"We'll pass on cocktails right now. I need—"

She immediately felt the pain inside her body.

"Yes?"

"Just some napkins please."

"I can see why." She threw a pile onto the blanket and unlocked the cart and moved to the next row.

She felt his erection diminish.

"That was almost an unfortunate mistake. Now you need to get me back to where I was."

"Why Hector, are you going back to your assigned seat?"

"Unless you want your head under the blanket, put your other hand under there too."

She felt his fingers resume their in and out movement and she added her other hand to his balls and squeezed.

His fingers hurt her and she released some of the pressure. She heard the rolling cart going up the aisle and she exchanged glances with the stewardess. The stewardess must have seen her with both her hands under the blanket.

I'm really not a tramp, but I wonder what I will be like in a few years after Chavez is done with me. There was only one person's prize possession she wanted, and she hoped her crazy sister wasn't going to cut if off.

Chapter 83

They headed slowly down the street.

"She looked at the page from the white pages. This isn't the right street. What are you doing Chris?"

"I'll tell you in a minute Alexis. I need to pay attention."

"Let's see your wound Scott."

The car turned suddenly to the left and she was thrown away from Scott.

She watched as Chris pulled the car into the very long driveway and parked it on the far side of the two car detached garage. "What are you doing?"

"Nobody is home here."

"How do you know that?"

"There are at least three days of newspapers on the front lawn. This is Newton. Nobody neglects their yards. If I'm right, his house is that one behind the garage on that side."

It was still early afternoon. It was a hazy and humid day. "Let's go."

"Wait. I want to see if Scott has stopped bleeding."

"You and I both know that is not what you want to do. Come on. Let's go before someone spots us in the car."

"Saved by the hair on your chinny chin chin, or your balls. That won't be the case for long though."

The garages were all detached garages in this neighborhood and backed up to the ones on the next street over. Their car was pretty much blocked from view by the high hedges and the garage. You could see only the rear fenders and bumper.

"I'm impressed Chris. I know you couldn't have planned this, but you did a great job of hiding the car," Alexis said, pushing Scott ahead of her. They headed for the high hedges behind their target house. Once inside the hedge line, the two of them studied the property.

"Alexis, there are lights on in the kitchen and in some rooms upstairs. There is also a bulkhead that leads to the basement. I'm going to see if there's a lock on it, or if I can get into the basement. Why don't you entertain yourself with Scott, which I'm sure you're dying to do, and if it's unlocked I'll wave for you to come over."

"Isn't that nice that you gave me permission to entertain myself with Scott, and to also come."

"That isn't exactly what I said and you know it."

She watched as Chris kept himself low to the manicured grass and moved quickly towards the cellar bulkhead. "I can't wait to get both of you naked again." She reached between his legs and pictured what she had seen only an hour ago. "I've only seen three naked men, with the exception of the doctor's nudist magazine. I would certainly put you up against the best of them. However, I'm going to enjoy putting you up against me again."

"Are you really going to kill Chris?"

"That cost you the last time you mentioned that. Why do you care?"

"He seems to really like you. Haven't you killed enough?"

"Scott, I wish I had hours to explain why I'm so upset. I missed the best part of my life, thanks to the deceased doctor. I had a family and an entirely different life, but I was taken from it. Maybe Melanie wouldn't have been as screwed up if I was with her. There's more, but Chris is waving to us. Until later." She touched him between his legs and then spun him around and pushed him towards the grass area.

Chris was emphatically waving them over and alternately pushing his hand towards the ground to get low. Once they were at the bulkhead, they entered the basement slowly and quietly. Chris pulled the outside bulkhead doors down blocking some of the light. He closed the inside doors to the steps leading up to the outside.

There was enough light in the basement to see. "Tie him to one of those columns over there."

Alexis watched him as he tied Scott to the metal column. Once Scott was gagged and tied to the column she could feel the tightening in her groin. She liked the thoughts of him tied to the column and wondered how soon she would be back to entertain herself. She quickly put her hand behind Chris' head and kissed him hard and probed his mouth with her tongue.

"I can tell you're excited," Chris whispered.

"Yeah, but you're the one with a screwdriver in your pants. Drop them. I want to suck you in front of Scott."

"All in good time Alexis. We need to do what we came here to do."

She continued rubbing her hand across Chris' now increasing erection. "You want me to do that as much as I do."

"Yes, but let's do what we came to do first." He cupped between her legs and she emitted a low rattle.

She listened to his plan.

Chapter 84

I knew where we were. I heard what Chris planned to do. I hope Mercedes wasn't in the house. It was obvious Alexis was planning to kill her father and then either Chris or me. I could warn Chris, but I had already done that. If I do it again, it might tip the scale and I'll be the one she kills.

I remembered what the doctor's face showed when she changed him into a woman, and then his expression when she slit his throat. My only hope of staying alive for minutes, if not hours, was to play along with her. Her sister had tried to kill me, and really couldn't bring herself to do it, but that was because of the circumstances and Melanie's complicated split-personalities.

I tried not to think that these might be my last minutes alive. The thoughts of Mercedes in captivity were not the best thing to be thinking about right now. She was why I wanted to live and without her, what would I do?

When they headed here I knew it was Stephen's house they were going to. Alexis wasn't here to introduce herself, although she may do just that, but was really here to punish him for what he had done to her life. I had seen Stephen make business decisions. He made them quickly and with conviction. Thinking about why he committed Alexis to the care facility I could understand why he did it.

His wife was weak at the time. If she knew she gave birth to a deformed child it would have been crushing to her. So, he made the best decision he could, given the circumstances. It wasn't what I would have done, but I can see him weighing the consequences and he decided it was best to hide her. It would have worked if Alexis had remained a deformed child. However, she turned into the same beautiful twin Melanie was.

I thought of my captivity by Melanie. She made me do things I wanted to resist, but she was too good at getting my body to react to her persuasions. However, cutting the arrow went too far, but I remember her eyes looking elsewhere, and I was lucky in hindsight.

I can understand why Mercedes was so upset by my nightmares. Our disagreement happened only a few days ago but it felt like weeks.

Mercedes I love you. I want you and I need you. Please God don't let her be hurt. I promise I will never ever do another investigation. I've learned my lesson. I want to be with you for the rest of my life. If you still do investigations, I will support you. However, we both could find something else that would be less threatening to our future. I want to have kids and make you the happiest person in the world.

I knew it was pointless to say my prayers. What was going to happen was going to happen. However, I didn't have much to lose by saying them.

I heard a loud thump above me and wondered what it was.

Chapter 85

They were walking up the sweeping staircase to what must be the upstairs bedrooms. She could feel her heart beating in her chest and looked down to make sure she wasn't bleeding since it was pounding so hard. Chris was behind her and letting her do her thing.

At the top of the staircase there was a long hall with several doors leading off it on the right. There was a railing on the left side overlooking the lower level and two more doors beyond the railing's end.

She stuck her head in each room, but they were obviously unoccupied. She could hear some muted classical music playing in one of the rooms down the hall. However, she kept checking out each room. She stopped when she heard the sound of someone moving in the next room to her right.

She put her hand up to have Chris stop and she moved quietly to the room she heard the noise in. She stood at the doorway and saw a woman, maybe in her fifties, sitting at a bench in front of the dresser mirror, brushing her hair. This must be her mother. She put her hand up again to Chris who was still staying right where he was. She entered the bedroom.

The woman's eyes were closed and she was lost in the brushing. This could have been someone who loved her, but her dad never let her know she existed. She slowly opened the straight razor and took another step towards the woman.

The woman must have sensed her presence since she opened her eyes. Her expression was one of confusion and of shock. She dropped the hairbrush and turned in the seat towards her. "Melanie?" She grabbed her throat and started to get up. Then she grimaced and grabbed her chest.

Alexis realized her mother was having a heart attack. "How nice to see you mother," she whispered. She closed the straight razor as her mother collapsed onto the bedroom floor.

She heard the sound of heavy footsteps out in the hall. She turned to see her father enter the bedroom and stop dead in his tracks. He dropped the small glass he was holding onto the bedroom floor. "Alexis…what have you done?"

"I haven't done anything. I was just going to say hello to my mother when she collapsed."

He was already moving to his wife's form, but they both saw how blue her face was. He pulled the bench away and started to blow into her mouth and press rapidly on her chest. "You don't seem that surprised to see me, Dad. Is that what I should call you? Or should it be Stephen or Mr. Strong? I think you're wasting your breath. She needs more than you can give her now. You know what…I needed a lot more from you too."

She opened the straight razor. "Couldn't you have called me once, or even visited me once while I was hidden away. Dad, I needed you more than you could ever know. I had a family and you kept me from it. Why? What did I ever do wrong to you?" She hated the fact she had tears running down her face. For the first time she realized Chris was standing inside the bedroom door. "Dad, why didn't you care about me? I was a real person and although I was ugly for many years…look at me now…I'm not that way any longer. You deserve to die for what you did to me."

She lunged at him with the open razor, and he ducked out of the way. He went running towards the door and Chris grabbed him. She watched them fight and was frozen in position. She wanted to move, but couldn't.

Her father made a move with his leg and both arms and Chris went flying onto his back. She saw her dad run out of the bedroom in his stocking feet and turn down the hallway. She was still frozen in position holding the straight razor when she heard a crack, followed by a loud crash.

They both left the bedroom to find the railing broken. They looked down and her father was lying in a growing pool of blood. He had obviously landed on a glass top table which had a metal frame. One of the metal frames was sticking out his back.

She dropped the razor and turned and buried her head in Chris's chest.

"I'm sorry Alexis. I'm sorry you didn't have the family you should have had." She felt his arms tight around her.

"I think I saw some love in my mother's eyes, but she only knew my image as Melanie's. I didn't even have time to tell her who I was. They're both dead now." She couldn't stop her sobbing, and wondered why she was so upset they were gone.

Minutes later she had calmed down enough to get her thoughts together. "Chris what do we do now?"

"Well, there's only Scott and Mercedes left," Chris answered as she felt him push her away from his body. She bent and picked up the razor. She noticed it still had some of Scott's blood on it. "Lick it Chris." She watched as he studied her eyes and licked the razor with some force.

It would be so easy to kill him right now. "I need you now Chris. I need you to lick me like you did that razor." She dropped the razor and started running down the hall, stopping periodically to remove a piece of her clothing.

"What about Scott?" he asked.

"What about him? Do you want him to watch us?"

"No, not really."

"Good. You can have Mercedes if we get the chance and we'll let Scott watch. Then I'll have Scott willingly because he will be trying to protect her. Then we'll kill them both. You and I will start a new set of trophies. I know what parts I want of Scott's, but you need to think about what you want of hers." She smiled a wicked smile. "Maybe you just want her long red hair."

She pushed him and removed the last article of her clothing and jumped on her parents' king sized bed. She watched him bounce when he took his briefs off. "Something has made you really excited." He started to climb onto the bed.

"Wait. I want you to do as I say. You'll get me, but you will be even more ready. Now do what I originally told you to do."

She watched his brain trying to remember, and then his recognition. He started towards her. "Slowly Chris...do everything very slowly."

Chapter 86

As soon as I saw them I knew I was in trouble. They were both naked and Alexis had her straight razor in her hand. She looked miles away.

"Scott, did you enjoy your time alone with your thoughts?" Alexis asked grabbing the front of my shirt and ripped it open. "Answer me."

"I wondered what was happening upstairs. But I guess I can tell now that you both are naked."

She couldn't pull the shirt completely off since my hands were tied behind the column. I heard the razor cutting through the cloth of my shirt. "Better," she said.

I could feel my heart beating a mile a minute and wondered if she was going to kill me right here. She leaned her ear against my chest with the razor right in front of my eyes. "I wish your heart was beating because you were excited to see me, but I know you remember what I did to the good doctor and worry about what I'm going to do to you. Right?"

I knew I better respond. "Alexis, your sister was much more of a romantic. She was mean in many ways, but she treated those in her captivity with some form of love."

"What does that mean? Do you want me to make love to you?"

"I don't know how to explain it to you. And no, I don't want you to make love to me." I hoped that was the back of the razor between my legs.

"I got your attention again didn't I?"

I looked over at Chris who was enjoying my predicament, and probably glad it was me instead of him. "Yes."

"Chris, come over here and untie him. Let's bring him upstairs to one of the bedrooms. I'm not finished with him yet, and I'm not going to make this easy on him by killing him here. Oh, and by the way…Stephen and his wife are both dead."

* * *

Chris had a cord around my neck and my wrists were still tied behind my back, but it felt strange to be the only one of us with clothes. I'm sure that was going to change very soon.

When we got upstairs I saw the pool of blood and the metal frame protruding through Stephen's back. I knew he was dead. It was hard to comprehend his being dead. I just talked with him a few hours ago. I'm most likely going to be the next person killed, unless she does Chris instead of me. That gave me an idea. Chris pulled on the cord and it was hard to breath. Is he going to kill me instead?

We stopped at the entrance to the master bedroom. Mrs. Strong's body was on her back and there was no question she was also dead. "Chris, drag her body into another room. I don't want to look at her lying on the floor," Alexis said as she motioned with the razor.

She pushed me over to the four-poster bed which was almost three feet off the floor. "You get up on the bed."

I backed up to the bed and lifted myself up so I was seated on the bed. I didn't like how Alexis was looking at me, and I just stared back.

She stepped closer and ran the back of the razor down from my forehead, across my nose and rested it on my lips. "Open your mouth." As soon as I did she had the razor laying flat against my tongue. "I should have had Chris take the rest of your clothes off before he left the room." Chris came in almost as if he was called.

I looked at his expression as he watched what Alexis was doing.

"Chris, give me a hand." However, he just stayed where he was. "Chris, please. Come over here and help me." He hesitantly came over and stood beside her. "Take all his clothes off and make him more comfortable."

He hesitated. "I thought you had some investigation stuff to do…we're wasting time."

"The sooner you get him tied up again, the sooner I can get on with what I was going to do. Besides, wouldn't you like to be mean to him, so I could be nice to you?"

I watched her other hand reach between his legs and then wrap her fingers around him. "Chris, remember all the fun you had doing the things I made you do in my bedroom? Now, hurry and do what I asked you to do. You're right, we're wasting time."

I knew once they had me tied to the bed and naked again, I had at best only a few hours left to live. I also realized I might not want to be alive for whatever she was planning. I made a quick move off the bed and started to run out of the bedroom. I heard Chris' bare feet pounding on the floor rushing after me.

It was hard running down the stairs with my hands tied behind me, but I was several steps ahead of him and headed to the front entry. I got a glimpse of Stephen's body to my right as I passed at a full run. What I didn't see was the blood on the floor. My first step into the blood and my feet went out from under me. I landed on my back and saw Chris' fist headed toward my face.

* * *

This was getting to feel like a broken record and I was the record. I could feel the pain in my back, but my extremities hurt just as bad. This time there was no play in the cords around my wrists and ankles. I opened my eyes to see Alexis sitting on my body. She was still naked and I was now too.

"You are getting to be a real problem Scott. I think Chris' suggestion to just kill you makes a lot of sense. Give me one reason I shouldn't just slash your throat right now." She looked down my body and ran her fingers lightly across my stomach. "That's one reason." She busied her fingers lower and I could feel my body slowly responding.

"Are you going to do the research you had planned on doing?" Chris asked from the chair he was sitting in.

"I am doing research right now. I like how both of your bodies respond to my touch. In Scott's case even when he's trying his best to ignore what I'm doing."

"Alexis you promised me."

"Yes, you're right...I did promise you. Okay Scott, you have a few more minutes to think about how you are going to be punished for trying to escape again. I know I'm getting tired of it, and I can tell Chris is getting annoyed with your presence." She got up and then planted a kiss right on my penis.

"Let's go do our investigation Chris."

Chapter 87

She knew Chris had one thing on his mind at the present time and it wasn't her…he was intent on finding anything of monetary value. He told her he was sure Stephen kept cash on hand. He couldn't have gotten ten thousand dollars out of the bank, as it was Sunday. It would keep him busy. She, on the other hand, was trying to understand why her father sent her away. She knew she was an ugly child, but there had to be more to it.

It was somewhat strange to be walking around her parents' house without any clothes, but who was going to see her, or them? She avoided looking at her father's body in the foyer and went to the living room.

The room was tastefully decorated in reds, whites and some light blue. The two main couches were a light blue and the other smaller one was a cream color. The red curtains were drawn and hung down almost to the floor. There were nautical paintings on the wall along with some photographs of sailboats. There was a grand piano in the corner with many framed pictures.

She made her way over to the pictures and saw an older man with two girls. One of the girls looked like her when she was that age. It was Melanie her twin sister. The other she imagined was Mercedes, who was only a few years younger. They all looked like they were enjoying being together.

There were many other family shots but Mercedes' Harvard graduation picture caught her attention. She could see her features were similar to hers. She was extremely attractive, with long red hair pulled down over one shoulder accenting the swell of her breasts beneath the gown. *She wondered what it would have been like to grow up with her sisters. Would she have attended Harvard too? Would her sister have been so screwed up?* She wanted to know more about Melanie.

Chris was moving pictures in the room now looking for a safe. "Find anything Chris?"

"I found one safe upstairs but I don't have the combination. Are you finding anything interesting?"

"Just some interesting family pictures. Is there an office upstairs?"

"Yeah, all the way down the hall, the last door on the left."

She went over to Chris and grabbed both of his ears and forced a kiss on his lips. She purposely invaded his mouth with her tongue. She felt his body coming to life. "I was wondering who the person was in here with me...I didn't recognize his lifeless protrusion." Her hand was busy coaxing a proper salute. "There's my Chris. Would you rather I went up and played with Scott instead?"

She felt his hands grab the cheeks of her ass and pull her body tightly against him. Her head was against his chest and she turned and bit his neck.

"Owe. That hurts."

"You love the attention and you know it."

"Don't you feel badly that your parents are dead?"

"Not really...I didn't know them, and they obviously didn't know me. My father didn't care enough about me to tell my mother I existed. He never ever asked about how I was doing."

"What about the doctor?"

"What about him?"

"Aren't you upset that you killed him?"

"He deserved what he received more than anybody else. I wish I had more time to have him feel the pain of what I did to him before I slit his throat. He treated me like a piece of meat." She pushed him away and rushed out of the room.

* * *

It took her quite a while to find what she was looking for, but she found it. In her father's desk she found false bottoms in both the left and right hand bottom drawers. In the drawer on the left she found Melanie's diary. In the other drawer she found something more upsetting.

In that drawer were pictures and reports from Doctor Adler to her father. As she read through the reports it was obvious her father was very much interested in her progress. The doctor was the one who was delaying her release back into her family's life. Her father even requested meeting with her to explain what had happened.

Doctor Adler replied that she wasn't quite ready for the shock and he was gradually introducing more and more of the outside world to her.

He was not doing anything of the sort...in fact he was treating her more like a sex slave. She thought of what she did to his body and wished she still had those parts...so she could cut them into tiny pieces.

Now she was truly sorry her father wasn't here. In his own way he loved her and wanted to bring her back into the family. However, he was worried what it would do to her mother since she was in a fragile state. There's no going back and undoing what had happened. I'm sorry dad...I really didn't know how you felt.

She read every piece of correspondence and how the doctor purposely twisted the facts to maintain her presence. If it wasn't for Chris she might not have learned about all of this. She put the material back in the bottom of the drawer and put the wood cover over it, and then the other material on top of it. *Why the hell am I doing that?*

For the first time she felt the leather of the chair. She was sticking to the leather and lifted herself and heard the noise her skin made. She sat back down and picked up Melanie's diary.

* * *

She looked to where the writing stopped and there were not that many blank pages left. She started at the beginning of the diary which dealt with her childhood. There was a pattern to the entries. Many dealt with going with her grandfather on his boat. Mercedes and she were close, but it was obvious, based on the comments, that Melanie tried her best to garner more of her grandfather's praise.

She was not reading every page, but glancing at the content. She could feel eyes on her and looked up to see Chris standing in the doorway. "I brought you something." He was holding a gray Harvard T-shirt. She smiled at him and he brought the shirt over. "You look like you could use a cover. What are you doing?"

She put the diary down and put both arms up and he put the shirt over her arms. She stood and pulled it down and it was long enough to cover most of her bottom. She did a pirouette and he smiled. "I like it," he acknowledged.

"Why Chris, don't tell me you are getting embarrassed by my naked body."

"No not at all. I just found it in your father's closet and thought you would like to wear it."

"You just want the thrill of taking it off. Do you think it's too short?" She pulled it up a little and made him smile.

"I think you look very sexy in it. From where I'm standing it looks just the right length."

"Judging from your body's reaction I would say you're correct. I wonder if Scott will react the same way." She could tell he didn't like her comment. "Don't worry...I won't ignore you or your body." Her fingers touched him.

"So, what did you find?" He looked down at the book.

"You just want to change my focus."

"No, you know I'm more than ready whenever you are. I haven't found anything else anywhere, and need to get this safe open."

"I found some material my dad had hidden regarding my progress. He wanted me to come home, but was concerned about whether my mother could handle the shock. We now know his concern was justified. I wish I had known how he felt. This is my twin sister's diary. It could get very interesting, but I'm reading about when she was a teenager right now."

"Are you hungry Alexis? I am."

"Not really. I'm going to read her journal. If you want to sit on the desk I can do two things at once. How about you sit there and I'll read what she wrote. You might just get more excited."

"I can see you like the feel of the material against your body, your nipples are swelled."

She lifted her T-shirt and watched his eyes focus, the corner of his mouth gave a hint of a smile, and she saw his erection twitch. She pulled him down and pulled his head to her chest. "Oh that feels so good. I'll give you a day to stop."

The phone's ring made them both jump.

He stood and she swiveled back and they both stared at the phone. They looked at each other trying to decide whether they should answer it. Her thought was if someone knew her father was home, along with her mother, and no one answered, it might alert whoever was calling there was a problem.

She lost count of the number of rings, but it stopped. "Chris, not answering the phone could be a big problem, especially if someone knew both of them were supposed to be home."

"Alexis, it's a Monday after a holiday weekend. Your father should be at work…I would think. I think I better keep looking for that combination."

"Yeah, it looks like the ringing took all your excitement away. I could change that, but I agree, keep looking for the combination. I want to finish reading her journal. Oh, how is our guest doing? Do you want me to check?"

"No. I think I should be the one who checks on him…that is if you want to make progress on your reading."

"You really are jealous of him, aren't you?"

He didn't immediately answer. "I didn't like the fact the doctor had you for extended periods, and thought it was going to be different when he wasn't around any longer. Now you seem to really enjoy Scott…or more appropriately, Scott's body."

He is jealous. "I'll try not to ignore you when I'm entertaining myself. Besides, you were going to punish him for his escape attempt. I would like very much to watch that, but if you want to hurt him…just leave enough for both of us to enjoy punishing him together."

"Maybe I will do that. If I do, I will try not to focus on the parts you seem to enjoy so much."

She watched his naked ass as he left the room and she reached for the diary to finish reading what her twin wrote.

Once again I have two attractive men to entertain myself. There will be only one soon. I haven't made up my mind yet who the winner is going to be. Our next session should help me make a really tough decision, but it will be even tougher for one of them. She remembered the doctor's shocked expression when he realized what she was going to do with the razor.

She couldn't hold back her smile.

Chapter 88

"Paddy, I don't like this at all," Mike announced.

"What?"

"I just called the airline and Mercedes' plane is being diverted to Miami. They wouldn't say why. However, what really surprises me is that there is no answer at Stephen's house."

"Didn't you just talk with him this morning?"

"Yes, and he hung up on me when he heard a click on the phone. I think his wife heard what he was talking about."

"I think we need to have the precinct do a drive-by to see if they see anything out of the norm, and see if his car is in the driveway."

"Okay, you do that and I'm going to check with Paul to see if there is anything new on spotting Sullivan's car."

He tried but Paul was not available and they indicated they would have him return the call shortly.

"Hi Mike, this is Paul. I was busy trying to track down a report of two men and a woman checking into a hotel in Burlington. As best we can tell by the condition of the room it was probably them. That means they are staying in the area. What's up?"

"Thanks Paul. This might tie in with that report. I personally talked with Stephen Strong this morning and he was going to be at his home all day. I just tried his home and there is no answer. At this point I'm a little worried. Do you think you could have a unit swing by to see if they spot anything strange at his home?"

"We do have a surveillance unit there. Let me touch base with them to see whether there is anything strange. Do you want to try him again on another line to see if you can reach him? In the meantime, I will get in touch with the unit. I'll stay on the line. Give me a few minutes though."

"I'll try Stephen again."

"Paddy, Paul thinks the three people put up in a Burlington hotel last night, but they are not there now. He is going to have a unit swing by Stephen's house to see if they spot anything strange. He wants me to try Stephen again."

He watched Paddy put two coffee cups on his desk. He quickly dialed Stephen's number again. "Thanks for the coffee."

They let the phone ring about ten times. "No answer." He hung it up and picked up Paul's line. "Paddy, I think this is an indication something is going on at Stephen's house. I just hope we're not too late. They have already killed one person, and they know we know who they are…they have nothing to lose killing Scott."

"Mike, yeah it's me. The unit is making a swing by the house now and will make a second swing a minute later and will contact me directly with what he observes. Any word on Mercedes?"

"As a matter of fact her plane is being diverted to Miami and we are trying to find out why. At least she is headed home."

"Hold Mike."

He could hear Paul talking in the background. "Okay, here's the story. There is no car in the driveway, but without checking the garage Stephen's car could be in there. There are lights on in what looks like the kitchen area and lights on upstairs."

"That doesn't sound right when the phone isn't being answered. I suggest the unit check for a car in the garage and anything out of order around the house. I don't need to tell you, that if Scott and the abductors are in the house and spot someone checking the property…well it could get messy."

"I understand. I'll have them park out of sight and check on foot. Anything else? How about checking the neighborhood while he is at it?"

"Sounds good. How can we reach you?"

"I'll just stay by this phone until I get the results."

"We'll be here as well."

"Paddy, Paul is going to have the unit check out the property on foot. You know all that material at Doctor Adler's house would give them Stephen's address."

"You're right Mike. If Alexis has any of her twin sister's genes, she might want to revenge what has happened to her for all these years. We saw what she did to the doctor."

"I just hope she doesn't want to hurt Scott to get back at her other sister, Mercedes. I think if Scott makes it out of this alive, he will surely keep his distance on any future investigations."

Chapter 89

There was a familiar smell to the creep beside her. It must run in the Chavez family. There was no way she was going to go back into Captain Chavez's captivity and she would take her chances when they landed in Miami. She really didn't have any choice.

She also couldn't wait to use the ladies room when they landed to get rid of this dirty feeling she had from his hands. This whole strange blanket thing brought back some memories of going to the drive-in with one of her earlier boyfriends. It was a way not to get pregnant and to get the rush connected with a climax, whether it was his or hers.

If this wasn't so serious she could crack up over what he had made her do, and not just once. She wished she had more napkins, but made do with what she had.

She had her plan and wondered if she could actually pull it off, no pun intended.

Hector was almost falling asleep and wasn't playing with her body like earlier. She heard the announcement that they were starting their descent into Miami's International Airport and they would be landing in twelve minutes. It was just about the right amount of time she needed.

She only had one hand under the blanket, but she knew it was going to be enough. A couple of quick squeezes and some fingernails brought Hector back to life. She could tell by what was happening under the blanket.

He turned and looked at her, smiled and said, "You really are everything my cousin said. You will make him a very rich man indeed." Unfortunately it brought his fingers back to life as well. "I am really going to enjoy being in your company when I can put that where it belongs, and some other places where it will wipe that smile off your face." She squeezed with all her strength. "Owe, take it easy."

The stewardess was coming down checking each passenger's seat backs and tray tables. When she got to their seats she asked, "Would you like me to take that blanket? I'll take it after we land and make sure it gets washed." She shook her head and continued down the aisle. A minute later she made the trip back to the front, but not before she checked what they were doing.

"This is the pilot speaking. We will be on the ground in three minutes. Crew prepare for landing. Passengers, please remain in your seats. Authorities will board the aircraft to conduct an investigation. We will resume our flight to Boston when the plane is released."

She clenched her legs together to prevent his further access to her body, and his body was lifting out of his seat and ready to pop. The plane touched down and swayed slightly and she heard the brakes being applied. He let go and she pulled her hand away and brought her elbow into his nose as he was leaning forward due to the braking.

Hector went out like a light and from the sound she knew she had driven part of his nose into his head. His head slumped forward and she realized the blow had probably killed him. The same stewardess had never taken her eyes off them and saw her strike him.

She saw the stewardess unbuckle and head quickly up the aisle while the plane was still taxiing. "What is going on here?"

"This note will explain what is happening. As soon as the authorities board the plane, I need to talk with them. Hector here is the one who killed your associate and he was planning on abducting me when we arrived in Boston."

She started to lift the blanket to cover his face. I suggest you don't do that. I would get a different blanket.

"Thank you Agent Strong. Then you were being forced to do what you were doing?"

"Look at this loser...what do you think?" She noticed the flashing blue lights as they came to a stop. The plane was not at the terminal. Instead, they were parked on the tarmac.

* * *

She explained everything to the investigators, displayed her credentials, then told them what had happened to the stewardess. She showed them the note she received in the terminal before she left Venezuela. She was taken off the plane by two of the investigators and minutes later they were in a security office.

"Look, I need to call my director in Venezuela to tell him what happened here and update him. He probably knows Ralph was abducted by now, but we have only a short time to find him or they will most likely kill him. I'm sure Hector was going to call when I was in custody in Boston."

It took several minutes to reach Max Gordon, but she was relieved he was on the phone. She started to convey everything and Max told her to hold up a minute. "Look Mercedes, I'm glad you're safe, but so is Ralph. Long story short, when he was taken, one of our contacts saw where he was taken. He is now safe and back in the hospital. He is okay, but they worked him over pretty well."

"Max, I know this is not the time or place for this…but I am going to be submitting my resignation when I get back to Boston."

"I'm not at all surprised, but would you like to take a few days to reconsider that? You've had a very difficult couple of days."

"Thanks Max. However, I've had some time to consider what I want to do with my future, and I want a family."

"Okay Agent Strong, we will meet in my office when we return. Do you want me to tell Agent Reynolds anything?"

"Please tell him I am very happy he is safe, and tell him he is a great agent and I enjoyed working with him."

"Will do. I understand they are holding the plane waiting on whether you are going to join them or not. I take it you want to get back on the plane?"

"Yes, I've got some unfinished business in Boston I need to address right away. Goodbye Director Gordon."

"Goodbye Mercedes...I guess I have to get used to calling you by that name now."

"Yes, you do Max."

Chapter 90

I was very uncomfortable on the bed in my condition. Several people were dead, and I might be her next target. She was flipping the straight razor open and then pushing it closed on the mattress. It was much too close for my comfort.

Chris was sitting in a bedroom chair and just watching Alexis read passages out of Melanie's diary. I could tell he was getting impatient with Alexis' proximity to me and how she was reacting to her sister's entries. If Alexis didn't kill me, I'm sure Chris would love to take me off her hands.

"Alexis, I thought we were going to punish Scott for trying to escape."

"I'm enjoying my sister's entries and it is starting to get interesting. She's out of the nut-house. Everyone thought she had resolved her issues, but she promised her psychiatrist that she would continue to sleep with him if he got her released. I can't believe we both went down that same path. You heard what she did to him, and the authorities thought the boat blew up by accident."

Alexis looked over to me, and I was not at all happy with where she was looking especially with the straight razor so close.

"Chris, listen to this entry. 'Yesterday the four of us cemented plans to have each of our tormentors kidnapped and brought to the warehouse. It was going to be costly to have each one kidnapped, but it would be worth it. We decided to pay the Calumet gang to kidnap each one. They would deposit each one down the coal chute. We were concerned the gang would find us to be a better target and rape us instead. However, the money was a great incentive and would help them buy more guns."

She flipped back a few pages. "I think I missed something." She put the razor on the bed and tried to find whatever she was looking for. "Here it is."

She picked up the razor again. 'Bob Sullivan came over while my parents were gone for the weekend. It was just like the other weekends. I had just turned sixteen. I fell asleep after we made love and when he woke me up we weren't alone. Three of his friends were in my bedroom. They tied me up and raped me all weekend. Bob threatened me when they finally left and told me if I told anyone, he would get my younger sister and they would rape her.'

She flipped ahead a few pages. 'I continue to try to avoid Bob, but he makes rude comments to me. I could kill him.'

She flipped ahead. 'Today I tried to burn down the house next door with Bob in it. They told me that I had gone too far and I was being committed to the asylum for observation.'

Another flip of pages. 'We had our first prisoner last night. All four of us are getting revenge for what Paul Maloney had done to one of my friends. It was exciting to strip him and hang him upside down. We were all naked and cleaning him in the shower with our brushes and the ice-cold water. He was covered in coal dust and we were very happy to clean every inch of his body. The most exciting part was when the guillotine cut the rest of his body apart. She had already taken the best parts. Seeing his head, hands and feet along with his best parts in the trophy case caused me to almost wet myself.'

"I'm not going to read anymore of this out loud." She read pages and pages and it was only going to be a short period when she finally saw my name in Melanie's diary. "Holy shit…you were one of my sister's captives. Chris, Scott was one of my twin sister's captives." I watched her excited look as she read entry after entry.

"Wouldn't you know it…my other sister almost saved your ass? She busted in the door, but Melanie got the best of her and tied her up too. You were rescued by some people on a task force, but Melanie says she jumped in the freezing water. She obviously survived."

Chris was now sitting beside her on the bed and Alexis couldn't control herself and was skipping all over the diary now. "Chris, listen to this. 'I managed to get plastic surgery in England and didn't pay a dime. My surgeon loved my body and changed my look to make me even more attractive. He served his purpose and I cut his manhood off and put the parts in a large jar in his office. He wasn't going to be using them any longer.'"

She flipped to more pages. 'It was hard work and hot work in Bermuda and it took about a year to complete but the rooms are finally constructed. Now, all I have to do is to stock them with some attractive men. With my assets it shouldn't be hard to do.'

"Chris my sister was worse than I ever imagined." She flipped to more entries. 'I enjoy making the rounds to the men downstairs. They try their best to resist my attention, but my naked body and my focused attention to their bodies always gets me the results I'm looking for.'

"Holy shit...listen to this. 'Scott has come for a visit and I'm finally whole again. He tries harder than all the others but I've showed him what can happen to him if he doesn't obey me. I carved an arrow into his lower body and I could tell he was worried I was going to cut those other parts off. He wouldn't be much use to me, if those were gone.'

She closed the diary and jumped onto the bed and wound up sitting on my thighs. "All of this could be a novel, or even a couple. Did you like what she did to you and your body?"

I didn't answer and paid an awful price. "Okay, Chris...he's not cooperating. Why don't you take out some of your frustrations and make him regret he tried to escape...not once, but twice. If you need any help, just let me know." She climbed off my body and Chris came to the bottom of the bed.

It was bad enough having Alexis all excited about what she was reading, but I didn't like Chris' expression or what

I saw in his hand. I also saw the look in Alexis' eyes and she looked exactly like her sister Melanie when she was going to kill me.

* * *

I tried to think of Mercedes while he used the belt and the electric cord on my body. I was beyond feeling the pain and just prayed that Mercedes would be safe. I could feel myself losing my will to stay alive. Alexis' urgings were getting further and further away like she was in a tunnel.

At one point I looked over and Alexis looked like the emotion of the day had caught up to her. I saw her eyes watering and wondered what she was thinking. However she wasn't going to let anyone see her cry and Chris was hell bent on leather.

This was how it was going to end. I hoped if she was going to use the razor that I would be out of it.

There wasn't any new pain but I could hear the sound of the belt on my body. However, it stopped suddenly. They must have been looking to see if I had passed out.

"Alexis, I just saw someone look in the garage out back." I heard his bare feet on the floor. "Shit, shit…it looks like the guy might be a cop. He doesn't have a uniform, but he moves like a cop. He's going over to the bulkhead. We need to leave."

"Chris I don't think we're going anywhere. Let's just kill Scott and make a stand here."

"What about using him as a shield?"

"Alexis I just wanted you and you deserved your father's money. Let's make a run for it and take Scott with us. He might be a good bargaining chip for later."

"Okay, why not. I ran across something in my father's files we might be able to use. Untie Scott and let's get dressed and out of here."

Chapter 91

Her plane finally landed in Boston and it was getting close to midnight. It had been a long day and she really wanted a hot bath and a good night's sleep, but more importantly, a safe Scott would be better than anything.

She was trying to decide where she was headed right now. She needed to reach her father before she did anything else.

"Mercedes!" Mike yelled to her as she was headed away from baggage claim.

"Mike." She felt strange putting her hand out to shake hands, but he came up to her and hugged her.

"Welcome home Mercedes. You must be pretty tired."

"I am, but I feel relieved now that I've landed."

She watched him take her suitcase and he had his arm around her waist and was moving her toward some seats.

"Mike, some thing has happened...hasn't it?"

"Mercy, we need to talk. Please, let's sit down here."

"Oh Mike, please don't tell me Scott is hurt or dead."

"I'm sorry Mercedes, but it involves your parents."

"My *parents*?"

"Yes...they both passed away this morning."

"That can't be...I talked to my father this morning."

"Did he tell you anything at that time?"

"Yes he told me Melanie had a twin sister Alexis, and she was one of the abductors who took Scott."

"Well they went to your parents' house and as best we can tell, your mom had a heart attack, most likely when she saw what she thought was Melanie's ghost. Your father looks like he either fell or was pushed through the banister and died in the fall."

She closed her eyes and tried to get her arms around what she just heard. *Please God don't let the only other person I love be dead too.* She took a deep breath and asked, "What about Scott?"

"As best we can tell he is alive and was there with Alexis and a caregiver by the name of Chris Sullivan. They managed to get away, but we have every town in Mass looking for their car. Mercedes, I'm really sorry about your parents."

"Thank you Mike. There was a plot to kidnap me when I landed in Boston, but I managed to deal with the man on the plane who was involved. However, he killed an unsuspecting stewardess. That is why we were diverted to the Miami airport. The same group kidnapped my partner, Ralph Reynolds, but he was rescued."

"We know about Ralph. Paddy has been in contact with Richard Damelio's brother Robert in Venezuela. He was the angel you and Ralph needed. He was working with the Venezuelan military trying to find the missing kidnapped citizens. They raided all of the addresses Richard had in his files and we don't have the final count of the number of people rescued but it is staggering. They also captured many of the gang."

"By any chance, did you happen to hear a Captain Chavez's name mentioned?"

"He wasn't immediately captured, but one of the men captured made an arrangement and told the authorities he was leaving on a plane bound for Boston. They tried to arrest him, but he and two other men were killed in a shootout at the airport."

"That is too bad, but good riddance. I would have enjoyed testifying against that slimy piece of shit."

"I'll take you wherever you want to go."

"I can't do anything for my parents at this point, but maybe I can do something for Scott. Mike, I gave an informal resignation to my boss. I'm not going to work for the FBI any longer, effective immediately."

"Do you want a job?"

"Mike…I really want a family. Finding Scott is critical to that direction. How can I help?"

Chapter 92

He was headed to the Brattle Street office and Mercedes looked like she could use a good night's sleep. He let her rest her eyes as he made the thirty minute trip.

"Mercy we're here."

"This used to be home when I was on the task force."

"It can be again if you want to work for Paddy."

"I'll give it some thought, but I really want to enjoy settling down with Scott and hopefully raising a family."

"Let's go inside. You know you can do all of that. I need to keep Scott away from future investigations, and having you at the office here, might just provide that result."

"Mike, this is the third time one of my sisters has him hostage. I sure hope he is going to be as lucky as he was the last time, but I'm really worried. My sister has nothing to lose at this point. I'm sure she would like nothing more than to hurt me by killing Scott, or killing both of us."

They entered the old colonial building and were greeted with the smell of fresh brewed coffee. "Paddy, look who is here."

"Mercedes welcome. I'm so sorry about your parents. Are you okay?"

"I've had a very trying few days, but I'm okay...tired, but okay. I need right now to do everything I possibly can to save Scott's butt, so I can pound the shit out of him."

"I think you could really do that too."

"Paddy, any news? Mike asked.

"I have the coffee in the conference room. Why don't we go in there and discuss what we have, and what we should do next."

The coffee tasted very good, and he noticed Mercedes finished her cup immediately, and poured another.

Paddy got up and went over to the blackboard. "I made some notes, but let me explain. After the unit spotted your dad's car in the garage and the bulkhead clasp broken, he reported he thought they might be in the house. Many of the lights were on. We dispatched many cars to the scene, but when they got inside, the abductors and Scott were gone."

He continued. "They found your mother in the master bedroom and confirmed she died of a heart attack. Your father died from a fall from the upstairs balcony. Neither one of them suffered from what we can tell. There were traces of blood on the master bedroom bed, but nothing life-threatening. They found electric cords, one with the end cut which might have been used to torture Scott."

"What condition was the house in?" Mercedes asked.

"It was obvious they were looking for valuables, and found the safe, but never got into it. We found a page from your sister Melanie's diary. It was about you and her sailing on your grandfather's boat. It looks like it might have been ripped out in a rage, most likely by Alexis."

"What kind of car were they driving?" she asked.

"They are in a '63 Pontiac Tempest...gold in color. However, the thing that all of us are surprised at is that with all the towns on alert, there hasn't been one sighting of their car. We can't figure that out, unless by chance they changed vehicles."

"Anything missing?" Mercedes asked.

"Well the diary is missing and something from the top of the desk, but we don't know what it was. Any idea?"

"My dad kept a neat office. What side of the desk are we talking about?"

"The right side, why? Do you think you know what it was?"

"Was his address book there?"

"I don't know. Let me make a phone call." Paddy left the conference room.

"Mercedes are you hanging in there?"

"Yes and no. Scott and I had words a few days ago about him going to see Maggie dance."

"Yes, Scott told me."

"He did?"

"Yeah. He was frustrated one night and went to watch her dance. Why?"

"Nothing else?"

"If you mean did he spend any time with her privately…absolutely not."

"Then I guess his other bad news was about him doing the investigation."

"What do you mean other bad news?"

He saw her let out a deep breath. "No, it was just Scott's way of not lying to me, but I took it the wrong way."

Paddy came back in the conference room. "Paul confirmed there was no address book on the desk or anywhere in the office."

"What are you thinking Mercedes?"

"I think I know where they might be headed. One of the pictures on the piano was of our New Hampshire camp."

"Do you know the address?"

"Yes, but better. I know how to get there and some other potential info if that is where they went."

Chapter 93

She had a tough time convincing Paddy and Mike not to call the New Hampshire State Police. Their points made sense, but the biggest trump card she played is that she knew the area, the camp and she was still an FBI agent. Since they might have taken Scott across state lines it was now a federal offense.

Her parents bought the camp when she was in the third grade. They used it in the summer months. Her mom would go up for the entire summer, and her dad would come up on Friday afternoons, and leave early Monday morning. It was hard not to think about all of the good times she had. The special times were when he took three weeks vacation in July. *It was hard to believe they were both gone. Saving Scott is what she had to do, even if it meant putting her life in danger.*

It was a long drive to Ossipee New Hampshire. She took the opportunity to sleep during the drive. It was easy to do, since she hadn't slept for a long time and the motion of the car was like a cradle. Mike was driving well over the speed limit, but at a safe pace. She could hear the engine's roar and the extra sway when he pulled out to pass.

Periodically she was not asleep, and could hear their conversation.

"Paddy, are we doing the right thing?" Mike whispered.

"I think we might be just a few hours behind them, but I agree with Mercedes in this instance. I think we have a better chance of freeing Scott from her sister. Sullivan is who scares me the most. He has gotten himself way in over his head. Blackmailing was one thing, but now he is directly involved in a homicide. He can't go back and undo it, and he might just become a cornered rat."

"What is the plan when we get there?"

"Based on the information Mercedes shared about the location of the cabin, on one side is the lake and the other is the long driveway which leads down from the road above. She said you can't see the cabin from the road, which gives us a way to approach the cabin without being seen. When we get there I'm going to let her tell us her thoughts on how to proceed."

"She's had quite the last few days…being abducted once is bad enough, but twice and then a third attempt. I can't blame her for slamming the guy's nose into his brain. Then on top of that to find both of your parents dead and the love of your life kidnapped. She is one amazing person. I would love to have her working with us. What are your thoughts Mike?"

"I'm all for it. It is strange that this is the third time she is attempting to save Scott's life from one of her sisters. If she does save him this time, she is probably going to kill him herself for getting involved in this whole thing."

"It's not 'if' Paddy, it is 'when' I save him. You better believe on one hand I'm going to thank God we rescued him, and on the other hand…well, it won't be pretty." She leaned over the seat and announced she was now awake.

"I hope you got some sleep. Mike and I both have weapons, but I know you don't have one. Here, take this backup piece."

"Thanks Paddy." She examined it briefly and put it in her waistband behind her back. We're going to find the cottages busy this time of the year. If they make a run for it, we need to be very careful that the vacationers are safe. Should they indeed run, there aren't many roads that they can escape on. When we get there is there any way we can then alert the state police to what is going on?"

"We have the radio and we should be able to reach them…good idea. I think we should wait until we assess the situation though."

"Right. Mike, this is the turnoff you need. Take a right here, it leads to the lake and to Maine."

"Maybe we should alert the Maine State Police," Mike said.

"Let's let New Hampshire handle that call. How far now Mercy?"

"About five minutes. We're looking for Leavitt Road I think, but it has been years since I've been up here. I'll know the turnoff when I see it. The camp is on the Leavitt Bay area of the lake complex."

Mike was still exceeding the speed limit. "There it is...that's it right there." Mike braked the car and the car went into a skid, but he managed to turn the wheel and correct it. The car bounced when it hit the dirt road. "Mike we have only a short distance to go. When we go by Broadbay Road we need to find a place to turn off this road. We shouldn't go much further in the car."

The night was giving way to the light of morning, but Mike turned off the headlights to be safe.

"That's Broadbay Road on the left, the next place you see to park take it."

A short distance later there was a home being constructed on the left and he pulled in off the road up to the newly poured cement foundation.

"This is it. The camp is about ten down on the right. It is a cape-style-two story house, red in color, with a detached garage. Once again you can't see the house from the road, or couldn't, back the last time I was here," Mercedes announced cocking her newly acquired piece.

* * *

Paddy whispered as they studied the property. "I don't see the car. What if the camp is occupied by someone else?"

"You know my dad's real estate firm could have rented it for the summer. Good point Paddy," Mercedes said softly. "There's no windows on the garage, so we can't check for their vehicle. If they took the large key ring from my parents' house, the keys to everything my parents own are on that key chain," Mercedes added.

"There aren't any windows on this side of the house…strange," Mike mentioned.

"Not really if you know my dad. This is the west facing side, and he purposely didn't want any windows as there is no A/C in the camp," Mercedes offered.

"What do you suggest Mercedes?" Paddy asked.

"Here's the layout of the camp. The left side of the camp is the original camp. When you come in you come onto the porch. The porch goes the length of the lake side of the camp on the old section. There's a door which leads to the kitchen and bath, and the living room is where the large chimney is.

"The entrance to the newer two-story addition is through the living room. There is a bedroom to the right of that entrance, and another sitting area to the left. The stairs to the second level are on the far side of that sitting area. Upstairs there are two bedrooms facing the lake off a common hall along this side of the camp."

"Any thoughts?" Paddy asked.

"Well, if they are here, Scott could be either in the bedroom in the new addition, or in one of the two upstairs. If they want to keep an eye on Scott while they get some privacy of their own, my money would be on the upstairs bedrooms."

"Can we see any of those rooms from the ground?"

"Not unless you are way out on the lake, or on that island out there." She thought for a minute. "There is a window in the downstairs bedroom, which is on the right hand side of that addition. We could check that out first and it would confirm they are upstairs."

"You're forgetting one important point…we don't know if they actually came here," Paddy said, but he wasn't smiling.

"Mike it is getting light out. I suggest you climb up on the garage roof to see if you see anything in that lower bedroom."

He started to move toward the camp.

She grabbed his arm. "Mike, one other thing…my dad had two shotguns and a rifle in the downstairs gun case. I have no idea if they are still there, or locked up some other place."

"Thanks, I think."

* * *

A long fifteen minutes later Mike came back to where they were hiding. "Okay, there isn't anybody in that room. There's a light shining from the far room, which might be that living room area you mentioned. What now?"

"Here's what I think we can do next, but it won't be very pretty, and I can do it. The old camp portion has a crawl space under it. I could crawl under it to see if I hear any voices above it," she said as she started to move away.

"You're not going anywhere pretty lady. You have had enough tight situations the last few days, and there is no way you are crawling under that house. But, it is a great idea. Just give me a few minutes," Mike said and was already bent over headed to the back of the garage.

"Mercedes, you're shaking," Paddy said putting both his hands on one of hers.

"I can't let Scott get killed. He's my future. My family is gone, well except for this nut-case sister, and all I can think of is the blood that you mentioned was on the bed at my parents."

"Mercy, if he is in that house, I promise we will get him out alive."

"I surely hope so. There are only two reasons he's there. Either they need him as a hostage, or I don't like the other reason at all. I saw what her twin did to him, and she confessed she loved Scott. This twin doesn't have any of that history. I'm a profiler, and I don't like what my gut is telling me."

Chapter 94

He saw Alexis' eyes when she told him to go in the first
bedroom and get on the bed naked. However, she took
Scott down the hall into the other bedroom and he worried
what she might be doing.

When they backed the car into the one car garage, Alexis
spotted the box of ropes and took several of them with her.
Her comment was something along the lines of being safe
and being prepared.

Now in the bedroom and naked on the bed he couldn't
hear what was going on in the other bedroom. Although it
was early July, it was still very early morning and the camp
was cold. He resisted the urge to cover himself with one of
the Army or Navy blankets piled on the only chair in the
room.

His mind was reeling from what they, or more
specifically Alexis, had done. Three people were dead and
he expected her to kill Scott. It wouldn't surprise him to
have her ask him to kill Scott. He could hurt him, but he
knew he couldn't kill him. He saw what she did to the
doctor, and there was no doubt in his mind whether she
could indeed kill again.

It had been at least thirty minutes and it was getting even
harder to ignore the blankets so close by. He heard a door
close and looked over to the bedroom door and saw Alexis
standing there with ropes in one hand, a razor in the other
and a huge smile on her face.

He had also seen her naked many times recently, but
observing her leaning against the door frame twilling the
ropes made his heart beat faster immediately.

"Chris I'm sorry it took me longer than I expected. Scott
needed more coaxing than previously, but he eventually
gave me what I wanted. When I left him he was quite
uncomfortable, but happy to still be alive. He also

confessed some things about his love of Mercedes that I found interesting."

He watched her stop swinging the ropes and head to the side of the bed. "You look like you're cold. Would you like me to warm you up?"

"Yes, I would."

"That's not a very respectful answer. Try it again."

"Yes master, I would like to be warmed up."

"That is slightly better, but it will do." She immediately climbed onto his body and licked his ear, and then nibbled it.

Feeling her hot body against his was extremely enjoyable and he could feel his reacting to hers.

"I can feel you getting excited." She wiggled her body against his and he continued to grow. She jumped off him and went over and opened one of the brown Army blankets. She came back over and continued to stare at his excitement. "You're much too distracting, so I'm going to cover you while I tie you up." She didn't immediately move to do that but watched his body twitch even more.

She finally spread the blanket from his neck down to his lower legs. She picked up a rope and tied it around the hole in the headboard, and did the same with another rope. "Put your hands up over your head." She wrapped one rope around his wrist twice and then tied a knot. She climbed onto the blanket covering his body and did the same with the other rope.

When she had both of his wrists tied above his head she offered a breast to his mouth. He closed his eyes and sucked on her breast and then her nipple, which immediately became enlarged and hard. She pulled away and offered the other. He had never seen her nipples so large. "You like this don't you?"

"I like it as much as you do Chris." She got off him and went to the bottom of the bed and pulled him down. She tied a rope around the left footboard and then spread his legs and tied the other end to his ankle. She did the same for the other leg, but she pulled the rope as tight as she could.

"That's too tight Alexis."

"What did you say?"

"Would you please loosen that last rope?"

"No."

He saw something he didn't want to see. She picked up the straight razor off the blanket and opened it. If it wasn't for her expression, he thought she might be going to cut the rope. However, he was trying to assess whether she was playing a game with him. She came over to the side of the bed and slowly pulled the blanket off him. The room felt even colder than just minutes earlier.

When she climbed on the bed and sat on his thighs it was like a frying pan was placed on them.

"Here's the same old Chris…standing at attention and waiting for me to give you a big reward."

He watched her studying his body from his hair down to the junction of his thighs.

"What do you want me to do Chris?"

He took a big intake of air, but didn't dare say anything.

"I'm sure Scott has recovered by now, I can go back to him. If that is what you want then so be it. Now is your chance Chris…tell me what you want."

"I want you to put down that razor and take me in your mouth."

She smiled at him. "Details, details." She put the razor down on his stomach, grabbed his erection, bent and put her mouth around it.

When she swirled her tongue he instantly grew larger. He could see her eyes looking up at him with the open razor in his line of sight.

She let her teeth drag along his length as her mouth left him. "Let's see now, put the razor down and take you in my mouth." She was still holding his erection and admiring it.

She changed hands and picked up the razor with her now free hand. She smiled at him and in one swift motion lifted his penis and sliced it off. She put the end in her mouth.

He immediately screamed feeling the incredible pain and the blood running down between his legs. He felt his chin drop to his chest and felt the next wave of pain. She still had his best part in her mouth when she reached down and took what was left of his best parts.

He couldn't deal with the pain. She stuffed his penis in his mouth and the last thing he saw was the motion of her arm.

Chapter 95

She watched blood spraying everywhere from his sliced neck. His eyes told the whole story of disbelief.

"Chris, if you can still hear me, that is for coming into my bedroom and reading my private diary. You had no right to read that. You and the doctor now can enjoy your time together in hell. I wanted my family. He kept me from it and you took them away."

Tears were cascading down her face. She reached out and slashed his face with the razor. She tried to stop, but she couldn't stop hitting him with the razor. Seconds later, she could no longer recognize him.

She was covered in his blood. She realized he really didn't deserve what she did to him, but she had Scott to herself now. There was only one member of her family left and she now had a way to get to her too.

The razor was still in her hand when she left the room and headed quickly to Scott's bedroom.

It was obvious by the look on Scott's face he knew what had happened to Chris. Chris' screams and the blood covering her body were a dead giveaway.

She moved quickly to the side of his bed and studied the two arrows pointing at her target. Her twin was dead, but she had managed to pick up where she left off. It was just Scott and her now and she was anxious for him.

She watched his eyes travel the length of her naked body and then fixate on the bloody razor in her bloody hand.

"I hope you're happy to see me, but I can tell by how deflated you are that you're not. We can fix that." She climbed onto his body and sat on his thighs. She ran her free hand across his face and slowly downward. "I read in my sister's diary that you tried harder than any of the men to resist her attention. However even you eventually gave in to her. I have all the time in the world, and like her, I will get what I'm after."

She moved the razor to her sister's arrow and traced the scar with the back of the blade. She looked at Scott's eyes and smiled. Then she moved the back of the blade to her own arrow, which was showing the first signs of healing. The razor was leaving traces of Chris' blood on his body.

"This isn't acceptable." She moved the razor to Scott's mouth. "Lick it clean or I will put your own blood on it."

She watched as he carefully licked the razor. She moved her free hand down further between his legs. "That's clean enough."

There was a loud crash downstairs and she realized that somehow they had been found. She wanted Scott to see what happened next and cut all four of his ropes freeing him from the bed. She climbed off Scott when she heard the pounding of footsteps on the stairs.

Chapter 96

Mike had crawled under the house and both of them were waiting for him to come back to let them know whether there was anyone in the house.

The early morning calm was split wide open with a man's tormented screams. They all had their answer and someone was being killed. She looked at Paddy and he was in shock. "Paddy, my God you're having a heart attack."

"I'll be fine with one of my pills. Go, Mike may need some help."

She jumped out of their cover, pulled the gun out of her waist band and ran to the camp and onto the porch.

She thought of Scott being killed by her sister which was enough adrenaline to give her the strength to kick the door and shatter the frame. The door banged off the wall and she ran to the stairs leading upstairs.

She reached the top of the stairs and caught sight of the blood on the floor. When she entered the bedroom she saw what was left of Scott on the bed. He had been cut apart and his face was a bloody pile of mush.

There was a loud thump and the sound of someone rushing down the hall. She didn't care about her sister or the guy with her. She moved away from the bed and slipped on the floor falling to her knees and dropping her gun. She leaned her head down and felt her insides coming up. She heard the noise beside her and looked up to see a naked woman about to swing a razor at the back of her neck.

She was covered in blood but the blade was shiny. It was all slow motion.

Then she thought she saw Scott behind her. However, it was too late. The razor was behind her sister's head and in one quick motion she was going to be killed.

Scott reached out and grabbed her wrist, but her wrist was covered in blood and he couldn't hold onto it. She saw

Alexis spin and kick Scott between his legs and he immediately doubled over. Alexis turned and rushed towards her again with the razor raised.

The room exploded and Alexis fell over her onto the bed. She looked at the bedroom door and it was Mike standing there, pistol pointed where Alexis had been.

* * *

The area was swarming with police as the medic was treating Scott. She thanked God he was still alive. Minutes ago she thought her life was over in many different aspects. If had been a tough few days, but it was over now. She wanted so much to yank the blanket covering Scott and show him how much she loves him. However, there were too many people around.

"Scott, I thought the body on the bed was yours and one of my sisters had finally taken you away from me. I'm so thankful you're safe. I'm so sorry we had the disagreement on the phone and I doubted you."

"Mercy, I love you and want to be with you for the rest of my life. I promise I'm never going to do another investigation."

"Well I accept all of those commitments. I have given my notice with the FBI. More importantly, I want you with me for the rest of my life too."

"Do you like the sound of Mrs. Scott Tucker?"

"Do I detect a proposal?"

"You really would make a good detective you know."

"That is all behind me now. If you are serious about never doing another investigation, I like the sound of being your wife."

"What will you do?"

"I think the first thing to do right now is to start practicing on how to make a family."

"I'm up for it right now."

The medic had already finished tending to his wounds. She pulled the blanket open and looked at his body. "I can see you are working on it, but you look like you need a little more assistance. How about we get out of here and start practicing?"

They watched Mike come over to them. "You two look like you've made up."

"Mike, am I needed here any longer?" Scott asked.

"No, we have your preliminary statement, but they will need a more detailed statement later."

"Is tomorrow okay?"

Chapter 97

It was Mercedes' final day at the FBI. A meeting had been set up for the end of the day, but she wasn't told what it was about. She figured it was going to be a goodbye session.

Ralph was back at work for a week and he took her out for lunch. "Mercedes you were incredible to work with, but I would like to still be friends. Would you mind having lunch with me every once in a while?"

"Ralph you are a great agent. You will have a great career with the FBI. We can still be friends and I would like very much to enjoy lunch with you once in a while. I have to thank you for respecting me…you could have made it more awkward."

Later that afternoon they both headed to the large conference room. The door was already closed and Mercedes knocked. The door opened and Max was standing at the front of the room.

"Welcome you two. The attractive young lady is Mercedes Strong. The young man with her is Ralph Reynolds. Please have a seat over here."

He waited for them to take their seats near the front of the room. "Today is a sad day as we are saying goodbye to one of our agents, Mercedes. She has been an asset to our agency and we will miss her very much. However, the rumor has it that she is going to be married very shortly. Congratulations Mercedes. It is also a special day as we are welcoming Ralph back to our agency and he is now a Special Agent. Congratulations Ralph."

Max continued after the polite applause. "We have some special guests in the room that I would like to introduce to both of you. We have two very thankful young ladies, Marie Quinlan and Helen Scott. They and many others were rescued from their abductors."

There was polite applause as well for them.

"Next to them is Richard Damelio who was also rescued. Because of his excellent record keeping we located all of the US citizens and with the help of the Venezuelan military rescued *all* of them *and all* of the other abducted women from other countries."

Once again the room filled with applause.

"Seated beside him is Robert Damelio, Richard's brother. None of you knew about him. Mercedes, you mentioned that you must have had a guardian angel watching over you...I'd like you to meet him in person. Rob, and a former member of the Venezuelan military, were the key investigators in Venezuela. Through their combined efforts they discovered where his brother was, but more importantly who was behind the abductions. They also stayed with it long enough to pinpoint the leaders behind the slave trade."

She got up and went over and hugged him. "I have my life thanks to you."

Max resumed, "Rob as I mentioned in the invite, many many people are free today because of your investigation."

There was a loud applause.

"This envelope contains an offer of employment with the agency, and I would be very happy to have you on our team. You can read the details later, but Mercedes and Ralph were more than just agents here...they were friends. Thank you."

The room erupted again.

"The rest of the story is that Captain Chavez was the leader of the gang, along with Jose and Hector Hernandez. Chevez was killed when he resisted arrest while attempting to board a flight to Boston. Mercedes introduced Hector to her elbow and his body was returned to his native country. Jose and the other members of his gang were arrested in a large number of coordinated raids by the Venezuelan military. The military has since learned the names of the people associated with similar gangs operating in other parts of Venezuela."

"In addition, the president has sent a communiqué to the Venezuelan president thanking him for the excellent work of the Venezuelan military in rescuing our kidnapped citizens. There is still an investigation now being conducted by the Venezuelan government to recover the vessels that were taken illegally."

She watched as Max picked up a small gold-wrapped package on the far credenza. "Mercedes this is just a small token of our appreciation for your years of service."

She stood and opened the package. She read the inscription on the plaque-

'In Recognition of Your Excellent Service
Thank You Mercedes Strong!
From Your FBI Family'

* * *

It had been a busy two weeks. There was the funeral for Mercedes family members including Alexis. Mercedes was waiting until after she left the FBI to deal with all of her parents' personal affairs. She was considering managing her father's real estate entity. There was a right hand person handling the development side of his business, and she was planning on giving him the reigns.

I was making us a shrimp scampi dinner when I heard the door open to her former apartment which was now our apartment. I had suggested we go out to dinner to celebrate her last day at the agency, but she wanted to celebrate privately.

I saw her smiling face first and then the box she was carrying. I went over to greet her and smelled the sweet scent of Gardenia. "Welcome home honey."

"It's nice to hear that when I come through the door."

"You look like you had a good day today. Did they give you a nice sendoff?"

"Yes they did, and I was quite surprised by it."

"Would you care for a drink?"

"A glass of white wine would be nice." She sat on one of the counter stools. "My guardian angel came to a meeting at the end of the day."

I handed her the glass of wine and touched my small glass of bourbon to hers. "Cheers."

"Cheers."

"I don't fully understand…guardian angel?"

"Well the 'Readers Digest' version is this…when we were in Venezuela both Ralph and I seemed to be rescued before anything serious happened to us. It was like we had a guardian angel watching over us. I met him."

"Him?"

"Yes, him."

I listened to her explain what happened at the meeting. The more excited and animated, the more I detected the scent of Gardenia. Although she had lost her parents she seemed to have the weight of the world lifted off her shoulders. I stirred the scampi, but wanted to turn it off. I couldn't wait to get something off her shoulders and elsewhere for that matter.

Right in the middle of her telling the story, she stopped. "Are you listening to what I'm saying?"

"Every word of it."

"Then why do you have that expression?"

"Can't you guess?"

"Are the Indians getting their bows and arrows ready?"

"I don't know about the Indians and the bows, but the arrows should be pointing at something."

"That's not the only thing that's pointing."

As we passed by the stove I turned the scampi off and followed this beautiful creature. She was easy to follow, leaving a trail of clothes along the way. When we reached the bedroom she was on the bed totally nude and holding her arms out to me. I had one last article of clothing left to remove and saw her big smile. "Let me do that for you." She slowly pulled down my briefs. "Do you have anything to say for yourself Mr. Tucker?"

"If you ever get lost there should be enough road signs along the way."

"Cute, but I don't plan to get lost."

"I think the more we practice this…the better we will get."

"Promises…promises. They say that practice does make perfect."

"Oh, wait Scott this is important. I talked with Maggie today and she is thrilled to death that she is going to be my maid of honor. However, we both agreed that she would bring a date to the wedding. I told her about this nice guy named Ralph at work. I think they will get on famously, don't you?"

"I'm sure they will. I talked to Mike and he's consented to be my best man."

"He might be your best man…but you're mine."

Made in the USA
Lexington, KY
06 November 2013